Dear Readers,

It's been a while since I published a major book, as I've been trying to get movie deals done, and I'm still working on that. There are far too many Black books that would make great films, including several of my titles. I'm determined to make that happen. I eventually want us *all* to be able to *see* why we fell in love with reading. When I first started writing *Flyy Girl* as a nineteen-year-old sophomore at the University of Pittsburgh in 1989, it was a young, urban book that opened the market for hundreds of new writers, millions of new readers, and made me a household name in Black literature. I'm a bit older now, and I know much more about the details of adult life to write about it, starting with my new book *Control*—a psychological thriller on the hot topic of mental health and our interpersonal relationships.

It explores the questions of how much control we have in our own lives, how much control we would like to have over our children and family members, how much control we would love to have over our mates or our bosses at work, and what would you like to control the most in your life? We can't control what everyone else does, no matter how hard we try—something I had to find out the hard way. We don't control life. We only live in it, and we do the best that we can with what we've been given.

Control features a Black psychologist, Dr. Victoria Benning, who has six clients, *all* with deep control issues that need to be resolved, including a young, female rapper who will do anything to sell her music to gain control over her money and career. A popular film director who needs to control the narrative about his personality and his masculine urges with beautiful young women aspiring to be movie stars. A used-to-be successful screenwriter who is out of control with everything to the point of needing pills, but refuses, thinking his lack of control enhances his creativity. A bisexual music producer who believes in the Illuminati and possibly gaining more control over her own career—even if a "blood sacrifice" is needed. A rich, White businessman who wants to control his guilty feelings over the atrocities done to Black people in slavery—including his great-great-grandfather on their family plantation in South Carolina. He's conflicted about race, class, gender, education, religion, and everything else. But he can't control himself. And finally, an overly emotional woman who can't even control her reality . . . or is she just crazy?

This all takes place in the historical city of Atlanta, Georgia, which has now become the new capital of Black Entertainment—in the A-T-L. Please enjoy it and spread the word!

Sincerely Yours,

Also By Omar Tyree

All Access
The Traveler: Welcome to Dubai
Pecking Order
The Last Street Novel
What They Want
Boss Lady
Diary of a Groupie
Leslie
Just Say No!
For The Love of Money
Sweet St. Louis
Single Mom
A Do Right Man
Flyy Girl

The Urban Griot Series
Cold Blooded
One Crazy Night
Capital City
College Boy

Anthologies
Unleashed: Provocative Short Stories
Dirty Old Men and Other Stories
Dark Thirst
Not in My Family
The Game

Proverbs of the People
Tough Love: The Life and Death of Tupac Shakur
Testimony

Original Ebooks
The American Disease
Psychadelic
The Traveler: No Turning Back
Insanity
Corrupted

Young Adult Books
Sneaker Kings
12 Brown Boys

Business Books
The Equation: Applying the 4 Indisputable Components of Business Success

Autobiographies
Mayor For Life: The Incredible Story of Marion Barry Jr.

Poetry
Poetry: For the Love of Black Women

CONTROL

OMAR TYREE

www.kensingtonbooks.com

This book is a work of fiction. Names, characters, businesses, organizations, places, events, and incidents either are the product of the author's imagination or are used fictitiously. Any resemblance to actual persons, living or dead, events, or locales is entirely coincidental.

To the extent that the image or images on the cover of this book depict a person or persons, such person or persons are merely models, and are not intended to portray any character or characters featured in the book.

DAFINA BOOKS are published by

Kensington Publishing Corp.
900 Third Avenue
New York, NY 10022

All Kensington Titles, Imprints, and Distributed Lines are available at special quantity discounts for bulk purchases for sales promotions, premiums, fund-raising, and educational or institutional use. Special book excerpts or customized printings can also be created to fit specific needs. For details, write or phone the office of the Kensington special sales manager: Kensington Publishing Corp., 900 Third Ave., New York, NY 10022, Attn: Special Sales Department, Phone: 1-800-221-2647.

Library of Congress Control Number: 2023952649

ISBN: 978-1-4967-4804-1
First Kensington Hardcover Edition: June 2024

ISBN-13: 978-1-4967-4806-5 (ebook)

10 9 8 7 6 5 4 3 2 1

Printed in the United States of America

Dude wrote a lot of books . . .
He must have a lot of shit on his mind.

What the streets say
about Omar Tyree

PROLOGUE

Dr. Victoria Benning

I'm in con-trolllll / never gonna stop.

Friday, February 2, 2024

"CONTROL," BY JANET JACKSON, PRODUCED BY JIMMY JAM AND Terry Lewis. I was a little girl when that record first came out, and I immediately fell in love with it. I just understood what she meant. Every little girl would like to have more control over her life. It seems like we have a million restrictions compared to the boys.

Lotion up your elbows and knees. Comb your hair. Straighten out your dress. Cross your legs. Put some baby powder on your neck, your underarms, and down in your tush. Don't you get dirty. Put down them rocks. Get out of that water. Don't play with them boys. Don't you touch that damn dog. Don't you hang out on that street. Get off that corner. And you watch your damn mouth when you speak to me, girl! You hear me? Now get in the house! Good girls ain't supposed to be out this late.

That's why I went out of my way to be a tomboy. I didn't ask to be born a girl. Raising a girl seems to present extra challenges. Your parents and family are always in protection mode. Like the boogeyman is always out to get you.

Anyways . . . back to Janet Jackson. She had six older brothers and two older sisters. But I was always more interested in her parents, Joe and Katherine. As much talk as we hear about Joe being a control freak and a dominator, I would always study Katherine Jackson as the woman who allowed it. As a Jehovah's Witness, she was actually as strict as Joe was with her children. I've been around Jehovahs before, and I wouldn't want to be one. It seems like they have a whole lot of repression going on.

Then I thought about Katherine's limp from polio and how that may have affected her confidence and ego when up against a man like Joe, a wannabe boxer. Katherine was an absolutely *gorgeous* woman in my humble opinion. And Joe . . . he reminded me of a 1970s horror movie called *Blacula.* It's just something about his eyes, his hair, and his eyebrows. He was just a spooky man to look at, almost like hypnosis in his eyes. I could only imagine the constant voodoo he put on Katherine, and the countless women he had jump-offs with as the father and manager of one of the most famous singing groups in history. But Katherine stuck by her husband and her kids no matter what. I have to honor her for that.

I've always been fascinated by control issues, who has it, who doesn't, and how we all respond to its absence or its gain. I know one thing, kids have a lot more control today than we ever had when I was growing up in Camden, New Jersey, in the 1970s. We were right across the bridge from Philadelphia, but I was never allowed to go there by myself in my teen years. So, I snuck over to Philly as much as I could and paid for it with a strap to my ass whenever I returned home and got caught.

I honestly didn't mind it though. As the old saying goes, no pain, no gain. So, I took my ass whoopings in stride and maintained my wild side.

Then I went away to college to study psychology at Clarke Atlanta University before earning my doctorate at Georgia Tech. My dissertation was all about the psychological elements of control.

What it all boils down to is *power,* really, who has it and who doesn't, and how that power, or the lack thereof, affects our desire to control whatever we can at all costs, while stressing over the things that we *can't* control.

I've now put in twenty-five years in the field as a professional psychologist in the Atlanta area, counseling stressed-out employees, corporate bosses, actors and directors, musicians and managers, and plenty of couples in relationships, whether they be married or just dating. I've even counseled a few "side chicks" which we have an abundance of in Atlanta now.

A lot of these girls would rather be connected to someone with money and power than be alone or with a man who doesn't have it, which places them right back under the control of a man who has it. So, I've advised women young and old on how to deal with the side chick disposition mentally and spiritually.

There's a lot of everything going on down here in Atlanta. This place has become full of drama, with people moving here from all over the country and the world, especially people of color. And it ain't all good either. Some of these new clients have taken my career to the edge of madness.

Typically, you're not supposed to talk about your clients. It's against the code of ethics, confidentiality, and professionalism. But over the past *week*, I've had *five* fatal cases with my clients and one on the brink of insanity. And it's all left me unhinged and in need of a vacation. So, I'm gonna break protocol here and talk about these six clients of mine as a part of my own therapy.

Shit, I'm human too. My doctorate degree doesn't absolve me from the drama. We all get caught up in life. So, I'm gonna start off by reflecting on Mrs. Melody, the youngest of these six clients at twenty-three. She was an up-and-coming rap star who I took on in the fall of last year. She was a gorgeous girl from Florida with a mouth on her that was *atrocious*. . . .

MRS. MELODY

Reflection 1

"THAT'S NOT A TYPO. I CALL MYSELF *MRS.* MELODY BECAUSE I'M married to the game," she told me. "I got no husband, no boyfriends, no managers, or none of that shit. They all just get in the fuckin' way. Jealous motherfuckas. So, I do a lot of shit on my own."

She sat down in my office wearing a lime-green, wraparound one-piece with golden heels that made me think of the character Poison Ivy in *Batman*. But her style and body were ten times tighter. And she looked biracial with smooth tanned skin, dark, almond-shaped eyes, and slippery, dark brown hair that moved easily on her scalp, the kind of hair that guys loved to touch to make sure it's real.

I asked her, "How long have you felt that way?"

"About three years. I just got tired of motherfuckas catching feelings and fuckin' up the business. So, like, I get in the studio to record. And the producers be feeling me to the point of wanting to give me free tracks or whatever. But then your dumb-ass boyfriend or manager starts tripping on some jealous shit.

"They pulling you aside, like, 'I'on like how he looking at you. We here strictly on *business*.' So, then the motherfucka charges us a thousand dollars and shit, when I could'a got the shit for *free* myself."

"But it *is* business," I reminded her. "You're not getting my services for free."

She glared at me with her dark, sexy, piercing eyes that I'm quite sure she's used a lot with the guys. But I was a professional, old-school woman from up North, who didn't go that way. So, she smiled and shrugged.

"I mean, some things you gotta pay for. But you don't charge nowhere near as much as these producers," she commented. "So, I ain't sweatin' it. Fuck it. I need somebody to talk to who won't judge me. Right?"

She eyed me again to test what my professional ethics were.

"I may not be here to judge you, but I am here to *help*, and if I can offer you a better suggestion on how to conduct your business, I will," I told her.

"That's fair. That's what I'm here for. But I get a lot more done with my career by myself now, and I just take *friends* with me. Because the reality is, guys are always gonna catch feelings for a pretty girl, particularly if they think she's available. But once you have all these other motherfuckas in the way, they start changing their minds on deals and shit."

"Okay, but"—I chose my words carefully to nail the point home to her—"business is still *business*. I mean, how would you feel if a handsome guy expected to get your restaurant cooking for free, just because he looked good?"

She pierced me with her eyes again. "I mean, that would be my *choice*. I could tell a motherfucka, 'No, you gon' pay for it.' Or I could give it to him for free. That's my *choice*. But if somebody else jumps in the fuckin' way, then it's *not* my choice. You know what I mean? I just wanna be in control of my own shit now. That's what I came up here to do in Atlanta."

I nodded to her, acknowledging her point. "Okay. I get that. But we all give up *some* control to people who can make better business decisions for us."

"Did you give up control of your shit?" she asked me.

"When I first started, yeah. I had to build my own client base and reputation. Nobody's gonna go to a girl fresh out of college."

"But once you had your own clients, you did your own shit, right?"

Cunning. She was a chess player, looking for her checkmate. I nodded to her from behind my desk. "Of course. We all want control once we know what we're doing."

She grinned. "Well, I know what I'm doing now. And what I found out is that guys are always looking for a hookup if they think they can get some. It's like a trade-off. And it never stops. I'm talkin' 'bout from the twenty-five-year-olds to the fifties. They all want some of this bright yellow pussy. And if you don't know how to manipulate that then shame on you."

I smiled, even though I didn't want to. I was sending her the wrong message. So, I quickly rebuked her logic.

"That actually feeds right into the Neanderthal philosophy that 'boys will be boys' and makes situations worse for young women and not better. We need more men to *behave*, and not act out like that."

She frowned immediately and said, "Please. You really think that women's lib shit is gon' stop guys from being guys? Music is the wrong fuckin' business for that. If you want guys to keep their dicks in their pants, then go be an elementary school teacher. Ain't no guys in there but math and gym instructors. But in the rap game . . . these guys out here all want pussy, and that's the rappers, the producers, the managers, promoters, fathers, uncles, cousins, you name it."

She counted them all off on her fingers, and I failed to hold in my chuckle. This girl, Mrs. Melody, was that raw with hers.

"Now tell me I'm lying," she challenged me.

"You may have to change your profession," I joked. "No, but seriously . . . you can actually set young women back by agreeing to those terms, because then they'll expect the next girl to do the same."

She frowned and disputed it. "No, they won't. Just like us, guys *choose* who they want to fuck with for free, and who they wanna charge. And if the next bitch walks in with her boyfriend, her manager, and her mother, and they're not attracted to her anyway, then they gon' charge the bitch.

"Everybody ain't getting shit for free. Please don't believe that," she continued. "It's just like at the clubs. The pretty bitches get in for free, and the ugly bitches gotta pay. Unless they come *early* or bring the pretty bitches with them. Then they get an ugly-bitch-for-free pass."

I mean, this girl *here* . . . What else could I say?

"If you have it all figured out already"—I opened my palms to her in surrender—"then what do you need me for?"

She shrugged. "Just somebody to talk to about my career. I mean, you don't cost that much. I got a hundred dollars for an hour."

I grinned at her, deviously. "Or, you could get one of your guys to pay for it, right?"

"Exactly. And I'll just tell him it makes me feel better. It's my therapy."

I continued to listen to her and pull it all together. "So . . . what happens when all of these freebies want a payoff?"

Mrs. Melody didn't flinch. "Then you fuck the ones you need. But you don't ever fuck 'em all. 'Cause see, some guys give you *more* before you fuck 'em, and other guys give you more *after*. You just have to figure out which ones are which."

At that point, my professionalism flew out the window. I just wanted to talk to this young girl and see where she was really coming from.

"What does your mother think about all of this?"

She looked appalled. "My *mother*? I don't talk to her about my shit. She got a regular job doing regular shit. And I would never wanna be like that. There's way too much in this world to do."

I was confused. Most kids follow in their parents' footsteps, unless she wasn't raised by her mother.

"Were you around your mother coming up?"

"Yeah, my mother and my older sister. They do what they do, and I do what I do."

Wow! Where was the remorse? Where was the guilt? Was it my job to make her feel guilty? She had me working.

"So . . . I don't know what to say," I admitted.

"Don't say anything, just let me talk," she responded. "That's therapy enough. Sometimes you just need to talk about shit."

"So, you *do* feel guilty if you need to talk about it," I concluded.

She paused. "I mean . . . not *totally* guilty, because these guys are what they are. I just need someone mature enough to bounce shit off of, because my girlfriends be on some other shit sometimes, and can't really relate."

"And you think *I* can relate?" I questioned her.

"I know you can," she answered. "In your profession, I know you hear a lot of crazy shit in here, so what I'm saying ain't new to you. You've heard it all. Right?"

"Not exactly. I hear new situations all the time," I explained.

"And each time you hear something *new,* you have to deal with it like a professional. That's what I meant by 'mature enough.' Some people just aren't built to deal with it. But you are. That's why you went into this profession. Right?"

She had a point. I could take it. Whatever she had to dish out to me. That was my job. She was right.

"So . . . what's your ultimate career goal, to get shit for *free* and fuck your way to the top with the right people?" I wanted to be as frank and as crass as she was.

She nodded and said, "Basically. I got three hot-ass songs out now, all because I made the right moves with the right people. And yeah, you're right. I *do* feel guilty about it sometimes. Sometimes, I'm like, 'What the fuck am I doing?' But then I think about the alternative of not getting shit done and not having hot songs out, because you turned motherfuckas down, and I don't feel guilty about it anymore.

"You know, you gotta do what you gotta do to be where you wanna be," she assessed. "And if not . . . then go get a regular fuckin' job. So, I don't complain, I just explain, and it's water down the fuckin' drain, with no strain on my brain . . . You want me to say that *ah-gain*?"

I smiled at her. The girl had me. I wanted to protect her and to be her big friend.

"Am I gonna be the one you tell everything to now?" I asked, still grinning.

She grinned back at me. "I'm trying to see. So far so good. But umm . . . I just feel more in *control* this way. Like . . . when a guy *thinks* he's gon' get some pussy, he'll wait for you. But if he don't think there's a possibility, then he's more likely to move on to the next bitch, and you lose the power of that moment. Then you're starting all over again. And I just got tired of that starting all over again shit.

"So, I learned how to say yes to the right people," she concluded. "And that changed everything. Shit really started happening for me."

I nodded to her. What could I say? The girl got me to put my professional guard down. She made a lot of sense. But I was still concerned about her. And she was right, I knew a lot about everything, maybe *too* much. So, I warned her.

"I hear your logic and philosophy, and it may have gotten you farther along than before, but life forces us to keep making the proper adjustments. And there's gonna come a time, very soon, when you don't *need* to do what you're doing right now. When you get on that Cardi B, Nicki Minaj, Megan Thee Stallion level, that's when sleeping around becomes a problem more than a method of advancement, because every industry guy will want the same treatment from you. You feel me?"

"Well, they're not gonna get it," she quipped with a chuckle. "But once I get on that Cardi, Nicki, and Megan's level, then you're right. I'll use more of my *money* to control shit. I'm doing more of that now. The more money I get, the more I pay for the shit I wanna pay for. Just like the guys do."

That was my first meeting and session with Mrs. Melody. And I felt really comfortable with her, as if I could do her a lot of good. She had climbed into my mental space.

CHARLES CLAY
Reflection 2

IN HIS MID-THIRTIES, CHARLES CLAY WAS THE VERBAL OPPOSITE OF Mrs. Melody. He didn't curse much at all and was a rather bland conversationalist. But his lack of conversation didn't matter. He was a highly sought-after film director in the Atlanta area that everyone wanted to work with. And he had landed in *my* office, of all places. I honestly had to stop myself from fanning out and stick to business. However, I at least had to tell him that I was an admirer.

"Ah, before we get started, I just wanted to say that I love your work. You're a special filmmaker. I really feel like I *know* the characters in your movies."

He grinned and nodded from my client's lounge chair. "Thank you. I appreciate it." He sat up tall and straight and crossed his legs.

He looked smaller than I imagined him from TV. And younger. He looked more like twenty-something than in his thirties. I could imagine him getting carded at the twenty-five-and-up nightclubs and bars. He even dressed like a younger man. He was overly neat, like a recent college grad who was trying to fit into the real world by wearing layers of what he thought was professional attire with freshly ironed shirts and sports jackets.

He had that look of heading over to the Gap to find the

cheapest professional shirts and khakis, while being intimidated by the stuffiness and high prices of upscale department stores.

I could imagine his entire outfit costing him less than a hundred dollars. He even wore the no-thrills Vans shoes that the skateboarders liked to wear. His shoes were a three on a man who was considered a nine. Charles Clay was that well respected in the film circles. But you wouldn't know it through his clothes.

"So, in our first conversations, you were saying that you wanted to figure out why people were taking you the wrong way," I began. We'd had a couple of phone calls before our first scheduled session, face-to-face.

"Yeah, I think I just need to talk more, actually," he responded, and chuckled. "You know, I tend to do more watching than talking. So, when I *do* talk, I don't really understand what they expected me to say. It's like, my conversation is different from what they expect."

I nodded back to him. "Yeah, that can happen a lot when people have expectations of someone they planned or hoped to meet. In other words, if they didn't know you and never planned to meet you, they wouldn't have any preconceived expectations of your conversation. But in your position, if you're in a room of twenty people who all want to meet you, and you don't get a chance to address them all as a group, then each person will have their own ideas of what they expect.

"You know what I mean?" I asked him. "I could expect you to be one way, and the next person will expect you to be another."

He stared at me before he commented, as if he was studying my face. "Yeah, but that puts a lot of additional pressure on *me* to read each person's mind."

I shook it off. "Not necessarily. You don't have to be what everyone expects you to be. Just be yourself."

He chuckled, awkwardly. "Yeah, but that seems to be the problem. I'm never in line with what they expect."

I paused. I needed a fresh example from him. "Okay . . . so, how do people respond to you? Explain it."

Before he answered, he looked around my office. "Would you happen to have a bottle or a cup of water?"

I paused. His sudden request for water annoyed me. I was ready for him to answer my question, not ask me for water. Nevertheless, I obliged.

"Oh, sure, I'll get you some water." Unfortunately, I didn't have any water in my office, so I had to walk out to the vending machines in the hallway and buy him a bottle. When I returned with it, he asked me if I had any lemon.

"I'm sorry, I meant to ask you when you walked out."

I nodded and handed him the bottle of water. "Okay, we have lemons in the cafeteria with the tea and coffee."

The problem was, the cafeteria was a farther walk than the vending machines. So, I began to think about the *time* as I walked. We hadn't really gotten into our session yet, and eleven minutes had gone by. By the time I returned to the room, we had burned sixteen minutes.

"Thank you." Charles poured the water into the coffee cup I handled him and squeezed fresh lemon juice into it. He seemed to take his time with everything.

When he finished his first sips of lemon water, we were at eighteen minutes.

"Okay, so . . . what I was asking you is how do people typically respond to you when you meet and talk to them? I need a clear example to work from."

He nodded and studied my face again. "This is really good water . . . But ah . . . I don't know. People don't tend to say much at all. They just listen. It's like, they don't know *what* to say, really. But then they'll make these little comments to my friends and associates."

"Comments like what?"

"Ahhh . . . well, he's really different. He's ahhh . . ."

He stopped and poured more of his water into the cup and squeezed more lemon juice. I had given him three lemon slices on a small paper plate. He took another sip as I continued to wait for him. We were at twenty-one minutes and still waiting. Suddenly, I found myself staring at the cup in his hand.

Would you stop it with the fucking water? I'm trying to do my job here! I fumed in my head. It was as if he was trying to infuriate me on purpose. I know that wasn't the case, but that's how it felt. His water distraction was wasting our time!

"Okay, so, what kind of comments are typically being made about you?" I pressed him.

He nodded and exhaled, but he still didn't answer. Not immediately.

"Ahhh . . . well, a lot of people say . . . he's arrogant. And it seems like he's not listening to me. And I don't know, I just have a lot going on in my head. So, maybe I'm *not* listening. And they're all just there in front of me."

I felt the same way with him. You feel like you're a production assistant waiting around for him to tell you what to do for his next movie scene. His meditative pacing and dismissiveness were mechanisms of control. And it made you feel insignificant, as if his time and thoughts were far more important than yours. Maybe it was unfair to think of him that way, but you did it anyway because he's a popular and successful director.

"Okay, I can *feel* what's going on now," I told him. "You need to do more than just talk to people, you need to be fully engaged. But if you're gonna walk around in your own world and not hear what they're saying to you, then you're gonna keep getting what you've been getting. And it's not about what you say, it's more about how they *feel.*

"If you make people feel like they're not important in the little time they have with you, then yeah, they're gonna make their negative comments, because many people are insecure, particularly when up against a person of your stature," I explained. "So, in their defense, they are going to think negatively about you, because you made them feel small, which damages their egos."

He nodded to me, taking it all in. "I see. That's fascinating. So, they're judging me based on how they feel about themselves."

I didn't agree with his overly simplified logic. It sounded self-serving in defense of his own ego. So, I added my professional spin to it.

"Not necessarily. People come to you looking for positive affirmation. They're not looking to be negative. They admire you. So, you want to give them a *positive* experience and not a *negative* one. And that takes work. That's why network marketing people talk about working the room," I told him. "That's essentially what you're doing. And you have to keep that in mind when you meet new people."

He stared at my face again. "So, I'm *working* at my public events and appearances?"

He sounded puzzled by it, as if he had never heard of the idea of working a room before. Any media training would teach you that managing your public perception is important, particularly if you're a public figure. And he was a popular public figure.

"Have you had media training before?" I asked him.

"Of course, I've had media training. But this is about the general *public*, not the media," he argued.

"Well, who do you think the media does their jobs for?" I questioned.

He continued to search my face for answers and shrugged. "I guess the editors, program directors, television producers . . ."

His answer was unbelievable. He totally missed my point. I was rapidly losing respect for this man. Was he really the director, Charles Clay, or a look-alike imposter?

I cut him off and said, "No, the media does their jobs to benefit the general *public*. Newspapers, radio, and television are all reporting to the *people*, not to themselves. Otherwise, what is the point?"

I don't know if he had somewhere else to go, but when he looked down at the gold watch on his wrist, he continued to irritate me.

"You have another appointment after this?" I asked.

He nodded. "I do."

At least I had gotten to the bottom of his issue, and quickly. I nodded back from my desk and said, "Okay. Well, you have *work* to do," I emphasized.

He looked confused again. "We're not done yet, are we?"

Actually, I was done. I didn't need to hear anything else from him. We were thirty-five minutes in, and I had heard enough. I wanted to get him out of my office before I became rude.

"Is there anything else you would like to tell me?" I asked him.

"Well, we have an *hour*, right?" he complained, still eyeing his watch.

"Not if we already know what the issue is. We can wrap this up right now. You want a twenty-five-minute discount?"

I meant it too. I'd had enough of that man. I could see why people called him arrogant. He had rubbed me the wrong way while I was trying to help him.

Charles looked at me and chuckled, as if he got a kick out of my candor.

He said, "I like you. You're straight to the point."

"Did you expect me to be some other way?" I commented. "This is my profession. You're paying me to assess the problem and tell you what needs to happen to try and fix it. And I've done that."

He took another patient sip of his water and said, "Have you ever acted in a film before?"

The question surprised me. I wasn't expecting him to go there. I was prepared for a rant about respecting people's time and professions. I was even set to call him an *asshole* to his face if he forced me to. Regardless of my degrees, at the end of the day, I was from Camden, New Jersey, and we didn't *play* that disrespect shit! But once he asked me about acting in a movie . . . I backed down and went soft.

"No, I've never been in a movie before. Why?"

He continued to stare me down, as if looking through a camera lens. And it finally broke me. All of a sudden, I started wondering what he thought about me. I felt alone onstage with the lights and cameras in my face . . . waiting.

He said, "I'm just thinking. I could have a few different roles for you. You're smart and professional, but I can tell you have a *mean* streak in you too. Where are you from?"

I said it proudly. "Camden, New Jersey."

"Oh, right next to Philly. I've been there. Yeah, I could use that."

I froze with exhilaration and felt silly. After all of that, his ass had me grinning.

"And what did you think about Camden?" I asked him.

"It's a tough city. And with you guys being right next to Philly, it's like you have something to *prove.* So, I understand you much better now," he answered.

I was quite sure I told him I was from Camden on one of our previous phone calls. But maybe he wasn't listening again.

Anyway . . . once he started talking about me acting in his movies, it changed my whole disposition, and I forgot about how disengaged he was earlier. In fact, that's what he needed to do with everyone, make them feel special. But of course, he couldn't offer everyone a movie role . . . Or could he?

Charles looked down at his watch again. "It looks like we have another twenty minutes. What was your favorite movie I've directed?"

The man had directed at least a dozen films, but I had only seen six.

"*Catch a Fallen Star,*" I answered. "I could relate the most to that one."

"Ah, yes, Brenda Stewart. She had some tough times. Has your life been that tough?"

I paused again. How much of my personal story did I want to tell him? I became coy with a smile.

"You said we only had twenty minutes left, but that story would be two hours," I joked.

He smiled back at me and chuckled. He was extra handsome when he allowed himself to pay attention. He had me in there feeling like a cougar. He was at least ten years my junior, but like I said, he looked *twenty* years younger.

He said, "Well, we could start it. No great story is told in one sitting anyway. And we're gonna do this *more,* right?"

I had hoped so, but after our first twenty minutes of nothing, I wasn't sure.

I said, "It's up to you. If you need more counseling, I'm here for it. You just have to remind yourself to be more attentive when you're speaking to people. Giving someone your undivided attention can really go a long way. So, get *used* to that."

He grinned and said, "I will. And I can get used to you telling me what time it is from Camden, New Jersey," he added. "Sometimes you just need a person who can set you *straight* instead of kissing your ass all the time, if I'm allowed to be frank about it."

I chuckled and accepted it. "Go right ahead. That's what I'm here for. Give me all of your honesty."

He said, "Okay," and paused. Then he hit me with this. "You know, I've always had a strong attraction to older professional women. Even the nurses turned me on when I was a kid. And I'd be sitting up in the room with a hard-on under the sheets. It was so embarrassing, you know. But I couldn't help myself."

I froze. What the hell was I supposed to say to that? It was embarrassing for me to hear it, especially while sitting there thinking like a cougar. I started to wonder if he had a hard-on while sitting there in my lounge chair.

I mumbled, "Okay," and left his comment alone.

But he didn't. Charles added kerosene to an awkward fire.

"So . . . when do we do this again?"

DARK & MOODY

Reflection 3

When I left Camden and headed off to college down here at Clarke Atlanta University in the 1990s, we had plenty of older students and recent graduates who were all into the conspiracy theories of the Illuminati, the Rothschilds, the Rockefellers, and all of that kind of stuff. Of course, with us being at an HBCU (Historically Black College and University), surrounded by two others at Spelman and Morehouse, we all understood that America wasn't exactly about pushing Black people forward, but I refused to believe there were secret forces trying to hold every single one of us back. It just seemed like an impossible amount of work. How could anyone ever know exactly what Black person is going to be the most dangerous to White society?

People with the most potential to succeed fall off every day, replaced by those you would have never thought of becoming successful.

I look at both Jay-Z and Kanye West becoming billionaires as prime examples. Shawn "Jay-Z" Carter was your typical New York City drug dealer with a side interest in rap music. Or maybe he was an aspiring rapper with a side interest in selling drugs. Either way, guys like him die and go to jail every day. And their fatality and imprisonment has more to do with the regular jealousy, envy, competition, and drug turf wars in the 'hood than any secret force of White people out to get them. One could argue that the fatalistic elements of our inner-city neighborhoods are all set up by "the powers that be" to begin with, but so was everything else in America if you want to use that logic. So, where do the conspiracy theories end, and where does regular life begin?

Then you have Kanye West, a backpacking, hip-hop loner from Chicago with a tendency to spazz out at anyone or anything that he has a conflict with. You could see Kanye coming a mile away with his backpack and no bodyguards. He would be the easiest Black man to kill. Yet, Kanye was able to climb to billionaire status and date international models. Was it because he had sided several times with Donald Trump and the right wing, or did he offer up the "blood sacrifice" of his mother for his success?

I bring all of this up because my next client was into it all. She was a bisexual music producer who called herself Dark & Moody. She specialized in what she called "gothic funk" music, while refusing to give me her real name.

"What does my legal name matter? As long as I respond to you when you call me, it's all good, right? I could call myself Jack & Jill. What does it matter?"

I shrugged and said, "Okay," as she relaxed in my office lounge chair.

She was in her early thirties and a chocolate cutie with height. She had played basketball in high school and in college in Louisiana. She had been producing beats for eight years and had landed a few major songs. But she was unsatisfied with the pay and her production credit.

"The industry is always trying to steal your shit and not pay you what you deserve. Especially if you're a Black woman."

She wore a blue jeans denim outfit with her pants and jacket littered by record company logos. She had Sony Music, Warner Records, Universal Records, Arista, Def Jam, Bad Boy, Death Row, So So Def, Roc Nation, Aftermath, Shady Records, G-Unit, RuffHouse, Cash Money Millionaires, Rap-A-Lot, Murder Inc., you name it, all over her blue jeans jacket and pants. It reminded me of the old-school baseball jackets that spotlighted all of the Major League Baseball logos. I thought the idea was rather unique. So, I told her.

"I really like what you did with your clothes. You look like a walking billboard for the record labels. They need to sponsor you for doing that," I suggested.

"I know, right? But they don't care. They would tell me not to use their logos at all if it was up to them," she responded.

She had sent me some of her music to listen to, and it was indeed dark and moody with spooky organs and hammering drums. Most of it sounded like a loud, science fiction horror movie to be honest. It wasn't my cup of tea. But the young people would like it. They loved when the music was considered "hard." And that's exactly what Dark & Moody was cooking, hard and spooky beats.

I asked her, "Have you ever heard of Mrs. Melody?"

She nodded. "Yeah, I've heard of her. She's cute. I'd do her in a heartbeat," she added.

I grinned and left that alone. "What do you think about her music?"

Dark & Moody shrugged. "I mean, she does sex music. Everybody's doing that now. People just follow what they think they can make money off of with no originality."

I didn't speak up to dispute it. She was probably right.

"Okay, so . . . you're trying to figure out a way to cope with the frustrations of the music industry?" I asked her. That seemed to be her angle for our first conversation.

"Yeah, that and some other things."

"What other things are you dealing with?"

"Family, friends, bills, lovers, you name it."

"So, it's not just the music that you're concerned with?"

"Oh, heck no. The music is my sanctuary," she answered. "I love making music. I'm just trying to get more out of it in business. It's everything *else* that's fucking with me. So, I'm trying to figure out who I need to sacrifice to get ahead."

That comment got a rise out of me. "Excuse me? Who you need to *sacrifice?*"

She said it almost casually, as if that kind of talk was normal for her.

"Yeah, you've never heard of blood sacrifices and the Illuminati?"

I paused. I wanted to be extra careful with my words and my advice to this young woman.

"Ahhh . . . if you've ever gone to college, then you've *definitely* heard of it. But I wouldn't want to take too much of that to heart. Especially when you start talking about 'blood sacrifices.' I think that's all a bit extreme."

"You don't believe in it?" she asked me.

"What, the Illuminati, or the sacrifices?"

"Both."

I didn't like her line of questions. I didn't want to go there. But it was my job to investigate her mind.

"Is that what you want to talk to me about?" I questioned. "Because I'm not an expert on any of that. You may want to go see a tarot card reader," I joked. I was attempting to lighten up the mood.

She smiled and said, "I tried that before. I've tried a little bit of everything."

"And what did you find out?"

She continued to smile. "That I'm destined for greatness. All I need is one sacrifice."

When she repeated that, I was ready to end our session. But I felt a need to advise her against talking that way.

"Are you trying to fuck with me, or are you serious?" I asked her.

"Oh, I'm *dead* serious. Pun intended," she responded.

That was enough. I said, "Okay, I'm feeling very uncomfortable with this. Are you fucking crazy or what? This is not a *game.*"

"I know it's not. And I'm not here for games."

I studied her demeanor and she remained unnerved by it. That scared the hell out of me. This girl was *serious.* I said, "Well, I hope you don't think I'm gonna *condone* you doing anything like that. Why would you even tell me this?"

"I figured you could help me."

"Yeah, help you not to *do it.* But I'm not gonna help you with anything else if you're in here talking about sacrificing *people* and shit."

I was appalled. I sat there and stared at her from across my desk. I asked myself, *What would she say or do if I made a comment about the police? What is she thinking? I'm not getting involved in this shit!*

She said, "I'm really just trying to take things to the next level."

"By committing a *murder*?"

She paused and thought about it. "A blood sacrifice isn't necessarily murder. We could just *pray* on someone dying."

I cringed. "And you would be fine with that?"

She paused again. Then she said, "People die every day."

I asked myself, *Lord, what is this world coming to?*

"So, you would *pray* for someone else to *die* just so you could become successful?" I put it to her that simple so she could hear it out loud, because it sounded ridiculous!

Then she broke down and cried, sinking her face into her hands. "I just want it that bad. I just wanna be a success."

"You *are* a success," I told her. "You've graduated from college. You're doing your music. You've landed big songs. You just have to keep doing it with optimism and not pessimism. You have to *know* that you're gonna succeed without harming other people. That way you don't end up with a blood diamond that will never shine clearly.

"You understand me? You don't want a career like that," I told her. "What if someone wanted to sacrifice *you* for their success? Does it just go on and on? Think about it."

She wiped her tears away with her hands and sniffed. "I just . . . I just want it."

I continued to watch her carefully from across my desk. I said, "We all want it. That's the American way. You think I don't want things? But I'm not sitting here thinking about *killing* people to get it. That's *crazy*."

"We all are crazy. People just don't want to admit it," she countered.

There was a silence that swept through the room that I didn't like. I felt like I should have had an immediate response to her, but I didn't. Finally, I mumbled, "Yeah, but you can't act out on it. You have to try and keep your sanity. You have to control yourself. We *all* do."

She looked hard into my eyes as if sending me a message. "Control is what we all want. Even when you have *power* you have to control it. And if I had more control . . . then I wouldn't have to sacrifice people. I could just make shit happen. You know?"

There was silence in the room again. I didn't disagree with her. I had been studying control issues for most of my life, and for all of my professional career. And she was right. Control was everything. Who presses the buttons to make things go in life? Who ignites the fire? Who controls the algorithms?

That was Dark & Moody's point. She was willing to do anything to have it. And her hunger for it was admirable; I just didn't like her choice of method.

As I got caught up in my own thoughts, she asked me, "What are you thinking about?"

Could I be honest with her . . . or not?

"I'm thinking of how I could have more control in my own life."

Her frown slowly turned into a grin. "Okay . . . so, we have something in common."

I nodded. "I guess we do."

JOSEPH DRAKE

Reflection 4

THAT SAME EVENING, I LISTENED TO DARK & MOODY'S GOTHIC funk music while on a drive to my next session. This guy, Joseph Drake, was a venture capitalist, and because of his jammed schedule, he offered to pay me *double* to come out to him after hours. So, instead of doing my office at three, I was doing his building at seven.

While on my drive east on Interstate 20 for 285 North to Stone Mountain, the gothic funk music thumped in my ears like a soundtrack. There was this one particular production that became my favorite. Dark & Moody listed it as "Ghetto Opera" in her files. And that's exactly what it sounded like, thick, pounding drums, eerie strings, a rhythmic bass line, and female harmonies in the background, wailing like suffering angels on a street corner.

Dark, spooky, and addictive, I set the track on repeat and imagined myself traveling to Count Dracula's castle in a horse carriage after midnight in Transylvania. Maybe I shouldn't have been listening to this music before my first session with Joseph Drake. It was giving me the wrong vision of the man before I even met him. Or . . . maybe it was a prelude of things to come.

When I arrived in the parking lot of his twelve-story, gray-brick building, most of the cars had already gone. Fortunately, the front door was still open without me needing to be buzzed in. They had a lone security guard inside the lobby area next to the elevators. He sat behind a sign-in desk with an open booklet of names in front of him.

"ID please," he asked me. He was a Black man in his thirties, well shaved and groomed in an all-black security uniform. And he was licensed to carry a gun on his right hip.

I don't know if the gun made me feel safer or slightly alarmed. It didn't seem like a building or an area where you would need armed security. But I guess it was better to be safe than sorry. This guy was a venture capitalist with plenty of money, so maybe he thought someone would plan to kidnap him and hold him for ransom.

I blew off my trepidation and pulled out my ID to sign in to the building.

"Who are you here to see?" the security guard asked.

"Joseph Drake."

He smiled and nodded. "Okay, good luck."

Maybe I was reading too much into things, but the smile and "good luck" felt peculiar. Good luck for what? I wasn't asking him for any investment money on a project, and he had already paid me to be there for our first session. What else was I getting myself into where I needed luck?

The first question I wanted to ask Mr. Drake, face-to-face, was why he had chosen me to counsel with? I'm quite sure the multimillionaire's team had a full Rolodex of professionals in every field to deal with. He didn't have to do anything with me. But I was grateful for it.

The ride up the elevator to the twelfth floor presented more music, a soft instrumental featuring a very active flute. I grinned, imagining what Dark & Moody would have thought of it.

"That shit is *soft,* man," I could imagine her commenting. "That's typical White people music with no emotion in it."

I'd then remind her that rock, grunge, garage, acid, and gothic—without the funk—were all considered "White people music" as well. Those genres were not soft and were packed with emotion. But as I stepped through the opening doors at the top floor of the building, what the elevator music did represent was controlled mood. It was the music of a productive office, played to make you feel light, sociable, and optimistic, the opposite of heavy, antisocial, and depressed.

I felt optimistic myself as I walked up to a reception desk, where a pretty blonde in her twenties greeted me.

"Dr. Victoria Benning?"

I loved how respectfully she said my name. She made me sound so . . . *distinguished.*

"Yes," I answered.

She smiled. "Okay, Joe is looking forward to seeing you. Right this way."

She stepped out from behind her reception booth and led me down a hallway, while I continued to psychoanalyze everything.

From what she had stated, her boss, "Joe," was looking forward to *seeing* me as opposed to *meeting* me. Or maybe that was a simple misuse of her words.

As she led me down the hallway, I couldn't help staring at this White girl's firm ass in a beige skirt. She had more ass than I *ever* had, and it was perfectly round with no panty lines. She was either wearing a G-string or nothing at all.

I immediately wondered if Joe was fucking this pretty, young blonde receptionist with the perfect ass after hours. In my profession, I learned that humans were capable of anything and everything. And she seemed too chipper at seven o'clock at night for it to be strictly work related.

"She's here," she announced to him, while swinging open his office door at the back end of the hallway.

Joe was still on a phone call when we walked in. He was sitting behind a massive desk with a clear view of the 285 beltway below. With his window facing the south, he also had a perfect view of the sunrise to the left and the sunset to the right. I envied his office view immediately. My only view crashed into the walls of the building that stood beside me.

Once we invaded his room, he looked up and addressed his call. "Hey, let me reach you later. I have a meeting here at the office."

Joseph Drake stood from his black leather office chair to greet me. He was a chiseled, forty-something White man in a charcoal-gray suit with a white dress shirt and no tie. He had a mane of dark brown hair combed to the back, like an old-school Italian, but with blue eyes. Being from Camden, New Jersey—with a lot of time spent in Philadelphia—I knew the Italian look, and Joe had it. He even had a tan. He was physically imposing, handsome and rugged, like an assertive corporate golfer capable of playing a lot of rounds.

He extended his hand to mine and said, "Nice to meet you, Victoria."

I grinned, shook his hand, and responded, "Likewise."

"I'll be out front if you need me," his receptionist said as she walked out.

"Close the door behind you, Rochelle," he told her.

Rochelle did it without comment, and I immediately felt awkward inside the room alone with him. I was used to meeting clients in the comfortable setup of my own office.

"I guess this is awkward for you being on that side of the desk instead of this side, right? You wanna use my desk and have me sit over there?"

He was reading my mind, so I chuckled at it. "I don't know if that's going to make a big difference. I would still feel out of place in your chair. So, let's just . . . hold our positions and get through it."

He shrugged and said, "Okay," and retook his seat, while I sat in the office chair across from his desk and pulled out my notebook with his name in it.

"So, Camden, New Jersey, huh? How do you like it down here?" he started.

"I've been here for nearly thirty years now. It's home," I answered.

"Really? I still don't call this place home. I'm originally from Connecticut."

I nodded. "I figured you were from up North somewhere. Connecticut fits you."

"Yeah, UConn and Columbia to your Clarke Atlanta and Georgia Tech."

I guess he had done his homework on me. But I couldn't find much of anything on him. His website and social media links were all about his business, Capital Exposure Unlimited.

I said, "I'm assuming that you're very private, because I couldn't find anything on you online."

He laughed deeply and proudly, as if mocking the world. "Yeah, I like it that way. When you get to a certain level of income, résumés don't matter anymore. Either you know the business, or you don't."

"Do you think I know the business?" I asked him.

"Do you?" he asked me back.

"I don't know, I'm just wondering why you chose me?"

He frowned and said, "Why not? Why not you? You're capable. Would you rather I do this with someone else?"

White men had a confidence in business that was unmatched. And it wasn't viewed as arrogant or cocky with them, it was more natural. They had been in dominant business positions for years.

I answered, "No, I can handle it. Whatever you have for me," and chuckled.

"Good, so you won't mind signing my confidentiality form."

Just like that, he slid a legal document over his desk for me to sign. And it wasn't a big document. It was only two pages long, but it still surprised me. I just didn't expect it. Nevertheless, most of my work was in confidence anyway. So, I read his two-page document, signed it, and dated it.

Mr. Drake countersigned it and made a copy for me from his fax machine.

"Good, we got that out of the way. I just don't want any confusions about anything I may have to say to you. And it's all in confidence. All right?"

I smiled. We were dealing with that one word again. *Control.* There I was at his office, on his time, signing his paperwork, at his building. I began to wonder how much of that was planned, because it felt like *all* of it.

"It must be something heavy you're planning to lay on me," I joked. I felt like a pigeon in a cage.

He laughed hard and loud again, as if mocking me. He said, "I need a drink. You need one?" He stood and walked over to a minibar in the corner of the room, where he pulled out a bottle of Rémy Martin Cognac. Then he grabbed two glasses as if I had said yes already.

"You do drink, right?" he asked.

"Usually not at the office," I answered.

"Well, you're not at your office now. You're at *mine.* So, loosen up and have a drink."

He was a White man all right. They dictate all of the terms, even when they're trying to be nice to you. But what the hell? I wanted to see where he was trying to take me. I was curious.

"All right, I'll have a drink. I just hope I don't crash on my way home tonight?" I joked again. Sarcasm was my only defense.

Mr. Drake paused and eyed me with concern. "Wait a minute. You can't handle your alcohol? I'm not gonna have you drink a lot, just a glass or two to take the edge off."

"I don't have any edge to take off. I had a good drive over here and I'm feeling good," I told him.

He nodded and set one of the glasses down. "All right, no drinks for you. You're straight by the book and I don't want to ruin your comfort zone."

"I can have *one* drink," I commented.

He continued to eye me. "Are you sure?"

I grinned at him. "I'm not a *child.* I can handle a drink," I confirmed.

"All right." He picked up the second glass, poured me a quarter of Cognac, poured three quarters for his, and brought both drinks over. He even gave me a toast. "Bottoms up."

Joe drowned his drink like water before I could even sip mine.

"Someone's a little *thirsty* in here," I joked.

He looked over at me and nodded, pensively. "I see you have a sense of humor."

I took a sip of my drink and said, "Yeah, that tends to pop right out of me." *Especially when I'm on guard,* I thought. We hadn't gotten anywhere near starting our session yet. And before I knew it, it was 7:27, so I became pressed.

"So . . . what exactly do you want to talk to me about?"

As soon as I asked him the question, I felt lightheaded and dizzy. I looked back at my glass to see how much alcohol I had left.

That shouldn't have been enough to get me dizzy, I pondered. I began to wonder if he had spiked my drink with something. *This is very unprofessional,* I told myself. I was embarrassed and determined to pull myself back together.

Joe sat back in his office chair with the Rémy Martin out in front of him on the desk.

He said, "Okay, here's the thing," and took a sip of his *third* drink already. "My family was originally from South Carolina, and we owned a whole lot of slaves."

As soon as his words hit my ears, I regretted being there. *Here we go with this shit,* I told myself. A White man's confession to Black people is the last thing you ever want to hear. It's always awkward, typically forced on you, and it usually comes from out of nowhere. And how come they always have to be *drunk* before they decide to do it?

Joseph Drake rambled on about his family history in South Carolina, but I didn't comprehend much of it. Half of me ignored him, while the other half tried to recuperate from the strong shot of Cognac. But I did hear his ending.

He said, "Now I wanna try and see how I can get a bunch of Black businesses to qualify for this capital that I have. I feel like it's only right, you know."

The key word was *qualify*. It seemed like we never qualified for the big money, only for the smaller money. We only qualified for the pebbles and crumbs.

I told him, "Get the money for yourself and just give it to

them. Then you can deal with Black businesses directly instead of these unseen boards getting in the way."

I didn't know a lot about corporate business, but I knew enough. I knew how they played the game of passing the buck, so you never knew exactly who or what had turned you down. And when they operated on a checks and balances system, you could pass three checks and fail the fourth. The only way to get past it was to find a qualifying cosigner, and that's what Drake was if he agreed to do it.

He said, "That would put a hell of lot of responsibility on me."

"And," I responded, "you're the one sitting in here feeling guilty about the past, right? Well, do something about it. Talking about *trying* means nothing. You need to *succeed* at it. So, you take on the business responsibility and set up your own criteria."

He eyed me across his desk and started giggling. "You're crazy. I'm not gonna do that. That would jeopardize my whole career."

"Well, what else do you want me to say in here? You know most of these businesses aren't gonna qualify for that money. The ones who will already have it. And they are not gonna share with the ones who don't. It'll be the same nonsense all over again with the haves and the have-nots."

On the same day that Dark & Moody talked about offering up blood sacrifices to succeed in life, I end up in a counseling session with a guilty rich White man who had access to plenty of money but refused to do what was needed to get it. I couldn't believe I was even in that conversation with him. All he did was make me angry and more cynical.

It was that damn hard for Black people to get their hands on any money, even when these assholes felt *guilty* about it. So, once it hit eight fifteen, I stood up and was ready to go. That man had wasted my damn time and was getting under my skin. There was nothing else to talk about in there. Corporate America really was like Dracula. They sucked your blood out and turned you into zombies.

"Where are you going?" Joe asked me.

"I'm going home. I just gave you an hour, and you wasted most of it *drinking*."

"All right, let's follow up next week sometime. I need to think about what you said and the ideas that you have."

I turned and faced him from the doorway. "Are you really gonna consider it? Because I could meet with a few Black businesses and come up with *more* ideas, if you really want them to qualify. But if you're not gonna go out of your way to make that happen . . . then what's the point? And I'm not gonna sit in here for you to patronize me for two hundred dollars, while you're sitting over there on two hundred million."

He heard my number and cringed. "Two hundred *million*. Oh, we got a lot more on the table than that," he boasted.

I stared at him and shook my head. Maybe Dark & Moody needed to sacrifice someone like *him*. It all felt like a frustrating tease. If you're not willing to do what's needed, then why even bring it up?

Before I left his office, I told him, "I had no idea what you planned to discuss with me this evening, but I surely wasn't thinking *this*. And all you did was irritate me while pretending to feel guilty. So, I pray for you."

"Hey," he mumbled as I walked out. "Hey . . ."

When I reached Rochelle out front, she asked me, "How did it go?"

"How does it go with you?" I asked her back.

The blonde receptionist looked confused. "Excuse me?"

I waved her off with my right hand. "Don't worry about it. It doesn't matter."

I walked back to the elevators and pressed the button for down, hoping to get out of there as quickly as possible. I felt used and manipulated, but that wasn't the first time. There had been plenty of people who had used my kindness and curiosity for a weakness.

There are vultures in this world that you can't do anything about. And when they see you stranded on the side of the road with no food, water, or gas, they swoop right down to get you, and you have to fight them off to survive. So, it was a good thing I was from Camden. I still knew how to fight.

As I climbed back into my car to drive off, I thought of playing Dark & Moody's music again. I initially didn't like it, but as I continued to play it and think about my current circumstances, the music began to make a lot of sense to me, so I continued to listen to it. I guess I was in a dark and moody mindset myself.

TYRELL HODGE

Reflection 5

TYRELL HODGE WAS A FRUSTRATED SCREENWRITER IN HIS FORTIES, who had success early on in his career and not much since. He was another Black Hollywood boy wonder in his twenties, along with John Singleton, the Hughes brothers, and Matty Rich. But his early success as a screenwriter didn't translate into his thirties or forties, which left him irritated and mad at the world.

He said, "It's not that I don't have the *skills* anymore. I just can't get these producers to say yes to the new projects. It's almost like, if it's not their people doing it, then they wanna control *your* shit. But I already got my own ideas. So, I just need the money to hire my own people now," he explained in our session at my office.

That was less than a week after my skirmish with Joseph Drake, so ideas about getting Black businesspeople money was still fresh on my mind. And since I had already known Tyrell for a few years, I could be more relaxed and casual with him.

Wearing a black-and-white Adidas sweatsuit, with a young man's tapered haircut, Tyrell was in a dark and moody place himself, *very* moody. People joked that he was liable to snap at the mailman for not delivering his mail on time. He reacted to everything and everyone. He couldn't seem to help himself. He was on response overdrive to anything he perceived as negative energy, which transformed every conversation into a battle.

"Have you tried to find your own investors?" I asked him.

"Of course I have. But a lot of these guys want you to have the film started already," he answered. "Then they come in as the saviors to help you finish it, while trying to claim a big chunk of the project, because they know you need the money."

Still athletic from playing multiple sports in high school and college, Tyrell was one of those guys who felt he had an answer or an explanation for everything. He had been a point guard in basketball, a quarterback in football, and an anchor on the track team, so he was used to being the man in charge. But now he couldn't get out of his own way to get something done with other people, where he wasn't in charge.

I suggested, "How about giving up one of your less popular projects to see what the producers would do with it."

He said, "I tried that already. And you know what happened . . . ? *Nothing.* Because if you don't have a committed team to push it forward, it just sets there, like a bill on Capitol Hill, trying to become a law."

I smiled, reflecting on the Schoolhouse Rock! song and cartoon from the seventies. Tyrell and I were closer in age and from the same generation. But he was from the Chicago area with admiration for Eric Monte, the writer of the classic *Cooley High* movie. We had talked about it in our cell phone briefing before the session.

"Do you feel like someone is blackballing you in the industry?" I questioned. "How about writing for Tyler Perry or something?"

I was just reaching to see how he would respond.

Tyrell frowned and repeated, "Tyler Perry? Is Jordan Peele writing for Tyler Perry? Is Spike Lee writing for Tyler Perry? Is Keenan Ivory Wayans writing for Tyler Perry?"

I grinned and shook my head. He sounded obnoxious. "They all have their own deals already, but you don't. So, you need to *humble* yourself and work your way back up."

"I *am* humbled. Didn't I tell you I'm driving PDS every day now? How humbling is *that*?" he responded. "And there's plenty of people who recognize me here in Atlanta."

PDS was a professional driver service that catered to a higher clientele.

"Well, that's a good thing. People still know who you are," I commented.

He stared at me for a moment of silence. "Are you trying to be sarcastic?"

"No. It *is* a good thing that people still notice you. You don't think so?"

He paused and took a deep breath. "I just need the money to do *one* solid project, man. That's all I'm asking for. Then I can build from there."

"Well, that's not gonna happen if you keep arguing with people and being difficult," I told him. "Nobody likes that extra aggravation."

"I don't go out of my way to argue with people. People just rub me the wrong way by saying the wrong shit."

"And you're never able to just ignore it and move on? Because you really don't need to respond to *everything*. Every issue is not that serious."

He exhaled and nodded, agreeing with me. "Yeah, you're right. I'm just fucking *pissed* that I can't make shit go on my own. I'm just *tired* of needing all these other motherfuckers to make shit happen."

"Well, welcome to the world, brother. We *all* hate that," I told him. I was just about to mention Joseph Drake and his desire to allocate major capital to Black businesses, but I remembered to bite my tongue. He had me sign a confidentiality agreement, and I still needed to work with him on how to get it all done. So, I kept the information to myself.

I said, "It'll happen for you. You just have to stay at it."

Tyrell looked up at the ceiling in my office and mumbled, "I just feel like I'm running out of time. Everything is for these young people now."

"And you used to *be* one of them," I reminded him. "Now you're more seasoned. And you just have to stay on that bike, or that treadmill, and keep your cool until something pops for you."

Sometimes I sounded more like a motivational speaker than a shrink. I just wanted people to *win,* and Tyrell's frustrations were obvious.

He said, "Hell, I can't even get my lady to say yes to me now. Things are just fucked up all the way around."

"What did you do?" I asked him curiously.

"Got caught cheating," he answered. "You just feel like you need something extra to fill the void of so many failures, you know. So, every little victory counts to keep you going?"

I didn't comment on that. Far too many men still looked at women as conquests, like we were some kind of ego booster fuel. That attitude from men has gone on for a long time.

"How long has it been?" I continued.

"Man, she's *always* been that way. It's like the method she finds the most successful to control me. So, she puts her panties on lockdown. And I hate that shit! I don't try to control her like that. When she needs money, I just give it to her. If I got it."

He fell into another moment of silence. I could tell he was distressed. He was borderline manic-depressive, where you fluctuate from high, ecstatic energy to low, depressive energy. In fact, a large percentage of celebrities, athletes, and businesspeople suffered from it as a part of their everyday lifestyles. They were constantly up and down depending on the success and failures of their projects and aspirations, and they were more intimately involved in their careers than people who worked your typical nine-to-fives.

"Are you okay?" I asked through his silence.

Tyrell shook his head and didn't answer. Not immediately. Then he said, "Am I wrong for wanting what I want in America? That's the American way, right? We *all* want what we want. People just like to lie about it with that humble talk shit."

I grinned. At least he was consistent. I said, "Well, right now you don't have a *choice* but to be humble because you're not in the position you want to be in. And maybe when you're finally back in it, you'll be humble."

"Yeah, if I ever get another opportunity to do something to be humble about."

"Oh, you will. I have faith in you. Just be patient and keep working."

"And keep *driving* too," he added. "This PDS shit is the only consistent hustle that pays the bills. Everything else be sometiming."

As he continued to talk, all kinds of ideas began to flood my mind.

"Have you ever thought about working on a project with Charles Clay?"

Tyrell frowned as soon as I said the name. "Aw, man, that asshole ain't thinking about working on a project with anybody unless it's already paid for. That's the problem I have now. I save up just enough to shoot a short pilot, but not enough to keep it going. Then an asshole like him would tell me to get the rest of the money before he budges on it."

"What about writing and shooting a cheap horror movie? You could even cast a few of these rappers and singers who are all over Atlanta."

I was thinking about Dark & Moody's gothic funk music and Mrs. Melody's acting capabilities. I was certain that she could do it. Her personality was natural for acting. I had other clients and associates who were actors and musicians in the Atlanta area as well, who could fill out the rest of the cast.

Hell, I began to think like a producer myself. I was diving all into the possibilities.

Tyrell said, "No matter what you do, you're gonna need *money* to do it. And once you run out of it, ain't nobody else putting it on the table for you."

I said, "Well, how come these kids are able to get so much done? They don't have any money."

"Yeah, and what they're doing ain't quality shit, either. It's *potential*," he responded. "That's the reason why they worked with me years ago. You show your potential early, and they'll work with you. But that's only when you're *young* and don't know any better. They figure they can control you then. But they don't treat you the same when you're older. Now you're a problem because you have your own ideas and you know how you want to execute them."

"Well, didn't you have your own ideas when you were young? I don't understand the difference," I lied. I understood *exactly* what he was saying. It was always easier to control a kid just coming into the business with fresh ideas than an adult who knows the game already. It was similar to older men dating much younger women. These older guys considered it fun, easier, and much less costly than an older woman with kids, baggage, and lifelong issues. Guys with real money were the last ones to deal with all of that. And when they could afford a girl like Mrs. Melody, that's who they went after. She knew it as well.

All of these strategic dots began to connect in my head while counseling Tyrell that early afternoon in my office. Then he looked at his cell phone and stood abruptly from the lounge chair.

"Well, it's time for me to go. I gotta get back to driving. That constant pocket money is addictive. I just wanted to get in here and clear my head for a minute with all the shit I got going on."

"So, you won't mind me working on a few things for you?" I asked him. My brain was running a mile a minute on moviemaking.

Tyrell paused and shrugged. "Sure. See what you can do. I never stop people from trying to help me. They just stop doing it when they see how hard it is. But it's easy when motherfuckers just say *yes*. That's all they have to do."

I nodded, agreeing with him, while thinking about Joseph Drake again. I said, "I know exactly what you mean. A lot of times the right people are right there in front of you, but getting them to say yes . . ." I stopped and shook my head, just thinking about it.

"And those same motherfuckers will drop twenty-five thousand on a vacation, and a hundred thousand on a birthday party," Tyrell added.

I smiled and didn't disagree with him. The city of Atlanta was full of pompous people with money. But it was *their* money, so they did whatever they wanted to do with it.

"So, are we setting up another session, or . . . ?" I wasn't sure how he wanted to do it. But I wanted to help. I felt like I *could* help him. I was optimistic.

He said, "I'll call you up on it. And if you get anything working just let me know."

I nodded and said, "I will."

"All right, I'll catch you." He walked out of my office, and that was it.

As soon as Tyrell left, my brain exploded like a bomb. I started pulling all of these random ideas together and had no clue what I was about to get myself into. But that's life. Sometimes we don't know where it's about to take us.

DESTINY FLOWERS

Reflection 6

By the time Destiny called me that same evening—right before closing up my office after five—I was distracted by a full plate of ideas and failed to give her my undivided attention.

"Ah, I'm just about to head out of the office for the evening. Can you call back tomorrow morning at nine? That way, you'll be my first call," I told her.

"Well, I just wanted to catch you before you left. I mean, I know you close up after five, and I didn't want to call while you were still in a session. So, I called right after."

"Okay, well . . . again, you'll be better off catching me in the morning where I can really *focus* on you. I'm sorry."

"I mean, it's not gonna take *long*. I just wanted to talk to you for a few minutes."

I paused. This girl was really pressing me. I said, "Well, are you trying to schedule a *session*?" I didn't have time for free calls of rambling, and I tended to get that a lot when I allowed it. But at that moment, I was not in the mood.

She hesitated and said, "Okay, well . . . I'll just talk to you in the morning then."

That made it sound as if she wasn't prepared for a session. She just wanted to talk.

"Good, I'll speak to you in the morning then. What's your name again?"

"Destiny. Destiny Flowers."

I nodded. "Oh, okay, it's Destiny. My bad. The caller ID didn't pop up. But yeah, call me in the morning, nine AM, sharp."

"All right. Are you gonna be there?" she asked me, uncertain.

I grinned and said, "Why wouldn't I be? I'm here every day. So, just call me at nine."

"Are you there on the weekends too?"

I paused. Some people just knew how to rub you the wrong way. I answered, "No. I just meant the week*days.*"

"Oh, okay, because you said every day. And some people do work on Saturdays and Sundays."

"Well, I meant the week*days,*" I repeated.

"All right, well, I'll call you tomorrow then."

As soon as I hung up with her, I shook my head and grabbed my things to leave out.

"I don't know what it is, but something is definitely *off* with this woman," I mumbled to myself. Sometimes you can just *sense it.*

JOSEPH DRAKE

Reflection 7

AGAINST MY BETTER JUDGMENT, I CALLED JOSEPH DRAKE THAT evening to see where he was on what we had discussed in his office a week ago. But I already understood how businessmen liked to operate. It was all about them calling *you,* and not you calling *them.* But I didn't care anymore about the bullshit of protocol. So, I dialed his office number anyway.

"Capital Exposure Unlimited," his receptionist answered.

I smiled. I guess she was working after hours again. But it was only after five.

"Is this Rochelle?" I asked.

She perked up. "Yes, it is. Who's calling?"

"It's Dr. Victoria Benning. Is Joe available?"

"Oh, hi! How are you? Ahhh . . . I think he's finishing up a conference call, but I'm not quite sure. Let me check in with him and see."

"Okay, you do that."

She was so full of carefree energy. I really admired that. She didn't seem to be boggled down by any issues, like the rest of us. Or maybe that was just her act at the job.

"Okay, he said he can get to you in just a few minutes," she informed me. "Can you hold?"

I nodded while waiting at my desk. "Yeah, I can hold."

"Okay, great. I'll punch you both in when he's ready."

As soon as she put me on hold, I began to think about Destiny Flowers again. She was a thirty-something sister from Cleveland, Ohio. I had spoken to her a few times previously, and she was all over the place, a wannabe actress, singer, dancer, and a hopeless dreamer arriving in Atlanta eight years ago to try her luck at becoming rich and famous in the entertainment industry.

How original was that? Thousands of people wanted to become rich and famous entertaining in Atlanta now. And many of them were not successful.

When Rochelle clicked me back on the line with Joe, I was still daydreaming.

"Victoria, are you there?"

"Oh, yeah, I'm still here. I just zoned out for a second," I told her with a chuckle. "I got a lot on my plate."

"Don't we all," she responded. I wasn't expecting that from her. "Anyways, let me plug you back in with Joe."

"Thank you."

Joe was still full of bravado when he jumped on the line. "Hey, Victoria. I never thought I'd hear back from you again."

"Why? I thought we agreed to stay in touch and develop a real game plan for the money."

"I mean, yeah, we talked about that. But with the way you left, I wasn't quite sure if you still believed in it. You were pretty teed off at me."

"Well, I just know how difficult it is to *qualify* for money when you're not used to the process. It's like asking someone to cook a meal in a new-technology kitchen. If they don't understand how the stove works, even though they know how to cook the meal, they won't be able to do it in that particular kitchen, because they don't know what they're doing in it."

He paused a second. He said, "I see what you mean. That's a pretty good analogy. They know what they're doing, they just don't know your particular process."

"I'm just trying to make sure you understand me. Because we'll have a few people who can pay the right folks to qualify them, and others—who really need the money—who can't afford to do that. But if you could help prepare the people I bring to you . . ."

"Yeah, but that's really not my job," he said, cutting me off.

"You need to *make it* your job," I countered. "That's why I was upset when you introduced this to me. I already know where this is going, and you already know what's needed to qualify."

When he paused longer, I couldn't tell if that was a good thing or a bad one. Was it a positive pause of consideration or a negative pause of deliberation?

Finally, he said, "You're really gonna push *hard* for this."

That confused me. Did he take me as just someone to share his emotions with, or did he really want me to help him qualify minorities for millions, and maybe *billions,* in business capital?

I responded real calmly, "It seems to me that you just want to *talk* about qualifying people and not actually help them to do it. Was that your intent with me? You just wanted me to analyze your *feelings* about it?"

After all, I was a psychologist. Maybe I had taken his business conversation the wrong way. But he surely didn't introduce the idea to me professionally with the after-hours alcohol. So, I didn't know what to think.

He answered, "No, I'm not just here to talk about it. It's all gonna happen. We just have to figure out *how.*"

Once I had rooted him back into our previous conversation, I was ready to make my pitch. "Okay, so . . . you do know that we're in Atlanta, right?"

"Right."

"And you know that Atlanta's the new entertainment capital for Black people," I hinted.

"Okay. I get that."

I paused. ". . . Are there any considerations in having some of this money to finance a new minority studio that includes film, television, and music?"

He chuckled. "I see where you're going. You mean like a new Tyler Perry?"

"Well, not so focused on one person, but yeah, a film studio with music included."

"Ahhh, the entertainment thing is always risky," he whined.

I was waiting for him to say that. Many financiers viewed entertainment as risky. But not with *that* kind of money in Atlanta. So, I told him.

"Are you kidding me? When a certain market is hot for something specific, you jump in it and go with it. That's like saying oranges are risky in Florida. Vacations are risky in Jamaica. Or a Broadway show is risky in New York City. I mean, that's what those areas *do.* And Atlanta does television, music, and film now. They even have major tax breaks for it here. Am I *wrong*?

"Now, if I asked you to finance an entertainment studio in Camden, New Jersey, that would be a different story. That *would* be more risky," I added. "But it makes sense down here in Atlanta."

"Yeah, yeah, I know, I know. It's the reality show capital of America," he joked. "Do you have a certain company in mind to bring to the table?"

I smiled. "I'm working on that now. I just wanted to see if it was a possibility first."

He said, "Everything is a possibility if the numbers look right."

I nodded. That was positive. I said, "I'm already on it."

TYRELL HODGE

Reflection 8

IT'S FUNNY HOW SOME OF YOUR MOST CREATIVE AND TALENTED people are just . . . *off* sometimes. Kanye West and Kyrie Irving immediately come to mind as two creative and popular Black men who consistently get themselves into trouble with their eccentricities. They don't seem to view or respond to the world the way that normal people do—if there's even such a thing as *normal.* Dark & Moody had a valid point about that. We are *all* crazy. It's just a matter of what degree.

I had those thoughts in mind when I made a call to Tyrell Hodge that same evening after work. By that time, I was back in my car headed for home through Atlanta's rush hour. So, I was headed nowhere fast.

"Hello," he answered gruffly over his car's speaker system. I was using my car's stereo system as well.

"Are you able to talk?" I asked him. He was damn-near a full-time PDS driver now, addicted to the consistent money. He told me so himself. Driving was the total opposite of the slower, wait-for-it money of writing for hire. Not to mention the dozens of people who would renege on his writing jobs or not have all the money once he completed it. The PDS money came immediately, and as soon as his passengers hopped out of the car.

"Yeah, I got a minute," he answered. "You caught me right before my next ride. What it look like? How'd your day go?"

Since we knew each other off the clock, Tyrell would check in with me every now and then, and I did the same with him. He just wanted someone to understand what he was going through, and I figured I could help him to manage his disappointments. But finally, I had something *big* that I could share with him.

I asked him, "Have you ever talked to venture capitalist or hedge fund managers about funding any of your projects?"

"Ahhh, man, fuck them guys," Tyrell responded tartly. "You never qualify for any of that shit. Getting that money is like playing the lottery. You might as well play eenie, meenie, miney, moe with your toes, trying to get that shit. Now you got these Bitcoin guys talking their shit and can't even spend the money. What's the point in having a million dollars in Bitcoin money if you can't cash it and do something with it? But these guys are forever bragging about how much their coins are worth."

I had gotten used to allowing Tyrell to express his ire before I advised him on anything. That's just how he was, a talk-first and listen-later kind of guy.

I said, "I'm working on something right now, so I'm gonna need some of those creative ideas of yours."

"For a venture capitalist?" He sounded doubtful.

"I'll let you know when I get further along with it. Just start pulling out your best ideas."

He laughed and said, "Oh, so you must be going after some big-money people, because if you're asking me for my *best* shit . . ."

Tyrell may have been frustrated, but his ego was still intact. And he really could write. His work was fast and furious and still good. He just had to learn how to *pitch* and sell it better. And that wasn't going to happen with all of his ongoing frustrations.

I grinned and said, "I told you it's big money. But I'll handle it. Just start pulling your best stuff out."

"All right, well, forgive me if I don't hold my breath for it," he commented.

"I didn't ask you to," I told him. "I know how this process works. It's tedious. And if it wasn't, everybody would do it. But just start thinking about your best work."

"All right. Time to go. Next rider." He hung up without saying bye or allowing me to get in another word.

I shook my head, disappointed with him. "That damn fool," I mumbled to myself. "He needs to land something *good* to get him out of his *funk.*" I felt sorry for the man.

I continued driving, stopping, and going in Atlanta's rush-hour traffic on my way to Interstate 20 West, while thinking about my next call. And I could still imagine Tyrell picking up his next rider, all pumped up with frustrated energy. Based on the stories that he would tell me, I could see it all in my mind.

He would hang up the call with me, whip to the curb in his silver Chevy Malibu, and wait for the next rider to walk out of their home, their office, their apartment building, the grocery store, or a shopping mall, and he would bombard them with his assertive conversation as soon as they climbed in.

"Hey, busy day out here, huh? Where you headed to?"

He would ask them this before looking at the directions on his app, just to get them to talk to him. It was his way of dominating the energy inside the car, no matter who climbed in. He wanted to let them know that he was the boss, otherwise some of the riders could treat him like a low-level servant, which he was *not.* So, he went out of his way to establish control of the energy inside his car with strangers.

The problem was, some of the riders didn't want to be addressed that strongly. They just wanted to get where they were going in silence. So, Tyrell had a tendency of rubbing people the wrong way, causing them to retaliate with low driver ratings or negative remarks about him on their rider app, even though he would get them there safely.

Or, when he slipped into his sour moods, he would barely talk to the riders at all, with a rugged Chicago attitude that they could feel, which got him into trouble with low ratings and negative remarks again.

"I'm not like that all the time," he would tell me. "And when the PDS guys hit me up about a rider complaining on the app, I always tone it down to get extra friendly with these people. I'm not trying to lose my hustle over their pettiness."

"Complaining about bad customer service is not pettiness," I argued with him.

Yet, he would continue with his reckless, big-city attitude. "Bad customer service?" he repeated. "I still get these motherfuckers where they're going, safe and sound, every time."

Then I would promptly change the subject on him. "So, how's life with your girlfriend going this week?"

"Oh, it's still the same shit, complaining about this, that, and other things. But it is what it is. We used to each other."

"That doesn't mean you stay in a relationship that doesn't feel *right* for you."

"Yeah, well, that's where I'm at right now. Just like with my writing career. I'm waiting for something bigger and better to happen, and I'll see how she acts then."

Yet, when I bring an opportunity to the table to finally make something happen for him, he immediately shoots it down like he does with everything else.

That's the definition of the word *frustrated*. You start to get in your own way by always believing the worst, and overreacting.

I shook my head again, while driving and still thinking about him. "That damn fool needs a miracle," I mumbled. And he really did.

CHARLES CLAY

Reflection 9

THE NEXT PERSON I CALLED FOR THE PRODUCTION GROUP I began to build was the director Charles Clay. If I could get a great screenplay idea from Tyrell, could I then get Charles to direct it? I wanted to find out.

However, I didn't know the director like I knew the writer. And the director was in the prime of his career, which meant more phone calls to reach him, and a more nuanced conversation with details to get him interested. Even then, I wasn't sure what he would say. But I figured Tyrell was right in one regard. Any hot, in-the-moment director is going to ask about the *pay*, particularly from a new production team. So, I had to prepare myself with an answer for that.

I called Charles's cell number expecting to leave him a message to call me back at his leisure. I had no idea how busy his schedule was, but I definitely expected him to have one. To my surprise, he answered on the third ring.

"Dr. Victoria Benning. What can I do for you today?"

That startled me. "Oh, you have me on caller ID?"

"Of course I do. It's good to know who's calling you these days. And in perfect timing too," he commented. "We were just about to start our preliminary casting ideas for a new production. You must have been reading my mind today. I know you're a psychologist, but I didn't know that you were *psychic*."

I paused and thought about things. Charles was very different from Tyrell. He was soft-spoken, patient, relaxed, and smug, the opposite of frustrated. He made long money with big checks and didn't have to drive strangers around all day, while hoping for tips. However, similar to the writer, he was utilizing his own method of control by flattering me. I didn't know if the movie production he was referring to was real or Memorex, but this time I was more prepared for him and in a different state of mind. So, I blew off his flattering comments.

"Well, no, I'm not psychic. I *wish*," I stated with a chuckle. "Now I'm sitting here wondering if *you* are, because I had a project idea I wanted to pitch to you."

"Really? What about? Did you write it? Is it a psychological thriller?"

I paused again. I was very curious to see how he was going to respond to my next question. "Are you familiar with the screenwriter Tyrell Hodge?"

His response was immediate. "Definitely. His writing was *brilliant*. That was the explosive Black film era of the nineties."

That got me excited again. I said, "Black books were big in the nineties too."

"Yeah, well, things have changed now. You have a million reality shows, hundreds of podcasts, kids putting stuff out on YouTube. It's all about generating numbers now. You have to *prove* that you have an audience somewhere. And sadly, Tyrell is like a relic. He just doesn't have that new audience. The time has passed him by."

I hesitated, not wanting to respond too defensively. I went easy with him instead.

"Quality writing is still quality writing, right?"

"We all would like to think so. But the industry has decided to cater to the active viewers more than ever now," he responded. "And by *active*, I mean viewers who seek and follow things on their own without a lot of marketing involved. So, what Hodge needs to do is put something out on his own that goes *viral* to prove that he still has it with the new viewers."

I could imagine how Tyrell would respond to that.

"Every-fucking-body can't go viral! We still need marketing! That's why we're getting so much bullshit out here now! The masses are controlling the art instead of people who know what they're fucking doing!"

I grinned and reminded myself to remain civil. I had to keep our conversation easygoing. I was surprised I even caught up to Charles, and that he had time to talk.

I said, "How 'bout if you two worked on something together? You have that new audience now, and he's still a quality writer."

When Charles went silent, I knew what it meant. There was no confusion about his MO at all. He was ready to shoot the idea down.

"I've heard he's hard to deal with," he commented. "And it gets like that when you're no longer landing anything. So, I don't think my team would agree to that."

All of a sudden, he was talking about his *team.* He didn't speak about his team being in the way of his decisions with anything else.

I joked and said, "So, your *team* wouldn't mind casting me in a project as an amateur actress, but they would balk at working with a celebrated, veteran writer? Really?"

I tried to make myself sound more curious than sarcastic.

But Charles matched my wit with his. "Dr. Victoria, we live in an era now where *amateurs* have taken the world by storm. That's the American way."

"The American way is also respecting people who've already put in their *dues.* It's just like these athletes getting the second and third contracts for more money," I countered. "You don't pay a rookie what you pay LeBron James."

I couldn't help myself. I was getting a little agitated. I said, "Would you at least take a *look* at what Tyrell comes up with? Particularly, if we could get the money to shoot it?"

Charles paused again. He said, "Well, it still would depend on our schedule. And we have to *like it* first."

Funny how he changed his tune when I brought up the money. All of a sudden, a project with Tyrell seemed doable. So, I guess the frustrated Chicago writer was right again. And I bet for Charles's team to "like it" would have everything to do with how much money we could offer them.

Well, I didn't feel like talking to him anymore. Charles was rubbing me the wrong way again, like he had done with dozens of other people. All humans want to hear what we want to hear. I couldn't even imagine putting Tyrell in the same room with him. Of course, Charles would probably not be as forward with Tyrell as he was being with me.

"You seem personally invested in this," he commented.

I am! I thought without saying it. I was ready to put my own career and time on the line to do something for others. And maybe I needed something extra to believe in for myself.

"I guess you can say that," I responded to Charles. "Let's just say, I came across a group that have some capital to invest, but it has to be an *inclusive* effort."

It was important for me to add that because I know how film people like to find money for their own pet projects. But this was my show to run, and I wanted to make that perfectly clear.

"Okay, well . . . let's see what Hodge has to contribute, and we'll go from there."

I smiled and nodded, while making my way along I-20 West. It took a little bit of an effort, but we arrived in the best place to end our conversation. The only better result would have been a flat-out yes, which I wasn't expecting.

"Thank you. I'll be in touch." I figured it was the safest thing to say.

Charles chuckled and responded, "Everyone wants to produce a movie these days."

I paused again. He was being sarcastic with me now. So, I laughed it off. "I guess so." And I left it at that. I didn't want to ruin the great ending to our conversation.

MRS. MELODY

Reflection 10

I HUNG UP THE LINE WITH CHARLES CLAY AND STARTED PLAYING Dark & Moody's gothic funk music in my car again. The more I listened to it, the better the music sounded to me. I guess I was beginning to understand it.

But instead of calling her to check in and present my ideas of using some of her gothic funk in a soundtrack, I thought of calling Mrs. Melody and introducing my ideas to her first. I could even send her some of the music to listen to. So, I called her.

I had no idea what to expect as I waited for her to pick up the line. I had only spoken to her a few times, and her life seemed to be the hardest for me to comprehend. I knew what everyone else was up to, including Dark & Moody making her music while praying for success. But I had no idea what Mrs. Melody's typical day looked like. What do rappers do all day? Are they in studios listening to new music? I had no idea.

"Dr. Victoria. Oh my *God*! You called me at the perfect time. Where are you?"

She sounded rushed and secretive, as if she was whispering.

I winced and asked her, "What's going on?" It sounded as if she was hiding in a closet.

"I can't explain it right now, but are you near downtown?"

I continued to scowl while trying to figure things out. "I'm on I-Twenty West. Why?"

"I need you to come get me. Then I can tell you about it."

Was this girl out of her mind, or what? I wasn't turning my car around and heading back downtown in Atlanta. I had just made it out of there.

Nevertheless, I asked her, "Are you sure you can't call an Uber or a taxi?"

What about any of these music guys you deal with? I pondered. I couldn't understand why she was asking *me* to pick her up.

"If you can't do it, I understand. But I wanted to talk to you about it. I'm in between two guys right now."

She still sounded like she was in a quiet place, whispering. "You're in between *two guys*? Downtown?"

"Yeah, I'll explain it to you when you get me."

I paused. "I don't even know where you are?"

"I'll text you the address."

This girl was really being presumptuous, and she was about to get away with it. I was already headed for the next exit ramp to turn my car around.

I said, "I don't know what you're involved in, but you're gonna have some explaining to do. It sounds like you're in a damn *closet*."

She chuckled. "Almost. I'm in the fire escape."

"The fire escape? In a hotel?"

The plot was getting thicker.

"Yeah, I got one guy coming in and another guy going out."

I hesitated and asked myself, *What?* Then I shook it off. I would have to find out everything that was going on once I got there.

"Okay, we'll talk about it all when I see you."

"I'ma text you the address now. And pick me up at the side exit, not in the front entrance."

I hung up the line and shook my head. As I made my left turn up the ramp to get back on the interstate for downtown, I mumbled, "This is gonna be *good*."

I started smiling just imagining what this girl's life was like. She had the new audience numbers that Charles Clay was referring to as well. I believe Mrs. Melody was up to 450K followers on Instagram, compared to my 12K followers. That was nearly forty times more than my number!

That gave me another idea. *Maybe Tyrell and Mrs. Melody could collab and write something from her personal life for her to star in, with Charles directing it.*

What did I have to lose?

I arrived at the W Hotel in downtown Atlanta and pulled up to a side-exit door for Mrs. Melody and didn't see her. I called her number again and waited for her to answer.

"Are you here?" she asked me after the second ring.

"Yes, at the side doors."

"Okay, I'll be right out."

I hung up the line and looked around, wondering again what this girl's life was like. She rushed out the side door and jumped into my car as if someone was after her. She was dressed in orange and black this time and was extra sexy.

"What is going on?" I asked her immediately.

She looked around outside and said, "Okay, I'll tell you. Let's go."

Everything was rushed. I drove back into the downtown streets of Atlanta and didn't know where we were headed.

"Where are we going?" I asked her.

"I live near Buckhead."

As soon as she said it, I exhaled with grief. Buckhead was North Atlanta, but I lived on the far southwest side.

"This is gonna be a long night," I commented. "I live nowhere near Buckhead."

She said, "I'm sorry. But I'm glad you were here for me."

"Okay, so . . . what's going on?" I asked her again.

When I looked into her face, she was prettier than she was in my office. It was her flyaway hair being a touch messy that did it. It gave her more sex appeal, like a lustful scene in a movie. I could already see her on the big screen. She was perfect for a starring role. And she wasn't even acting yet. This was her real *life.*

She started explaining it all to me with her hands. “Okay, so, I was here to see Guy A, and then Guy B shows up, and they don’t like each other.”

I paused without comment. I could already imagine the scene. “And then you decided to run and go hide in the fire escape?”

“Yeah, these guys both got bodyguards and friends and all that shit. It could have been a real fucking *scene* out here. You know, people get *killed* over shit like that.”

That was what she told me. I said, “Well, why are you in the middle of it if you know this already? And put your seat belt on.”

She buckled herself in and answered, “But see, I didn’t know. Not initially. So, once I found out they’re like, *enemies*, I was try’na decide how to play this, and who gets exed out, because it’s too dangerous to fuck with both of them.”

“Yes it is,” I told her. Those Atlanta rap guys were crazy. Rappers in general were crazy. And she was crazy for dealing with them. But that was her world. “So, have you made up your mind yet?” I asked.

She exhaled before she answered. “Okay, so here’s the thing. The one that I decided to be with, I haven’t fucked with him yet. But the other one . . . I was already dealing with him. But he’s the one that I’m ready to leave.”

I shrugged. The problem was solved in my eyes. “Okay, so, just leave him.”

The whole time she was talking to me, her phone was going off. She looked at her incoming call and said, “Speak of the devil.”

“Which devil?” I joked. They could all be devils to me. Men were a different breed, young and old.

Mrs. Melody laughed and said, “I know, right? But this the one I just left.”

“Are you gonna answer it?”

“Not yet. I gotta get home and get settled first. You know, I gotta think about what I’ma say.”

I shook my head and grinned, glad that I didn't have her problem.

I said, "I figured you could get yourself into trouble by dealing with too many guys in the same industry. That's like dating two or three football or basketball players, while thinking they're never gonna find out. But these guys in the same industries *talk*. And Atlanta's not that damn big to begin with."

"I know, I'm finding that out."

I frowned at her. "You should have already *known* that. Look at how many rappers and singers collaborate in Atlanta. They're all gonna know each other here."

She nodded to me, while still fiddling with her cell phone.

"I guess both of these guys are worth it then," I commented. "Are they both worth your problems?"

She looked at me and froze. "Well, yeah, but the second one I didn't know I could get. So, that threw a monkey wrench in my plans."

She was so casual about it that it didn't seem to matter. "Well, did somebody see you there?"

"No, that's why I ran in the fire escape as soon as I saw him. But, you know, when they got friends and bodyguards and all that, all it takes is for one of them to see you. So, I had to hide from all of them."

"And what are you gonna tell the first guy? You just up and disappeared from him?"

"No, I had already left his room. But then I can't hang out with him, because he's gonna want to go out at some point, and I didn't want to be trapped in the room with him. So, my best decision was to leave. And that's when you called." She grinned. "Perfect timing," she repeated.

"For you, maybe," I told her, "but I was damn-near home already."

"My bad. But this the kind of stuff I get into that I need to talk about."

"No, you need to stop getting *in* this kind of stuff in the first place," I argued. "Talking about it after the fact is useless."

"Yeah, but then I wouldn't have anything to talk *about.*"

We looked at each other and laughed in unison. She knew she was crazy.

I said, "Anyway . . . I got some music I want you to hear. And you tell me what you think about it."

She perked up with that, as if she was ready to twerk in my passenger seat.

"All right, let me hear it. What you got, some old school?"

I smiled and put on Dark & Moody's "Ghetto Opera" track. I didn't even want to tell Mrs. Melody what it was. I wanted to see if she could figure it out.

She started listening to it and froze. She was really paying attention. She said, "The beat is dope. But it sound like . . . spooky horror music."

"Could you write something to that?"

She frowned. "If I'm doing a Halloween song. Who produced that? That's not *your* music, is it?"

I shook it off. "No, I don't do music. This is from another client of mine."

Mrs. Melody eyed me again. "She got a bunch of issues?"

"No more than *you,*" I told her. "She just wants to be successful like everyone else. That's what you want, right?"

"Hell yeah," she hummed. "But naw, the beat ain't bad though. It just got that spooky sound."

"All right, let me play you another one." I put on another beat that I liked, which was more up tempo. Mrs. Melody started nodding to it immediately.

"Okay, this one sounds like . . . we got a Halloween *party* up in here." She curled up her nails as if she had turned into a dancing zombie from Michael Jackson's "Thriller." And we laughed again.

"So, you can't do anything with this one either?"

"I mean, it's just not my style. Maybe if she took out all that spooky-sounding shit and just used a funky-ass bass line, I could do something with it."

I nodded and continued smiling. "What if I put you two together to work on some new stuff. Then you can tell her what you want."

Mrs. Melody went silent and stared at me in deep thought. "She's not real crazy, is she?"

I continued to smile at her. "Well, how crazy are *you*? What if she asked me the same thing about *you*? Because jumping around in the bedrooms of enemies in the music business is suicide. So, again, how crazy are *you*?" I repeated.

"I'm not crazy, I'm just try'na get mine," she responded.

"In any way that you can, which could be considered *crazy*," I stressed.

"No, it's just *determined*."

"Whatever you wanna call it," I argued. "So, would you meet up with her?"

She paused again. "Where? 'Cause I wouldn't want to meet her in the dark or at night or anything. I gotta meet her for breakfast when the sun is out. Like ten or eleven o'clock in the morning would be good."

"That's more like a *brunch*," I joked.

"Yeah, and that's better than *dinner*. I don't want her thinking about sippin' on some wine or nothin'. She might try to slip some blood in it."

"Would you stop? She's not like that," I lied. I didn't really know *what* Dark & Moody was capable of to be bluntly honest about it. I had to talk her out of thinking about blood sacrifices, and I definitely wasn't going to tell Mrs. Melody that.

"I'm just saying, man. If she's making that kind of music and she's already seeing you . . . Does she wear all black with thick black mascara?"

I shook it off. "No." *But she does call her music gothic funk*, I told myself. I said, "But she's already dark, so she doesn't have to do all of that with the mascara and makeup. She's a dark and *beautiful* girl."

Mrs. Melody smiled at me. "Sounds like you got a crush on her."

I chuckled. *I got a crush on you too,* I mused. "So, let's say I invite both of you guys to meet up at my office. Would you be willing to do that? Then you can see for yourself how normal she is."

Mrs. Melody wavered for a minute and then tossed up her hands. "All right. When you wanna do it?"

I continued smiling. Everything was falling right into my plans. I figured I would tell her about my movie ideas later. It was one step at a time.

DESTINY FLOWERS

Reflection 11

AFTER A VERY LONG NIGHT OF DRIVING, PLOTTING, AND PLANNING, I got back into the office that next morning closer to ten AM than my usual nine. I had forgotten all about a follow-up call from Destiny Flowers. But she didn't. Like radar, she called me as soon as I got settled in.

"You had a busy night last night, huh?"

"How'd you know?" I asked rhetorically.

"Because I *called* and you weren't in yet."

"Did you leave a message?"

"I don't like leaving messages. I'll just call until you get there."

Yeah, whatever, I thought. I could tell this woman was going to be irritating. But I didn't have a first session that morning until eleven, so I had time to let her pull my ear for a minute.

"So, what can I do for you this morning?" I asked her.

"Oh, I just wanted to talk to you about some of my ideas."

"Ahhh . . . you do realize that I set up professional appointments for my clients to come in and go through a full hour-long—or more—session for *pay,* right? I mean, that's my *job.* That's what I do. I just don't listen to people's ideas. You might wanna call up a think tank company for that."

"I know what you do. You don't have to explain that to me. I'm not stupid."

At that point, I was speechless. I never called her stupid. And I was hesitant to say the wrong thing to her. So, I mumbled, "Ahhh . . . okay . . . would you like to set up an appointment?"

"You charge a hundred dollars an hour?"

"Yes, I do. I try to keep my price even and affordable."

"Well, I can afford that."

"I know you can," I told her.

"How you know that?"

I paused. "If you're paying rent or a mortgage here in Atlanta, then you got a hundred dollars, 'cause if you don't, you can't live here. In fact, you need a hundred dollars to even keep a cell phone on."

"Oh, now that's *true.* These cell phones are getting more and more expensive. Then they keep trying to add more data and apps and stuff all the time."

I nodded, wondering when we would get to the beef of her conversation.

"Okay, so . . . do you have a certain day or a time in mind?" I commented.

"A day and time for what?"

I paused again. *This woman . . .* It was too early in the morning for foolishness. I said, "Excuse me—"

"Oh, oh, you meant a day and a time for your sessions," she said, cutting me off. "Well, let me think about that."

She was a real time waster, so I started eyeing my clock to take my mind off of cursing her ass out. I said, "Well, you need to think about that before you call here again."

"I need to set up an appointment just to call you?" She sounded offended.

"No, you don't need an appointment to *call,* but you do need to think about setting up a *session.* Otherwise . . . what's the point?"

"The point is, I just wanted to talk to you about my ideas."

"Okay, we already discussed that. And I am not a think tank. I'm a psychologist. I get paid to discuss people's personal issues."

"And I got a whole lot of 'em."

"That you need to set up a *session* with me to discuss," I told her. "Now, if you don't mind, I have another long day ahead of me that I need to prepare for."

She said, "Your first session is not until eleven o'clock. So, you still have time to talk to me."

"How do you know what time my first session is?"

"Well, you're not gonna start in between hours, are you? And right now, it's only ten twenty-eight."

I didn't want to give her more information about my work schedule, so I let her go on with her assumptions.

I said, "Well, you let me know when you have a day and a time in mind. Okay?"

"Are you getting ready to hang up on me?"

"I'm trying not to. I would rather be professional and civil. But . . ."

"I'm getting on your damn nerves," she filled in.

"Yes, you are," I admitted.

She started laughing. "Well, at least you're honest about it. I like that."

I had heard enough. I said, "Okay, look—"

"I know, I know. I need to make an appointment, right? I will. One day."

"Well, you let me know when, and I gotta get back to work now. Okay? Bye."

I waited for her to respond.

"Aw'ight," she mumbled. "I got you."

Then I hung up the line.

"That damn girl," I commented. "She gon' make me need some coffee."

DARK & MOODY

Reflection 12

ONCE THEY WORKED OUT THEIR SCHEDULES, I WAS ABLE TO GET Mrs. Melody and Dark & Moody together in my office that next week. And I was smiling away, just thinking of all the collaborations we could come up with.

"You two look like a new-wave Salt-N-Pepa in here," I joked.

They looked at each other, both dressed in their usual style. Mrs. Melody was extra sexy in a baby blue dress, and Dark & Moody was artistic in black denim with colorful jewelry and earrings.

Dark & Moody smiled at the reference. "I'm way darker than Pepa. In fact, they should have called them Salt-N-*Cinnamon*, 'cause Pepa's not all that *dark*."

Mrs. Melody grinned and chimed in. "I think the point was to use a familiar term like salt-and-pepper because everyone can remember the name. You know, it's catchy."

"I think it's catchier to use things that people *don't* know. Then you're like the only one doing it."

Mrs. Melody continued smiling. She said, "It's very hard to be the only one doing something these days. When you have no followers, that means you make no money."

"And we want plenty of those," I interjected. "You have nearly a *half* million followers now," I added of Mrs. Melody.

I hated to pick sides, but one of the things that could hold Dark & Moody back was her penchant for presenting the counterculture, which is only good when it works. The reality was, Mrs. Melody was the one who could take Dark & Moody to a new place in her career. So, I had to make sure we all got on the same page for something to work.

"Money doesn't always lead to longevity," Dark & Moody commented. "I'd rather have a long and productive career than a fast, overnight burnout because I was chasing the money. That happens to a lot of people in music now."

"They just need better producers," I countered. I had to make Dark & Moody feel important as well. She had 52K followers on Instagram herself, which was still four times as many as I had.

"So, anyways . . . what I haven't told either one of you yet is that I'm pulling together a possible film and studio project with a venture capital group that I'm hoping will say *yes* to the ideas. I'm trying to pull all of the pieces together now. And I was thinking something like a horror vehicle, or a psychological thriller."

Mrs. Melody grinned and said, "That makes sense for you. You deal with people and psychology all day."

"Exactly. And I was thinking about using Dark and Moody's music to create the *mood* that we want."

Dark & Moody heard that and grinned herself. She said, "I can see that."

Mrs. Melody added, "Yeah, but you don't want the whole *movie* to be like that. I mean, what if you have a love scene or something?"

Dark & Moody frowned at her. "I can produce regular music. I just prefer my gothic funk."

"Gothic funk?" Mrs. Melody repeated. "Sounds like some Batman shit."

"Well, Batman *is* the Dark Knight from Gotham," Dark & Moody countered.

I couldn't tell if these girls were getting along or not. It sounded as if they were both trying to establish their perspective.

"Well, I was thinking Mrs. Melody would make a great lead for that. What do you think, DM?" I asked the music producer.

She paused and considered it. "DM? I like that," she responded. She didn't say anything about Mrs. Melody's acting in the lead.

"Yeah, it's short for Dark and Moody," I told her.

"I know. People just haven't called me that before. They just call me Dark, or Tasha."

"Oh, so that's your real name?" I perked. She had never told me before. Maybe it had slipped out by accident.

She smiled and said, "Yeah, it's Tasha Samuels."

Mrs. Melody nodded. "You put T. Samuels on your music credits for publishing?"

She nodded. "Yeah. What about you?"

"I'm M. Anderson."

"Cool. So, we have Tasha Samuels, Melody Anderson, and Victoria Benning all sitting here trying to figure out how we can work together," I commented.

"On a movie?" Mrs. Melody repeated. "And these guys have the money?"

I paused. "They have it but getting it from them is the challenge."

Mrs. Melody frowned. "Getting the money is *always* the challenge. Welcome to the fucking world of America."

DM eyed her and said, "Well, I don't do everything just for the money. If it's a good project, I'm in."

"So, you would be willing to contribute some of your productions to the project?" I asked her.

She stared across my desk from her chair and said, "Definitely."

"Well, I really like the 'Ghetto Opera' track of yours," I told her.

She smiled immediately. "Yeah, that's one of my favorites."

Even Mrs. Melody agreed. She nodded and said, "That could be the theme song."

"But you said you couldn't *write* to it," I reminded her. It was the first track I had played for her in my car.

"No, I said it wasn't my *style.* But I can write to anything. Or freestyle to it. *Ma-fuckas say they wanna make a movie / it's all good if the money there to move me / I'm a stuck-up chick, I get choosy / start talking bullshit, and you'll lose me / but say the right shit to me, and we groovy / popping champagne bottles in Jacuzzis . . .*"

I was impressed. Even DM smiled at it. "But that's not the topic," she commented.

"I mean, whatever the movie's about, I can adjust to it," Mrs. Melody countered. "I'm just saying that I don't have a problem with writing. Especially if it's gonna be the theme song of a movie. But to use it as *my* music . . . I mean, my fanbase would be like, 'What the fuck are you doing?' You know? They ain't never heard no horror shit from me."

DM started shaking her head. "See, now that's the problem. When we start letting the audience control our careers, that's when we end up with a *job* instead of a *passion*."

Mrs. Melody persisted. "You can do whatever you wanna do with your career. You just won't make any money from it."

"Oh, I've made *money*. Let's not get it confused," DM responded. "My shit is that *good*. I'm just saying that I don't allow the audience to dictate what I do. We lead and they follow. Right? Not the other way around."

Mrs. Melody paused in deeper thought about it. Her answers were typically rapid-fire, so Dark & Moody had definitely gotten to her. And I was curious to see how she would respond.

"I mean, you can say that . . . but . . . if the audience is not following what you're doing, then you're just gettin' in the way, 'cause they'd rather hear something else," she argued. "So, move off the stage with that shit. That's when they start booing."

"Then that's not your audience then," DM countered.

Mrs. Melody said, "No, you could have *made them* your audience, but you fuck it up when you try to do *you* before they know you. You gotta *please* them first. Then you can do you, because they like you. But if you don't let them *like* you first . . ."

She had a point, so I turned to DM and awaited her response.

She said, "You want the right *ones* to like you. Because if you're just out here chasing any audience, your numbers and popularity will go up and down based off what *they* like versus what *you* like."

Mrs. Melody cringed. She said, "That's gonna happen anyway. I got songs right now that my audience likes way more than I do. But I don't get mad at them for that. I made all of it. So, I let them like what they like and keep doing it."

She said, "It's a give-and-take when you have an audience. It's not always about *you.* It's just like any other relationship. The other side has things that they're interested in too."

With that, I wanted to redirect the conversation. Since they both had very strong personalities and opinions, they could debate like that for hours.

"So, the movie idea would be a go for both of you guys?" I asked them.

Mrs. Melody answered first. "Sure. But you still don't know what it would be about?"

I nodded as they eyed me across the desk. "I have a *friend* who could write something based off of what you both are going through in your lives right now. Like, what would it take to push you over the top? And what would happen if you lost control of yourself?"

I was making it up as I spoke. Surely, Tyrell Hodge could do something with that topic. He was borderline losing control himself.

Mrs. Melody started grinning. She said, "You always have to keep your control. That's one of the only things you have left in this world. How do I control the shit I choose to do?"

DM was more pensive. She looked at me and said, "You know how I feel about that. We all want more than what we're allowed to have." She looked at Mrs. Melody and added, "Even you. You dress all sexy and do sex music to try and control the response of your audience. But in doing that, they end up controlling *you.*"

"Yeah, but then I'll have more control over my own *life* when I got more *money* because of the decisions I make," Mrs. Melody shot back. "So, you can be hardheaded and go your own way if you want, but then you'll end up complaining when you don't have the money to do the shit that you're really trying to do. Then you just end up complaining all the damn time."

She said, "I got girlfriends like that now, including my mom and my sister. They're always complaining about shit that they can't change, and I'm the only one helping them the fuck out. But yet they call *me* the crazy one!

"So, say what you fuckin' want. But I know how this real world works," she continued. "And if you don't work to please no-fucking-body, then nobody's gonna please you. And you'll be a lonely motherfucka out here by yourself."

I looked across my desk at DM and smiled. Of the two girls, Dark & Moody was the one brooding, and Mrs. Melody was the one shining. So, she knew what she was talking about.

DM grinned back at me and said, "So, the light-skinned Becky with the good hair gets to be the star of the movie, and I just make the music for it."

Mrs. Melody grimaced. "Oh, we goin' *there*? Is that where we're going now?"

Dark & Moody said, "It's the *truth*, right? That's what the people want. The light-skinned, mixed girl with the big titties, the big ass, the swimming hair, the yuck mouth, and the nasty-ass clothes up her ass."

I was ready to jump in and stop a full-fledged fight. That comment had nowhere to go but into unadulterated ugliness. But to my surprise, Mrs. Melody kept her poise.

She said, "I don't wear no nasty-ass clothes. But I know how to get nasty when I need to. Do you?"

She looked Tasha Samuels right into her eyes as the room went silent. And then they . . . started laughing, and it shocked me. I didn't know what to expect. I thought they were about to start throwing punches and pulling hair in there, because Dark & Moody had hair too.

She responded, "I know how to do what I need to do when I need to do it. Ain't nobody no little girls in here. I know how to handle mine."

Mrs. Melody said, "Okay then. Do you and stop hatin' on the next bitch. That's my motto. I ain't got time to be thinking about *Becky* or no other bitches. She ain't filling up my pocketbook with spinach. So, why am I concerned about what *she's* doing?"

I jumped right in and said, "Good. You shouldn't be. So, I'll start working on that movie idea and see if I can get my friend to interview both of you guys. Because it doesn't have to be about just one person. You both have interesting stories to tell. And that would make a more interesting movie."

TYRELL HODGE

Reflection 13

TYRELL WAS AT IT AGAIN ON SPEAKERPHONE, AIRING HIS FRUSTRAtions with an agent friend, while driving to pick up his next rider.

"They're only offering *two* thousand dollars? We waited all this time for *that*?"

"Look, Tyrell, you have to allow yourself to get back in. Sure, I know it's worth at least ten, but that's all they want to offer. So, take it, bank it, and write something else for tomorrow."

Tyrell yelled, "These motherfuckers! They're *toying* with me, man! They could've said that shit *weeks* ago. Why wait this long just to lowball me?"

"You're running out of options, Tyrell, you really are. Everyone calls you *difficult* at this point, and they're trying to see if they can even work with you. So, if you turn this down, they may never make another offer no matter what it is."

"Okay, so, I take the offer and keep writing for *pennies*? How does that help me?"

"It helps you by getting you back in. Then they could offer you four thousand for the next one, and ten thousand after that. Just give it a *chance*."

"Give it a chance to do what? To *rob me?*"

There was silence over the car speakers as Tyrell pulled up to his next pickup location outside a Walgreens drugstore. A tall Black man in his mid-twenties waited there for his pickup and checked the PDS app on his phone.

"Okay, that's him," the man mumbled as he began to walk toward the silver Malibu.

Tyrell remained focused on his call, oblivious to the rider walking up behind him on the passenger side.

The agent said, "I'm ready to just stop doing this for you, Tyrell. I put my neck out there for you and you don't seem to care. But I have a reputation to protect in this *too.*" He said, "I'm not getting anything from this two thousand dollars. I'm trying to help *you* out."

"Help me out how? By selling me into child labor, like I'm a damn *kid,*" Tyrell yelled into his car speakers. He said, "I write grown-man shit and I want a grown man's paycheck for it."

The rider froze just as he opened the back passenger door to climb into the Malibu.

Tyrell finally noticed him and was startled by it. "Shit! I ain't see you back there," he snapped with a smile.

The young man hesitated while holding the door open. "Is everything all right?" He didn't know if the older driver was talking to himself inside the car or not. And angrily too.

"Yeah, I'm just having an argument with a friend of mine. Everything's good. Come on in."

The younger man climbed into the back and sat down cautiously. Tyrell often put people on guard that way. And he liked it. It was his Chicago edge to rule his car no matter who sat inside it.

His agent friend said, "Okay, I'm done."

"Yeah, I'ma call you back after this ride, man," Tyrell told him.

"For what? You already told me you don't wanna do it, right?" the agent responded. "And I take *offense* to you saying I'm selling you into child labor. Why would I want to do that? If your price remains low, then my commission remains low. But at the same time, if you can't land *anything*, then what's the point in me trying to represent you?"

"Aw, man, that child labor thing was just a figure of speech. Stop gettin' all sensitive. I'll call you back later."

Once again, Tyrell hung up rudely to drive. He looked back at his passenger and said, "My bad, man. I got a lot of shit going on. How 'bout you?"

The passenger shook it off, not wanting to share his personal life with an angry old man. All he said was "I'm good."

"Yeah, well, that's good to hear. We all don't need fucked-up lives out here. Somebody gotta be doing good."

The younger man listened in silence. He wanted the ride to be over with as quickly as possible, especially when Tyrell kept talking.

"Yeah, man, motherfuckers try not to pay you what you're worth, and then they expect you not to be offended by it. Like, you're just supposed to take anything. You know?"

The younger man nodded and remained silent in the back. In his silence, he hoped and prayed that Tyrell would follow his lead and just drive without talking. The young man didn't care to hear the extra commentary.

"Aw'ight, let me see where we're going," Tyrell continued. He looked down at his cell phone, which was front and center with an attachment on the dashboard, and he made a hard right turn, following the directions of the app.

"Aw'ight, you just got nine minutes. I call them baby rides," he commented.

Finally, he got another response from the young man. "Baby rides?" He was confused about the context of the word *baby*. What did a "baby" have to do with his ride? Was the older man calling him extra young because of the short distance of his destination? The analogy didn't connect for him.

Tyrell grinned and explained it. "Anything under ten minutes is like riding a tricycle instead of a bike. So, I call them baby rides. You get it?"

The younger man grinned and mumbled, "Okay," He didn't want to lead the older man into another aimless conversation, but it was too late. Tyrell was already in a talkative mood.

"What about you, man? Would you keep taking less money

than you deserve on a job? 'Cause I've done that shit before and it didn't add up to nothing. Either they get happy 'cause they got you for a discount, or they keep trying to get more deals out of you."

The young man tried his hardest to mind his own business and make it home without conflict, but Tyrell was determined to push his point.

"I mean . . . it depends on the situation," the rider answered carefully. "But I'm not gonna *keep* doing it," he added.

It was the right answer. Tyrell got excited and said, "Exactly. And once you figure out these motherfuckers gon' keep trying to get you, you gotta cut off the well."

The rider nodded in agreement. "Yeah."

The problem was, Tyrell had cut off the well with his opportunities years ago by being so acidic in his responses. Of course he had a point about the value of his work and pay, but he had yet to understand that the majority of humans liked sugar more than spice. He still had to learn how to negotiate civilly. And it didn't matter how talented he was, how hard he worked, or how much writing experience he had, humans continued to value *charm* that Tyrell refused to utilize.

He had created the same issue for himself at home with his lady friend. He would drive all day and night, arguing about every issue that disturbed him, and then come home looking for healing. But she was tired of healing him, and tired of his toxic attitudes. He even walked into the house wrong.

"Yo, I'm home. Where you at?"

It was after eleven o'clock at night when most people are ready for bed. But Tyrell was wired like the strongest coffee. He was an all-night-long man, and it took a lot to deal with him. So, his lady slipped into the bathroom upstairs as soon as she heard him walk in, which was easy to do because he was so loud and predictable.

"What you got down here to eat tonight?" he yelled up the stairs. Without an answer from her, he headed into the kitchen to find food.

On the stove was chicken, broccoli with cheese, mashed potatoes, and buttered rolls, but it was all cold because she had prepared it all before eight.

"Aw, shit, I'ma eat good tonight," Tyrell told himself as he prepared a plate for the microwave. He had the same modus operandi, nearly every night. He'd walk in late with new, hard-earned money, while hungry and horny. Sometimes, he would bring fast food with him. Then he'd eat while watching sports highlights on ESPN inside the living room. Once he retired from that, he would expect to jump his lady's bones inside their bedroom, as if it was as easy as washing his hands. Yet . . . he couldn't understand why she had grown tired of it.

As talented as he was a creative writer, Tyrell was what relationship experts liked to call a Neanderthal. He just didn't get the basic need for change. And he was at his bad habits again that night.

He finished eating his food, watching the sports highlights on TV, and was still feisty with energy after midnight. But when he walked up the stairs, expecting to find his lady friend inside the bedroom, she had yet to leave the master bath that had now become her sanctuary.

Tyrell looked around and said, "Yo, you still in the bathroom? What the fuck you doin' in there?"

He took off his shoes and sat on the edge of their king-sized bed, which was peppered with magazines that she still liked to read and flip through.

"Hey!" he yelled again toward the bathroom door. "What you doin' in there?"

No answer. She had gotten used to ignoring him. But a Neanderthal would always pursue. So, he stood up and walked over to the bathroom door, expecting it to be locked, and it was.

"Are we doing this shit again? You gon' spend all night in the damn bathroom?"

"Did you put the leftover food away?" she finally responded to him.

"Yeah, I always put it away."

"No, you don't," she argued.

"Whatever. Just hurry up and get out of there."

"Why? Do you have to use the bathroom?"

Tyrell paused. They had a second bathroom out in the hallway, and a half bath downstairs. But he answered her anyway. "Yeah, I gotta go."

"And you have to use *this one*?"

It was fascinating how they continued to play a game of mental chess with each other, but it was what it was. And once those mental games had started, they continued going until someone or something would end them.

Tyrell realized that he was being ridiculous, and so was his lady. They were being ridiculous together. Yet, they continued with the charades.

"Why you always gotta paint your toenails late at night with the damn door locked? You can do that shit out here in the bedroom," he complained. He could smell the polish through the locked door. It was that pungent.

"No, I can't, because you're gonna *complain* and bother me."

"Well, why you gotta do the shit so late? You could have done it before I came home."

She ignored him again. She had explained it all before. Like anyone else with an active schedule, she was busy doing other things during the day, and she needed to be stable for her toes to dry instead of moving around. So, she chose to do them late at night, particularly when she didn't want to be bothered by him. She understood that the process of toenail painting gave her a perfect diversion. But when a man lives with a woman, he already knows as much.

"Yeah, I know what you're doin'. You try'na create another *excuse* not to fuck with me tonight. You ain't slick."

"Whatever," she responded casually through the door. No matter what he said, she was not opening it. He would just have to deal with himself. Tough cookie.

Realizing as much, Tyrell exhaled and thought about grabbing a beer out of the refrigerator in the kitchen.

"Shit!" he snapped. "Fuckin' playing these damn games all

the time." He walked off for the kitchen, still mumbling to himself. "Motherfucker work hard every day to pay the bills in this camp, and she wanna paint her damn nails all night. She knows my damn dick hard out here."

What could be said about the raw emotions of an unapologetic man? It was just *too much.* He may as well have gone out and grabbed a dinosaur bone and knocked his lady over the head with it. No self-respecting woman responds glowingly to that kind of denigration. He was fortunate to still have her. But you couldn't tell Tyrell that. He still lived on Mars, while his lady lived on Venus.

The man finally walked back down into the kitchen and grabbed two beers from the fridge. He sat back on the living-room sofa, clicked the TV on, and drank himself to sleep, while watching more ESPN highlights.

CHARLES CLAY

Reflection 14

"SHOW ME HOW MUCH YOU WANT IT. *SHOW ME.*"

"I want it *bad.* I want it."

"Then show, baby. Show me good."

Charles leaned back on a hotel bed and allowed a pretty, aspiring actress to perform oral sex on him.

"Mmm, hmmmm," she hummed in between the director's open legs.

"Is this how your boyfriend likes it?" he asked her.

"Yesss," she slurred. "Mmm, hmmmm."

"Then show me, baby girl. *Show me!*"

He gripped the pretty young woman by the crown of her curly head with both of his hands and pushed her down faster and faster.

"Show me. Show me. *Shooowww meeeeeee . . .*"

His climatic explosion squirted all over her face, her shoulders, and her hair as she closed her eyes at the foot of his hotel bed, where she had kneeled down below him.

Charles fell back against the pile of white pillows behind him, exasperated and panting. "My *God,* you're good!" he told her. "You need to be a *star*!"

The poor girl had a happy enough disposition to giggle at it, while wiping off the mess that he had made of her with a fluffy white towel.

She said, "I really do need to be a star. And I'm willing to do whatever it takes."

The young twenty-something was so beautiful she was hard to look at without feeling hypnotized. She had the thick, curly hair of a Latina, coupled with the smoothest peanut-butter brown skin you could imagine. She looked like a painting with no makeup needed. And Charles had ruined her.

He looked up at the ceiling and said, "I'm gonna see what I can do for you. I really am."

"Are you serious?" She said it as if she didn't believe him. Why should she? The popular director had lineups of *grown* women from all over the country wanting to be cast in his films. So, why would he need to promise a young hopeful *anything*? She hadn't even been featured in a music video yet, let alone a movie. But in America, people were taught to *believe* that anything was possible, no matter how unfathomable.

Charles looked into her young and pretty face as she stood beside him and continued to wipe herself off. She wore a hot pink top off the shoulders with ruffles, and blue jeans so tight she had to yank them up and peel them back off. Her colorful clog heels completed her stylish look. You could tell that she was into high fashion. All of that . . . just for him to ruin her.

The guilty director said, "Yeah, but you know we can never talk about this, right? This would be the worst way to start your career."

She grimaced as if it was the worst comment for him to make. "Oh, I already know that. My boyfriend wouldn't like that shit either." She grinned and added, "He would try to kill you."

Charles chuckled nervously. He didn't expect her to be so candid. That made him feel uneasy about her, as if she didn't know any better. They were the worst type of girls to try and keep a secret with. Naivety can be reckless . . . and dangerous.

He said, "Well, of course you would never tell him something like this, right?"

She frowned and said, "No, I'm not *stupid.* Why would I do that?"

Charles could think of five million reasons why. But he kept those ideas to himself. He didn't want to create what he was thinking by speaking it into existence.

Instead, he said, "Ah . . . I just wouldn't be too *loose* with talking about this, that's all." He grinned and added, "It's like *Vegas,* you know?"

She looked at him confused. "Like *Vegas*? What do you mean?"

Every word out of her mouth made him feel more anxious. "You know, what happens in Vegas *stays* in Vegas. You've never heard that saying before?"

The young woman continued to stare at him, as if she had no idea what he was talking about. "I mean, I've never even *been* to Vegas before. What do they do out in Vegas?" she asked.

Charles became so disturbed that he sat up in bed to think. "Ah . . . how old are you again?"

She started smiling. "Okay, like . . . I'm *legal,* but I'm not twenty-five yet. So, I can't get into, like, the *older* parties unless somebody lets me in. But I can get into everything else. I just haven't been out to *Vegas* yet . . . to do whatever the Vegas people do."

All of a sudden, the hotshot director felt like someone had tossed him into a frying pan with seasoning sprinkled on him. He was speechless, realizing that he had made a huge mistake.

He thought, *This girl's a complete freakin' airhead! What the hell did I just do to my career?*

But then she bailed him out of the fire.

"I'm just fucking with you," she admitted with another giggle. "You should have *seen* the look on your face. I should have taken a *picture* of it."

She laughed and said, "I'm twenty-seven, and I *know* what they do out in Vegas, I just haven't been there yet. They have legal prostitution there, right?"

Charles nodded, but he didn't think any of it was funny. She had left him speechless.

"That was a little, ah . . ." he mumbled, and stopped.

"Off the cuff, right?" she filled in for him. "I just wanted to show you some of my acting skills. You know, too many people look at me as just a pretty face and good hair. But I can really *act* though."

Charles didn't really care at that point. He was scared to death of her and didn't know what to expect. So, he shook his head and no longer believed anything she had to say. It could *all* be an act.

Did she just suck me off, or was I imagining that? he questioned. He started to believe it was an illusion to dismantle his feelings of anxiety.

He even told her so. "You know what? I don't believe anything. This could *all* be an act."

But it was not, and his pants were still down with semen dripping out of his penis to prove it. So, he quickly pulled his boxers up and zipped up his pants.

The pretty young woman looked down at him and repeated, "You don't *believe it*? What don't you believe? I'll do *anything* for this? Just *ask* me."

He said, "I *did* ask you. I asked you not to talk about this. And you turned it into a big old *joke.*"

"I just wanted to show you that I could *act*," she repeated. "I told you that."

The director had turned the tables on her and had *her* feeling anxious. She felt as if she had just messed up her big opportunity with him. And he could *tell.* So, he decided to use his new leverage on her.

"I don't know if you're *mature* enough for this business," he told her. "When people ask you not to do something, that's what they *mean.* Your coachability and protocol in this business is *everything.*"

She looked at him frantically. "I said I wasn't gonna talk about it. I told you that," she insisted.

Charles looked at her exotic frame of curves standing there inside the hotel room with her beautiful face, hair, and stylish clothes, and he wanted to test her, while testing himself. How much power did he really have?

"Okay, so you'll really do anything?"

"Yes." She didn't budge or waver.

There was a moment of silence, while he thought of everything he could ask her to do. But instead of going overboard, he kept it simple.

"Okay. Take everything off . . . and get back in bed."

She eyed him without a word and began to strip naked, starting with her top, as her pert breasts popped out in front of him. Next, she pulled and tugged and wiggled out of her form-fitting blue jeans, revealing a perfect shaved punany, and an ass as perfectly round as a basketball. Then she climbed onto the bed and slipped under the cool white sheets.

Charles watched it all in amazement, as if filming it for the big screen. The man couldn't believe his luck. He had been an awkward suburban kid with big, visionary dreams, who could never get the girls. But now . . . he felt like he could have them all. And he *loved it,* even though it terrified him to get caught.

I really shouldn't do this, he warned himself. *This could really come back to haunt me. I don't even trust this girl.*

But it was the *business.* And in the big leagues, there was no time to fear anything. Either you pushed ahead and got what you needed to get to keep going, or you got nervous and allowed yourself to get left behind. Or at least, that's what Charles had told himself.

So far, he had succeeded with the game plan of pushing himself ahead. So, he took off his clothes, clicked off the lights, and climbed back into the bed with this gorgeous, aspiring actress, with the intent of making her call him daddy.

JOSEPH DRAKE

Reflection 15

IMAGINE BEING INSIDE A ROOM WITH A GROUP OF VERY WEALTHY AND powerful White men. *Old* White men, the kind who don't apologize. It can be very stressful for a woman or a person of color, unless you feel like you're accepted by them, or you're doing a major business deal that they have to have. Because everyone and everything has a price. That's how they think about the world. It can all be bought.

Joseph Drake was a White man as well, he was just less wealthy and less powerful than the rest of the men inside the room. He was slightly younger too. So, he had to deal with the natural rules of the pecking order.

"Drake, go get me some more spinach dip."

That was Cunningham, a real estate tycoon in his seventies. He was holding out an empty plate for his young hedge fund partner to refill. He was all gray on top and smallish in size. He was the perfect example of a Napoleon complex, a little man with a big appetite and ego, who was buying, selling, and renting big buildings.

With Cunningham being in his seventies, Joe didn't mind catering to the older man. The more he catered, the more he imagined positive gains from their relationship. But he didn't feel that way about all of the men in the room.

"Hey, Drake, how long have you been a closet rapper?"

That was Wilton, a technology investor in his mid-fifties. He used the same joke from Joe's last name nearly every time they saw each other. Tall with a solid build and energy, Wilton was physical like a professional athlete. He reminded one of a high-school jock and bully who made life a living hell for any and everyone who was not on his level. And he continued to dye his hair to maintain a young and fierce business look.

Joe smiled and tolerated the man as he slid past him toward the table of finger foods that featured refreshments, beer, wine, and dip. But Joe didn't *like* the man. In fact, several of the men didn't like Wilton, particularly the older guys in the room who had less money. Sometimes, a younger man could be a little cavalier based on the size of his bank account. And they didn't like it.

"Hey, Drake, how's it going?"

That was Fincher in his sixties from Texas. He was a financial specialist who had written some of the biggest business plans in the country. He was also a gay man who wasn't bashful about it. If you were willing to be had, he was willing to have you. But Fincher typically dealt with younger men in their twenties and thirties. His boy toys.

Joe liked to keep his conversations short and sweet with Fincher. As a chest-thumping, type A man, he didn't want to accidentally say or do something awkward that may trigger the financial specialist to not want to work with him in the future. Fincher had been known for tuning guys out who he had a vendetta against, but he would never tell you. And Joe didn't want to sit on that side of the fence.

"I'm just staying on my best behavior and trying not to be too naughty," Joe responded with a grin. It was his code language, respecting the lifestyle of an opportunist, while slyly stating that he wasn't on the market for anything extracurricular.

Fincher smiled, realizing as much. "There's a time and place for everything," he responded.

"Don't I know it."

Joe filled the empty plate with more spinach dip and chips and was on his way back to Cunningham.

"Hey, bust a rhyme, Drake," Wilton teased on the way back. He was now flanked by Jacobs and Smith, two lackeys who smiled and laughed at everything Wilton said or did.

Joe decided to patronize the man. "*Ahhh, one and two / and I buckle my shoe / three and ah four / and I open that door / five and ah six / and I . . .*"

He laughed it off and kept it moving with the plate of spinach dip and chips in hand. But Wilton was feeling the improv rap and wouldn't let him leave. He even grabbed Joe's arm.

"Hey, keep it going, Drake. We'll make it rain for ya."

Jacobs and Smith howled laughing, while Joe held his tongue and his temper.

"Hey, I need to get this food back over to Cunningham. He's waiting for it."

Wilton looked in Cunningham's direction and frowned. "Aw, that old bat ain't going anywhere. Give us another rhyme."

Joe thought, *Jesus, I hate this guy! He's such a fucking asshole! And Jacobs and Smith are fucking cheerleaders! They need two skirts on with pom-poms!*

Nevertheless, he forced out a smile. "Maybe another time," he said, while brushing Wilton's hand away from his arm.

"Awww, party pooper," Wilton whined as Joe walked off. Humans could all be harassed and made fun of, man or woman, White or Black, rich or poor, Muslim or Christian. And we can all react to it the same way, *pissed*, while forcing ourselves to remain civil.

Then you have your no-nonsense leadership.

"All right, gentlemen, let's take our seats and dive into it."

That was Sampson, the lead domino in the room of nearly thirty White men. He was a hyperfocused computer software and games developer in his mid-sixties, who still had a lot of youthful energy. He was one of those guys who could find relatable conversations to connect to everyone. And he was no joke when it came to investing. So, even though he didn't have the most money in the room, he had the most *respect* and was very comfortable in leading their financial discussions.

The men all found their seats in five rows that stretched from the front to the back of the room, while Sampson continued to stand.

"Davis will lead with the updates of our goals and the status of our new efforts."

Davis was one of the younger men in the room with Joe, both in their forties. He was chubby and wore glasses, the kind of awkward, academic man who found solace in his expertise and research. He was most comfortable in what he could study and master, which did not include women. So, he was still unmarried and barely dating.

Davis took center stage in the room and said, "Our goal is to raise three hundred million dollars for the College Prep Initiative hedge fund. We are now at eighty-two million and change with two hundred and eighteen million left to go.

"So far, our new efforts have been . . . I guess *adequate*, but we could do a lot more," he concluded.

"You, ah, mentioned to me a few days ago, Davis, that you felt opening up the initiative to the Black and Hispanic communities could push us over the top a little bit faster. It that right?" Sampson asked him.

That question got Drake's full attention. How did the rest of the group of White men feel about helping minorities?

Davis nodded. "That's right. The increase of social media, interviews, and minority news articles could help take us over the top rather quickly."

"Yeah, but then they'll take over the fund. And it becomes a Black and Brown initiative instead of the red, white, and blue initiative that we all planned."

That was Allen, the tight ass in the room. He was slightly on the younger side himself in his early fifties with a pharmaceuticals, packaging, and distribution company. He was also one of the top three moneymakers in the room. He could finance the whole initiative by himself if he wanted to.

He said, "The problem with including the multicultural and minorities conversation is that they become *insatiable*. All of a sudden, everything becomes about *them*, and what they feel we should do, and how they feel the initiative should be run. And they just complain, and bitch, and gripe, and eventually they'll try to dictate what they feel we're supposed to be doing with *our* program when we're the ones who decided to help. You don't get to tell us how we would like to *help*. It just strikes me as being unappreciative.

"But if we continue to build this fund and initiative in secret, where we're not in the public eye, then no one gets bent out of shape, and we can include the number of minorities that we want to help, along with poor White kids, instead of having the Black and Brown dictate what we do," he concluded.

Joe looked around the room for a response and was itching to jump in, especially when he saw that no one outwardly disagreed. It takes *courage* to dissent. And Joe had to force himself to have it.

"You know, the problem that we get ourselves into when we do things in *secret*, is that the general public typically looks at that as if we're trying to *hide* something from them rather than us trying to help them," he commented.

Wilton smirked and said, "We *are* trying to hide it from them. But it's for their own *good*. It's like hiding the toys from the kids before Christmas. It's better that way. If you let the kids know where the Christmas presents are before you wrap them, they'll fuck them all up. You know that, Drake. Or maybe you *don't* know. You don't even have any kids."

Joe paused and thought about it. He *did* have kids. He just didn't let them know about it. In fact, most people didn't know about Joseph Drake's kids, not even his own family members.

Sampson broke the silence and said, "Wilton, are you comparing the African-American and Hispanic communities to *kids* on Christmas?"

Wilton held out his opened palms in innocence. "I'm just making a simple analogy about transparency. Sometimes it's *not* the best thing."

"I agree," Cunningham spoke up. "You have to allow the chef to finish preparing the meal before you start asking him for a taste test, because the meal is not officially *done* yet. Then you'll have people leaking out information and getting upset before we've had a chance to execute all of our plans.

"So, Wilton is *right*," he concluded. "Too much transparency, too early, can actually cripple a plan more than enhance it, particularly if we're referring to something more complicated and nuanced than what they're used to."

"Yeah, the main goal is to be inclusive of everyone, but that goal becomes compromised when the Black and Browns begin to view the funds and the initiative as only for *them*, which it is *not*," Allen argued.

"Okay, but we still need to inform the various communities that these funds are gonna be available for everyone. That way, they'll know when, where, and *how* to apply, and we'll get a significantly larger number of applicants who *qualify*," Joe insisted. "That's all I'm saying. There's nothing wrong with us doing that."

"Yeah, and we'll do that *after* we finish raising the money," Wilton countered. "That way they're not all *anxious* about it."

"But that would destroy the whole idea of us raising the money *faster*. Right, Davis?" Sampson asked for clarity.

Davis nodded again. "Yeah, with us publicizing the funds and the initiative—with the help of the Black and Brown communities—we would allow more people who *want* to help to know about it."

Cunningham said, "Now, are we also assuming that the Black and Brown communities are going to *contribute* to the funding themselves, because you know how they look at us. We already *have* the money, so they won't respond well to a bunch of rich, old White guys asking *them* to help raise more of it."

"And they're not going to *contribute* either," Allen argued. "These Black and Brown athletes and entertainers are only concerned about themselves and their *own* charities. They don't care about anyone else. It's all about *their* people. And they complain about everything we try to do that includes others."

Allen was really going in on it, displaying his honest emotions and true-blue colors, which made Joe's blood boil.

"Why are you talking about athletes and entertainers? They're not the only people who matter in the Black and Brown communities," Joe argued.

Cunningham answered, "But they're the only ones who have any *money*. What was there, *five* new Black billionaires over the past couple of years? And they're *all* in the sports and entertainment fields."

"That doesn't mean they're the only ones who can *contribute*. We have plenty of Black and Brown doctors, lawyers, and businesspeople who can contribute to the fund as well," Joe stated.

"Yeah, just not *enough* of them," Wilton countered, jumping back in. "And what are they gonna give, a thousand dollars apiece? That's not any money. I gave *two million*."

"Yeah, you have two million to *give*," Joe reminded his rich White peer.

"This is all what Allen and Cunningham are both alluding to," Sampson cut in. "Is it worth the risk and the public confusion to bring in these additional communities to help raise the funds if we *know* they're gonna prioritize their own personal or community concerns, which have nothing to do with our overall goals and mission to help *everyone*?"

After the leader spoke, there was silence in the room again.

He said, "So, how do we vote, yay or nay? How many people say yes, it's *worth* the risk?"

Not even Joe raised his hand. He wanted to see who else agreed with him in the room first. And outside of Davis, who came up with the idea, no one else raised their hands, so Joe joined Davis with his right hand up.

"All right, how many people say no, it's *not* worth the risk?" Sampson asked.

When the rest of the hands went up, Joe exhaled, nodded, and accepted the group's answer.

These guys don't give a fuck about helping outside communities, he mused. *It's all an ego stroke. Because if they really cared, they wouldn't have a problem with listening to how the people want to be helped.*

This fund is not about us. It's about them! he concluded.

At that point, Joe was ready to leave the room and not finish their meeting. But he couldn't. He knew there would be more important battles for him to have in the near future, battles that he wasn't too confident about.

Cunningham leaned into Joe at their chairs and mumbled, "You can't be so emotional about these things, Drake. We've done things the same way for a long time for a *reason.* And everyone can't understand those reasons, but at the end of the day, this is what we're agreeing to do, and we don't have to agree to do *anything.* So, they have to take what we offer them."

Joe continued to listen and nod, while settling back into his chair. And he understood. Rich White men were still in power, and they still wanted to control all of their efforts . . . even when they agree to help people.

DESTINY FLOWERS

Reflection 16

I WAS ON MY WAY BACK HOME ON INTERSTATE 20 WEST AFTER ANother late night at work when Destiny Flowers called me on my cell phone. Her name popped right up on the dashboard screen of my car with the phone connected to the stereo system.

"Hello," I answered, confused. I don't know how she got my cell phone number. I surely don't remember giving it to her. Why would I do that?

"How are you doing, Dr. Benning? You real busy now, huh?"

"Ahhh . . . how did you get my cell phone number?" I asked her.

"You called me from it after the last time we talked, and I just saved it on my phone. Why? You don't want me to have it?"

"I just don't remember giving it to you," I responded. "So, I called you from my cell phone?"

"Okay, so, you're that busy where you don't remember calling me?" she questioned.

I really didn't remember. When would I have the *time* and what would be the *reason* to call her?

"What did I call you about?" I asked.

"You were just following up with me after missing my call to you, because we're always missing each other."

"Missing each other? Did you sign up for a session yet?"

This woman had me so confused, I didn't know if she was making shit up or what. But she got my number somehow.

"Yeah, that's what we talked about last time, setting up a session. You didn't put me in your schedule book?"

"I don't have a schedule *book*, I just have a calendar on my computer."

"Well, you need to check that for both of us then," she told me.

"I'm not doing that right now. I'm driving."

"On I-Twenty West?"

How come this girl is always trying to guess what I'm doing?

"Does it matter?" I asked her curtly. She sounded like a possessive old boyfriend or something.

She said, "Why it seem like you always catch *attitudes* with me? Is that *professional*?"

It wasn't, but nor was calling me on my cell phone after work hours. So, I let her ass know.

"You know what? I have my personal time and my business time. And right now it's *personal*. So, excuse me for being quick-tempered, but I'm off the clock right now."

"Well, is this how you act when you're *off the clock*? Maybe you need to set up a session to talk about *you*."

"You got *jokes*?" I snapped at her.

"No, I got *facts*," she responded. "You're the one out here *trippin'* on me. I finally set up a session to get myself some help and this is how you treat me."

I *swear*, this girl could bring out the *worst* in me. So, I had to take a deep breath to gather myself before I responded the wrong way, which I definitely was about to do.

Instead, I said, "Okay, I'm almost home now. So, what I'm gonna do is check my appointment schedule to see about your session, then I'll email you to confirm it or send you a new link to fill it in."

"See that? Was that so hard to do? That was *easy*, right? That's all you had to tell me."

I stared out at the road in silence and shook my head. What else could I say to this woman?

"Okay. I got you. As soon as I get home."

"You're not gonna forget again, are you?"

"No. I will not forget," I told her. "Now let me go," *before I curse your ass out in here!* I snapped to myself. She was that irritating.

"How's everything else going for you? Do you have a hubby? You don't mind me asking, do you?"

"Okay, it's time for me to go. I told you already, my personal life is not part of the conversations."

She said, "Look, I'm just being friendly with you, 'cause it sound like you need a man. Is that who you're driving home to?"

"Excuse me?"

"I didn't stutter. I said, 'It sounds like you need a *man.*' "

I pressed my end call button and hung up on her. That was the end of that. Then she called me right back, and I ignored her. But when she called three more times, I had to set this girl *straight.* She was asking for a Camden, New Jersey, ass kicking. *For real!*

I accepted her fifth call and said, "Look, you are really *bothering* me. Okay? Now, at this point, I don't care if I help you or *not,* because obviously, something is very *wrong* with you."

"Well, *duhhh.* That's why I'm trying to get *help.*"

"Well, you're gonna have to find someone else to help your crazy ass!" I barked at her.

"That's not very *professional* for you to call me *crazy.*"

"And I'm not on my professional *time* right now, either."

"That don't mean you can't *be* professional. Your reputation is your reputation no matter *what* time you're on. It's still *you.*"

She had a valid point, which upset me even more. Before I realized it, I had drifted into the right lane as I drove.

BBBLLLAAARRRNNN!!!

"SHIT!" I hollered.

I whipped my steering wheel back to the left as a big-ass truck blew the horn at me.

"Watch yourself on that road!" Destiny warned me too late. It was *her* fault that I was drifting in the first place.

"Yeah, like you *care,*" I commented.

"I *do* care," she told me. "We didn't even have our first session yet. So, don't you *die* on me."

I shook my head again. This girl was liable to say anything. I called her a *woman* and a *girl* interchangeably because I realized that she was *grown*, but she still had a lot of immaturity about her, like preadolescent immaturity. I couldn't even call it high school. She had middle-school issues going on.

I told her, "Trust me, I'm not planning on dying anytime soon."

"Are you sure?"

What kind of a question was that?

"Am I *sure*? What the hell's wrong with you?" I asked her. "Are *you* planning on dying?"

"Eventually, we're *all* gonna die. You don't know that? You're not a *goddess*."

"And neither are *you*," I argued. "You're not a *goddess*, either."

Honestly, I didn't even know what she looked like. Based on her immaturity, I figured she was attractive and used to getting her way with other immature people. But I could have been wrong. Maybe she just *thought* she was attractive. And we had a whole lot of that in the world.

I had no idea how she would respond to me, but I was curious, so I waited. And then . . . she started laughing.

"Yeah, you *wish*. *Nerd*. I know who you are. You're that smart girl in school, who was scared of all the boys, 'cause you thought they were try'na get your oochie coochie. Now you all grown-up and try'na *help* somebody. Girl, sit down."

I paused. I hadn't heard that tone from her before and it startled me. That tone wasn't immature at all. It was deep, *grown-folks'* shit. And it reminded me of my *mother*. But how could *she* know that? Was it just a coincidence?

"Are you still there?" she asked me.

"Who am I speaking to?" I questioned. I was curious again.

"Who you *been* speaking to?"

"I was speaking to Destiny Flowers," I answered. "But it sounds like someone else jumped on the phone. So, I just wanted to make *sure*." Maybe this girl had multiple personalities in her bag of issues.

"You speaking to the right person. I just got different *moods*, like every other woman," she answered. "But I'ma let you go now, so you can drive home safely. And I'ma talk to you another time."

Instead of lingering on the phone and waiting for me to respond, she immediately hung up and left me confounded. I didn't know *what* to think. This woman was more complicated than I first thought.

"Okay," I told myself with a nod at the wheel. "I need to meet this woman to figure out what's really going on with her." So, I planned to check my calendar as soon as I got home to see if Destiny had actually booked a session like she told me she had.

DARK & MOODY

Reflection 17

IT'S AMAZING HOW PEOPLE CAN MAKE RANDOM COMMENTS AND LOCK something in your head that you weren't even trying to deal with. I wasn't thinking about men or relationships at all. I've been more focused on my job and my goals. Then you wake up and realize that you keep adding things to your plate that take the place of a man. Did I do that on purpose or was it all happenstance?

At any rate, I started thinking about Tyrell Hodge, of all people. He had a live-in girlfriend who he was having intimacy issues with. I wondered how things were making out with that. So, I continued to feel sorry for him. But one thing was for sure, he needed to calm down with all of his frustrations. That only made situations toxic with everyone else he dealt with. No one else cared about what he had been through or was still involved in. They all had their own problems to deal with and Tyrell needed to realize that.

By accident, I pressed on another one of Dark & Moody's tracks in my car that had very mellow music behind it. This track featured a harp and strings that actually fit the mood of melancholy that I was in.

You know those times when you feel a touch of sadness, while remembering the places, people, and things that are no longer in your life? I was having one of those moments, all because of Destiny Flowers and her different *moods.*

As I continued to listen to this music, I began to wonder about Tasha Samuels as well. Was she still thinking about sacrificing people for her success? Did she have a man, a woman, or someone to confide in outside of me? I'm sure she did. She had to have *someone.* But I didn't know and I hadn't asked her.

What I did know was that she had a real gift with picking instruments that colored her music perfectly, while getting an emotional rise out of you. And I wondered how she would work out with Mrs. Melody, who seemed to have an opinion about everything.

I shook my head and smiled, while turning into my exit. I could just imagine Mrs. Melody's *mouth.*

"She's gonna be real picky," I said to myself of the young rapper and her taste of music.

But I wonder what they'll come up with.

Sure enough, Mrs. Melody met up with Dark & Moody for the two of them to work on something new inside Tasha's bedroom studio. They were trying to find something they both liked. And Mrs. Melody was right on DM's case.

"Wait a minute. Why do *you* have to like it if *I'm* the one recording to it?" she complained, after Dark & Moody skipped over another beat that she liked.

"That beat's too simple," Tasha answered. "I wanna make sure this song hits more than just one emotion."

"Well, you *made* the beat. What were you thinking about when you made it?"

They were both dressed down for a change in sweats, but the sweat clothes that girls wore nowadays showed all of their curves. It was as if spandex had turned into the new silk, and women were wearing ass-and hip-hugging tights everywhere!

Tasha eyed Melody in her small bedroom studio and was bluntly honest with her. "An artist who has more lyrical *range* can take a song in different directions *without* the music changing.

But with you . . . I wanna make *sure* you do that by changing up the beat."

Mrs. Melody stared at her. "And what if I don't like how you're trying to change it?"

DM stared back. "You know, you don't have to have your way with *everything*. Let the beat do what it do and just follow behind it."

Melody took a peek at her cell phone and returned a text message before she responded. "How 'bout you let me do what I do on the beat and you just follow behind *me*."

DM shook her head and froze with a novel idea. "How 'bout we do *two* songs with a beat you like and a beat that I like?"

Melody responded to another text before she answered. "And I can use that same simple track that I already like?"

DM exhaled slowly. "Yeah, but you gotta keep your lyrics on topic, and it ain't all about just *sex*."

Mrs. Melody grimaced. "So . . . what's the topic?"

"Anything but *sex*. I mean, be *creative*, for God's sake," Tasha complained. "I gotta come up with something for you to *say*, too? I mean, I can do that, but I thought you wanted *control* over your writing and what you plan to say on it."

Another call came through on Melody's cell phone, the eighth call in less than an hour that they were together. Tasha took note of it.

"I guess you're real popular with the guys, I see," she commented.

Melody smiled. "When you got 'em, you got 'em." Then she stopped and thought about it.

"That's a song idea right there. I got 'em locked on it."

DM frowned. "That's the same old stuff you *been* doing."

"Yeah, but it's *catchy*. And girls can relate to it." She immediately started chanting the hook, *"When you . . . got 'em, you got 'em / when you . . . got 'em, you got 'em / when you . . . got 'em, you got 'em / when you . . . got 'em, you got 'em . . ."*

Melody stopped again and nodded to it, grinning. "Now, that's a hot record."

Dark & Moody shook her head in disappointment but she didn't fight the process. It *was* a hot record. She could hear it easily. The words jumped off Mrs. Melody's tongue. And if the words jumped off her tongue that effortlessly, they would jump off everyone else's tongues as well.

Nevertheless, DM had her comments. "I hate them easy-ass hooks like that."

"Whatever. Pull that beat back up."

Dark & Moody found the simple beat in her music files and played it loud through her speakers, while Mrs. Melody jumped on it in sync with the rhythm.

"When you . . . got 'em, you got 'em / when you . . . got 'em, you got 'em / when you . . . got 'em, you got 'em / when you . . . got 'em, you got 'em . . ."

Tasha nodded to Melody's vocal cadence and sat down in front of her keyboard. "Keep doing it, I hear something."

As Mrs. Melody continued to have fun with the hook, Dark & Moody played notes on her keyboard, adding attention-getting strings and a new bass line that fit right in with the groove.

Melody listened to it and smiled, broadly. "There you go! I knew you could do it!"

Tasha smiled back at her. "Yeah, but you gotta add *more* to that hook," she insisted.

Melody grimaced again. "Add more for what? You gotta learn how to leave stuff alone when it's already *hot.* Too many producers do that and end up overproducing a song."

DM ignored her and started chanting the hook herself. *"When you . . . got 'em, you got 'em / my eyes . . . got 'em, you got 'em / my thighs . . . got 'em, you got 'em / they rise . . . got 'em, you got 'em / these guys . . . got 'em, you got 'em / like flies . . .*

"Come up with stuff like that. And what I'll do is stack the first part of the hook on the edges, and place whatever you add to it down the middle," Tasha explained to her.

Mrs. Melody thought about it and nodded, while running the idea through her head, right as her cell phone went off again.

"God, would these guys leave you the fuck *alone* for a minute?

We try'na *work* over here," Dark & Moody snapped. "Put that shit on silence already!"

Melody laughed it off. "They can't help themselves," she bragged. "But let me call him back, 'cause he hit me up four times now."

Dark & Moody shook her head and barked, "Pressed!"

"And that's *exactly* how you gotta have 'em too," Melody responded.

"Whatever."

Mrs. Melody answered her phone as she walked out into the hallway to hear. "Hey, love."

"Yo, where you at?" a gruff, masculine voice asked her.

"I'm in the studio working on something right now."

"What studio?"

"A girlfriend of mine has her own setup."

Dark & Moody listened and watched from inside her studio room as Mrs. Melody started gyrating in sex moves. Then she bent over to touch her toes with her left hand, while holding her cell phone in her right. With the sheer material of the spandex, her ass looked like she was practically naked with multicolored skin. And DM took in every curve of her.

This sexy-ass bitch is getting to me, and she don't even know it yet! Tasha expressed to herself as she continued to watch and grin.

Melody was putting on a private freak show while on her phone in the hallway.

"What time you gon' be done?" her guy asked over the line.

"I'll call you," she told him, pushing his imaginary head between her legs with her left hand. She even tossed her head back and squeezed her eyes shut, as if she was in ecstasy.

Dark & Moody watched it all and kept grinning. *This bitch here!* she told herself.

"Aw'ight, I'll call you. But let me finish what I'm doing right now. This is how I make my money," Melody told her guy.

"You could make money over *here,* too. You know I got you on that. We got plenty of beats," he responded.

"I know, but I like doing my own thing. I don't like to *assume* shit," Melody countered, while bending over and touching her toes again.

Tasha had an urge to run out in the hallway and grab her erotic ass, while wearing her own spandex. But she restrained herself. Melody didn't know her like that . . . *yet.*

Yeah, she gon' make me get her ass in bed, DM mused as she watched.

"Aw'ight, well, let me get back to work. I'll see you in a minute," Mrs. Melody told her guy.

"You mean in a couple of *hours,* right?" he corrected her.

She grimaced. "Yeah, you know what I mean."

"Aw'ight, call me when you're done."

For her encore, Melody imitated a strong-armed man, stroking her from the back with violent thrusts, as she pumped her hips faster and faster, while holding on to an imaginary woman.

All the while, Dark & Moody continued to watch, shake her head, and grin, while feeling moist and slippery between her own legs.

Once she ended the call, Mrs. Melody walked back into the studio room as if nothing had happened. "Okay, where were we?"

"So, you can turn it on and off just like that, hunh?" Tasha asked with a snap of her fingers. She was amazed at how nonchalant Melody was about her sexuality.

She said, "I tell women all the time, you keep letting them old rules about sex control you, and you'll end up being *miserable,* like a million other girls out here. So, if I wanna fuck somebody, then I'm gonna *fuck.* And I don't get all bent out of shape about it. Nor do I let anybody tell me that I'm not supposed to feel *sexual.* Do your titties feel good when you rub 'em?"

Dark & Moody grinned. "Of course."

"Okay then. It feels good for a *reason,*" she noted. "Now, that don't mean you go out and fuck every guy, all day and all night, 'cause we got other shit to do like *they* do. And you ain't no open fuckin' door to give it to just *anybody.* But once you choose who you choose, stop fucking punishing yourself thinking you gon' control these guys with your pussy, because you're *not.* And all you're doing is creating a cat and mouse game that's gon' come back and bite you in the ass when neither one of you can stop doing it. Then you start feeling all *guilty* and confused about something that was given to us from *God.*

"So . . . I just do my thing and keep it moving," she concluded. "I don't add all that extra stress to my life. I don't need it."

"What about if a guy cheats on you?" Dark & Moody questioned. That was the elephant in the room that ruined relationships for a lot of women. If men could keep their dicks *at home,* maybe more women would feel better about being submissive instead of complaining.

But Melody's response to it was a giggle and a shrug. "Hell, I cheat too. I ain't married. And I never call any of these guys my boyfriend. So, don't get it confused. But anyway . . . so, you want me to add different comments to the hook that you're gonna mix in the middle, while the rest of the hook is stacked on the edges?"

DM nodded, "Yeah." She was impressed again at how Mrs. Melody was able to jump right back into business.

"Aw'ight, I can do that!" she agreed. She started freestyling with an abundance of energy. *"My eyes / my thighs / make nature rise on these guys / they vibe / then lie / trying everything to get inside . . ."*

Dark & Moody continued to smile, while enjoying every minute of their work, even while thinking of Mrs. Melody as a one-dimension sex fiend.

Well, it is what is, she told herself. *I gotta roll with the flow. She's fucking good at this! And she got me wet now too. But we'll deal with that at another time. Right now, we got songs to make.*

MRS. MELODY

Reflection 18

AFTER A COUPLE OF HOURS OF VIBING TO THE FIRST BEAT, DARK & Moody finished an easy sex song with Mrs. Melody, which was exactly what she didn't want to do. But the result was a hot record! She had to admit it herself. The song had a contagious swing and thump to it that was sure to get the strip clubs rocking.

"So, what you think?" Mrs. Melody asked, knowing what she already knew.

DM smiled. "It's nice."

Melody frowned at her. "Aw, girl, stop *trippin'*. You know that shit is *hot.* You can't even keep your *neck* straight. We'll finish your complicated song next time."

"And when is that gonna be?" Tasha questioned.

"Whenever the fuck it is. It could be tomorrow," Melody snapped with her foul mouth.

Dark & Moody nodded. "Okay. I'm gonna mix this one down, and we'll get to the next one whenever we get to it."

"Cool," Mrs. Melody perked, while gathering her things to leave.

"So . . . what are you about to do now?" Tasha asked her.

Melody looked at her as if she was crazy. "I'm 'bout to hook up with this guy. The motherfucka been calling me all night? You *forgot?*"

"That don't mean you gotta hook up with him," DM commented.

Mrs. Melody tossed her colorful pocketbook over her right shoulder and stood in the doorway. She said, "Why wouldn't I?"

Dark & Moody shrugged. "I don't like it when guys are all pressed like that."

"Well, you still got a lot to *learn* then. 'Cause when a motherfucka pressed like that, you can get whatever you want out of him," Mrs. Melody explained. "And that's exactly what I plan to do tonight. He gon' eat this pussy."

The girl was *shameless.* Tasha laughed at it.

I wish I could eat your pussy too. And have you eat mine, she thought to herself. Melody had that kind of wicked power over everyone.

"Well, be safe out there," Dark & Moody told her.

"Oh, I know how to handle myself," Melody commented. She even pulled out a colorful gun from her carry bag, like a comicbook movie. It was a .25 handgun that looked like a toy. But it wasn't.

Dark & Moody eyed it and cringed. "What are you doing with that?"

Melody stared at her. "What the hell you *think* I'm doin' with it? These guys are *crazy* out here, especially in the music industry. I ain't slippin'."

Tasha shook her head and was baffled. "You're getting more interesting by the minute," she confessed. And she *liked it!* She knew people who sold guns.

Mrs. Melody grinned and slid her gun back into her bag to walk out.

"All right, I'll talk to you."

Dark & Moody jumped up from her music station to lead her to the front door.

"I'll walk you out."

"You don't have to. I know where the door is," Melody told her.

"Yeah, but that's *rude.*"

"Not if I'm walking myself out. I don't need an escort," Melody argued.

It didn't matter because Tasha was already walking her to the front door. And Melody could tell that she liked her now. So, she teased her.

"I'll be safe out there, Mom. Don't worry." She even stroked her left arm, gently.

Dark & Moody nodded and smiled again. "All right. Call me if you need to."

Mrs. Melody returned to her car with bounce and swagger in every step. She looked up from the apartment complex parking lot toward Tasha's third-floor window and grinned, knowing what she knew.

"When you . . . got 'em, you got 'em / when you . . . got 'em, you got 'em . . ." She chanted her catchy hook again as she climbed behind the wheel of her car.

Then it was over. She got back on point and returned a call to her guy.

"Yeah, where you at? I'm done now."

"What happened to calling me back in a *minute*?" he questioned. It was damn near midnight. He had a point.

Melody paused. What was he trying to say? "You knew what I meant. I told you what I was doing," she barked at him.

"Yeah . . ." he mumbled. He sounded noncommittal.

Melody read it accordingly. "So . . . what, you ain't try'na see me now?"

He probably got a hoe with him, she assumed.

"Give me umm . . . a few minutes . . . I'ma call you back," he told her measuredly.

She nodded, knowing what she knew. "All right." And she hung up. "Fuck him! He must think I'm stupid!"

Then she thought of calling someone else. "I'on even feel like calling him," she commented. But she was already pressing his number on her cell phone.

"Hello," a calm voice answered.

"Hey, umm . . . what are you up to?" Melody asked.

He paused. "I thought you told me you was gon' pull back?"

Melody backed her car out of the parking space and was still confused about what she wanted to do. Sometimes it's better to do nothing. Just go on home and enjoy an evening watching television or reading a good book. But that's not what she wanted to do. She felt restless. So, she pressed the issue.

"I mean, if that's how you wanna take it. But . . ."

It was up to him. Either he wanted to take advantage of her moment of weakness, or he didn't.

"I ain't doin' nothing. What you wanna do?" he asked her calmly.

I wanna get my pussy ate, Melody thought with a grin.

She was ridiculous. But at least she realized that stating what she was thinking about would have been too forward, especially when calling a man on the rebound. She would have to ease him into her desires in person.

"I mean, it's whatever," she answered. She was already driving in his direction.

For whatever the reason, he understood that she was offering him a free pair of her panties after breaking off relations with him a week ago, and he wasn't going to turn the opportunity down. So, he said, "Aw'ight. I'm at the crib."

"Meet me at the Waffle House. I'm hungry," she told him. "I just came out the studio."

He paused again. The audacity of the girl. "Just order what you need to get and bring it to the house with you. I ain't going out there. I'm nice and settled."

Again, it was damn near midnight, and he was not out running the streets of Atlanta. Nevertheless, Mrs. Melody was ready to argue. Waffle House was right around the corner from him. But she stopped herself. Beggars can't be choosers, and she was definitely begging.

"All right. I'll call you when I'm pulling up," she responded with a cooler head.

She ended the call and was filled with trepidation on her

drive. *Should I do it or not do it?* Yet, she continued on her way to the Waffle House that was right around the corner from her destination.

Melody found an open spot in the Waffle House parking lot and pulled in. She then hopped out without her bag with the gun in it. She only needed a twenty-dollar bill to pay for her order, and she considered her northern area of Atlanta to be safer, where she didn't need to feel overly protective.

She walked in with her twenty-dollar bill in hand and headed straight to the counter.

"Can I get a Texas Cheesesteak melt with a side of hash browns?"

An older Black waitress wrote up the ticket and passed it on to the cooks behind her, while Mrs. Melody paid for her food and took a seat on a stool to wait for it. And as soon as she swung her head to the right, in walked trouble.

Shit! She panicked. Her guy BJ looked her straight in the eyes with a flirty female hanging all over his left arm. Medium brown and handsome with the solid build of a football player, he was shocked to see her sitting there right out in front of him.

"I guess that's why you didn't get a chance to call me back, huh?" Melody asked him sarcastically.

In his late twenties with money, BJ's gold jewelry glittered against his black designer shirt, and was shiny enough to blind you. "We just hanging out," he responded immediately. He looked ready to shake the woman off his arm too, but she held him tightly with a firm grip and a big body. She was a slightly lighter brown complexion than he was, and she looked like an oversized swimsuit model, the kind of girl who called her extra ass and titties "healthy."

"Look like you doin' more than hanging out to me," Melody quipped, eyeing them both.

The curvy woman's smile and giggle turned into a frown as she sized up the situation.

She looked BJ in his face and said, "You were supposed to call her back *when*? While you were with *me*? Is this the girl you were on the phone with earlier?"

As young people liked to say, the man was straight *busted*. He felt so exposed that he was ready to do away with both of them. And that's exactly what he decided to do.

"You know what? Fuck all of this." He pulled his left arm away and said, "I'm not about to be in the middle of no bullshit. So, y'all do what y'all gon' do." And he walked out without the woman he walked in with.

The woman looked around at everyone inside the Waffle House and felt embarrassed. All eyes were on *her*, including Mrs. Melody's.

"So what you gon' call, an Uber?" Melody asked the older, taller, and thicker woman. It was an authentic question, but the timing and reality of the situation made the Waffle House customers laugh.

"Oh, shit! She didn't!" someone commented.

The curvy woman stared Mrs. Melody down as if she was ready for a fight. But she stopped herself with a raised palm of surrender.

"You know what? I'm not even gonna go there." She walked back out alone with the intent of calling BJ back to come get her, while Mrs. Melody thought of calling him back herself.

"Matter fact," she told herself, while still seated on the stool, "he better not get her." She already assumed what the woman was thinking. She had no choice. BJ had left her there stranded.

"Hello," BJ answered on the first ring.

"You better not pick that bitch up. Let her catch a *ride* home," Melody demanded, spitefully. She had no idea how far the woman lived, nor did she care.

BJ had a nerve to chuckle at it. "You *cold*, man, you *cold*," he commented.

His response made it obvious where his loyalties were.

"You just couldn't *wait* for *two* fucking hours," Melody snapped at him. "*Guys*."

"Ain't it the *truth*," the older waitress responded with a chuckle. "They're *all* impatient." The Texas Cheesesteak melt with hash browns was ready. So, she slid it over the counter.

"Thank you," Melody told her, grabbing it.

"So, what you want me to do?" BJ asked her over the line.

Mrs. Melody stood up to walk out with her bag of food. "Meet me at the Ritz-Carlton," she answered out the doorway.

"The Ritz-*Carlton*? What, you got a room over there already?"

He sounded leery, as if he wasn't trying to *pay* for one.

Mrs. Melody read the conflict in his voice. "No, I just want you to meet me there 'cause it's close by. Then we'll figure out what we doin'. Just don't pick that bitch up," she repeated.

"Yo, I heard you the first time. And she blowin' up my phone *right now.*"

Melody climbed into her car and placed her food in the passenger seat. She said, "Of course she is. You got her out here looking stupid."

"Naw, *you* got her out here like that," he argued.

Melody pulled out of the Waffle House parking lot and smirked. "I didn't bring her ass out here, and I didn't *leave her. You* did that."

She drove right past the curvy woman who was *pissed* and standing out on the sidewalk, while still trying to call BJ.

"This motherfucker!" she yelled, up the street from the Waffle House.

Mrs. Melody looked the woman off with her new song still in mind. *When you . . . got 'em, you got 'em / when you . . . got 'em, you got 'em . . .*

Meanwhile, she forgot all about the second man she had called to see that night. Her rebound with him was no longer needed. She didn't even bother to call him back with a handy excuse.

Instead, she shrugged and mumbled, "Oh, well, you win some, you lose some," and went on with her business.

Mrs. Melody pulled up at the front entrance of the Ritz-Carlton in Buckhead, where BJ was already waiting in his car in front of hers. She climbed out to walk up to his driver's-side window as he stepped out of his car to greet her.

He immediately shook his head and smiled. "This a crazy-ass night, man."

Melody smiled back at him. "Ain't it though? So, where we going? Does that chickie know where you live?"

He shook it off. "Naw, I was ready to take her home after getting her something to eat."

"And then what?"

Melody was already assuming things.

"Then I was gonna call you," BJ lied to her.

"Yeah, right. You tellin' me you wasn't gonna do her tonight? Don't lie."

"I told you, we just hangin' out," BJ insisted.

While they continued their conversation outside his car, they were oblivious to being watched and listened to by an eavesdropper who stood right out in front of the hotel. The early-thirties Black man with a fully groomed beard jumped on his cell phone to report the incident.

"Ay Gary, it's Mike."

"Hey, what's up, man? What you doin' tonight?" Gary answered.

"I'm outside the Ritz-Carlton waiting for my lady to come down so we can go out, and I'm standing right in front of that rapper girl you mess with?"

"Who, Mrs. Melody? You *sure*? She was supposed to be on her way over here. She told me she was going to Waffle House," Gary informed his friend.

"Oh, yeah? Well, not only is she not getting Waffle House, she's out here with that promoter BJ you don't like. I just figured I'd tell you, 'cause that's a li'l bit *much* to be messin' with the same girl."

There was a long pause over the line. Finally, Gary said, "Thanks for tellin' me, man. Good lookin' out."

"You got it."

Less than a fifteen-minute drive away, Gary took a deep breath, exhaled, and looked down at his cell phone in muscular brown hands.

"Is this young bitch out here trying to play me?" he mumbled to himself. He called her number and waited . . . for no answer. Then he texted her.

Yo what you doing? You still coming through?

Again, there was no answer. Then she texted him back.

Something came up. I'll call you tomorrow.

Gary smiled and nodded, deviously. "Yeah, this young bitch must think I'm a *sucker.* Okay."

He stood up from his sofa, where he watched a Thursday Night Football game on a large flat-screen TV. He had clicked the volume on mute for his cell phone call.

Thick like a nightclub bouncer in a tight-fitting, dark blue T-shirt, he rubbed the knuckles of his right hand with sinister thoughts in mind. But he tried his best to shake them off.

"Nah . . . I'm gon' leave this girl alone . . . before somebody get hurt out here."

CHARLES CLAY

Reflection 19

CRIMES OF THE HEART ARE PARTICULARLY DANGEROUS, AND THEY are often committed spontaneously. When our human emotions get all twisted up, look out. We don't tend to think straight in those moments, while hit by a wave of anxieties that we don't know how to handle. So, we end up making reckless decisions out of fury that we live to regret. And sometimes . . . we may not live through it at all, depending on who we affronted.

But Charles lived, with a whole lot of nervous apprehension that he could have avoided with better decisions. And when he entered his studio office on Monday morning, he lacked his normal calm swagger, replaced by a skittish energy.

"Are we still on schedule for today?" his pretty-faced assistant asked from his office doorway.

"Huh?" Charles uttered with his head on a swivel. He wasn't ready to receive her that morning. His mind was still in a clouded haze from his recent events with women.

The thick-bodied assistant in her late twenties smiled and looked down at her watch. "You were supposed to have a conference call at ten thirty, and it's now a quarter of eleven. So, I was wondering if the schedule had changed."

"Oh, shit! Get me on that call!" he panicked.

His assistant smiled, calmly. "Okay. Not a problem."

She disappeared to her workstation to set up the call.

Charles took a deep breath and sat in his office chair, attempting to relax. "All right, new day, new money," he told himself.

As soon as his office line buzzed, he picked up the phone and got back to work.

"Charles, have you seen the new production budget?"

It was a Black woman, his co-producer on film projects, who was all about business with no small talk.

Charles hesitated. "What's wrong with it?" He hadn't seen the new film budget yet. He immediately opened his laptop on his desk to have a look, as the producer went into it.

"They are fucking us again! They always do this with Black films. I am so fucking *tired* of this!" she ranted.

Charles couldn't get his emails to open fast enough. "Well, what's the number?" he asked as he continued to wait for his computer to respond.

"Two point two million."

Charles listened and paused. "Well, that's not *that* bad. It qualifies us for the tax break."

"Yeah, and that's *all* it does. So, it's obvious that's all they wanted to do. They just wanna get their fucking *money* back! They don't care about this film," she continued to rant over the line.

Charles began to smile and returned to his calm swagger. His composure was a big reason why he had been able to sustain success as a Black filmmaker. He never allowed the drama over money or the smaller details to distract him from the bigger goal of directing a good film. As long as the money was there, and it was a good project, he was available to direct.

"Jackie, calm down," he told her. "Of *course* they want their money back. That's why they're investing."

"Well, we need to find more people who *like* what we're doing. We're not amateurs anymore. That's barely *half* of what he needed."

"And we'll make it work as always," he assured her.

"But I'm tired of that 'making-it-work' shit! We've been doing that for *eight* years now!" Jackie barked. "We need to move the hell up the ladder. That's like working the same job for eight years and never getting a *raise.* You gotta start thinking bigger than that, Charles. Or they're always gonna try to get us for *cheap.*"

Charles exhaled and sunk back into his chair. He was getting tired of hearing his partner's ranting over money and elevation. He figured they were both in their thirties and still had plenty of time to grow. But if she was in a rush . . . then maybe she needed to partner with someone else.

He said, "Making films is not all about the *hype*, the cars, fancy clothes, and all of that stuff. It's about the *craft* of getting a product done *correctly*. And that's what we've been doing." Then he paused, before he made an ass of himself. "Maybe you need to pull back on some of the extravagant expenses that you have. I mean, you didn't have to buy that *condo*, or the loaded Range Rover."

Jackie heard that and said, "Excuse me? Mr. Fuck Everything That *Moves.* I do very *well* with my money. Have you forgotten about my real estate? I got that damn condo on a *deal*! A *great* damn deal at that. And my *car*? Okay, I splurged on that. But I've been working my *ass* off for you on these films, and that's what you got to say to me for trying to move you up the ladder for bigger and better projects?

"You got some fuckin' *nerve*!" she blasted him. "All you seem to think about is *pussy* and getting your little ding-dong licked. And it's gon' come back to bite you in the ass. You think I don't know about these little fucking girls you keep dealing with? You gotta get that shit off your *mind* and get back to the *business.* But you so satisfied with getting *pussy* now, that nothing else matters.

"What, you couldn't get none in high school and college, so now you try'na make up for it in the film game?" she went on. "It's *sick*, Charles. And you need to get a *grip* on that shit if we all trying to be *honest.* I thought you said you was gon' go and get some *help* for that."

It got real quiet over the line as Charles felt hot and immobile in his chair. How much did his production partner know about his reckless jump-offs? He was even ready to ask her. But she didn't give him a chance to.

"Now let's do this conference call and get back to business. We're a half hour late now," she told him. "Hold on . . ."

Embarrassingly, Charles took another deep breath as he awaited the conference call connection.

"Okay, Renald, this is Jackie and Charles on the line," his partner announced.

"Hey, guys," Renald responded.

"Hey, Renald," Charles chimed in.

"Yup, we're all here," Jackie stated. She jumped right back into the business. "So, we took a look at the new budget, and it's like . . ." She left it open for Renald to explain it on his own.

"Yeah, we ah, honestly have multiple projects going on at the same time, and that's all we're able to allocate for this one. But we wanted to make sure that we had enough there to qualify for the tax break," Renald explained.

"Yeah, I see that," Jackie responded. "So, if we were to come back in another four to six months, what would that number look like then?"

"Ahhh, it would actually go *down* in four to six months. And we'd have to wait until the top of next year to do anything more than that."

"And how much more would that be? Because we'd really like to keep more of the *beef* on the project to get more of a return for *all* of us," Jackie countered.

"Yeah, I fought for that, but ultimately, we wanted to do what we could to get this thing moving *forward.* So, if you have any other partners you could bring to the table, we'd consider that, as long as they understand that we eat first," Renald negotiated.

"Oh, of *course,* you put the money up first. That's understood," Jackie told him.

"But one of the reasons why we agreed to work with you and

Charles is because of your experience in getting projects done under budget," Renald added. "We've heard nothing but great things about your productions."

"Oh, yeah, we do a great job. We're *very* proud of what we've done," Jackie commented.

"And we'd like to keep moving up," Charles decided to add, cheerfully. He was strategically letting his partner know that he agreed with her. It was time to elevate their product.

"At the same time, we value all of our new relationships," Jackie hinted. It was the game of the film business, and they knew how to play it.

"We love that. That's why we agreed to work with you guys," Renald responded.

Jackie said, "Yeah, we've really mastered the domestic film market at this point and look forward to a more *global* reach, where the numbers really become advantageous to our investors with international support. That's what Charles is really looking forward to."

"You gotta travel out of the country and get them to know and love your work up in Canada, over in London, Dubai, France, Africa, China. I'm ready to *travel*," Charles plugged in.

Renald chuckled and said, "Well, we'll ah . . . see how this first film goes and then see what we can offer for the next one."

"That's what we wanna *hear*," Jackie responded enthusiastically. "So, we'll crunch these numbers, see what corners we can cut, what favors we can call in, and what other partners we can bring to the table to get this thing done."

"Well, all right. That's what *we* like to hear," Renald countered.

Once they ended the conference call with the investor, Jackie spoke to Charles, alone again.

"Okay, we're gonna do this *one* deal with them, and if they don't up the ante on the next one, we move on. Because they have a lot more money than what they're offering us. And they're probably putting more on the table right now for their other deals. I guaran-*tee it*," Jackie insisted.

Charles nodded and agreed with her again. "You're right. I bet they are investing more in their other films."

"You *know* they are. That's a billion-dollar company playing the bullshit game. They're teasing us with a fuckin' *chicken bone*," she barked. "And I'm *tired* of it. So, that's *it*! We do this film to increase our reputation, and we move on."

Charles continued to nod in his chair, realizing that he needed her. His partner was a *beast* at the business! She always got it done.

"Okay," he mumbled meekly.

Jackie told him, "And I apologize for what I said earlier, but you have to realize who you're talking to. I'm not one of these little starry-eyed *girls* you're dealing with. I know how this shit really *works* 'cause I've been *doing it.* And it ain't fucking *magic*! It's a whole lot of hard work and compromising. So, *please* get your head out of your *crotch* so you don't fuck this all up. You have to learn to *control* your urges."

What could the man say? He listened to his partner's rant of truth serum and exhaled. "Okay. You're right," he mumbled.

"All right, I'll talk to you later. I got twenty more phone calls to make now to get this shit *done*."

Charles hung up the line and felt mentally and spiritually exhausted. He had no idea what he had coming to him that morning. Jackie had just jumped in his ass. But he deserved it and needed it.

He sat back in his chair and mumbled, "Yeah . . . I need to give Dr. Victoria Benning a call . . . and follow up with her."

JOSEPH DRAKE

Reflection 20

JOSEPH DRAKE BEAT CHARLES TO THE CALL THAT MORNING.

"Hey, ah, Dr. Benning, you got a minute to talk?"

I looked over at my schedule on the desk and grinned. "I got fifteen," I told him. Hell, I had an *hour* if he needed it. But I knew how to play the game like he did. The less time you had the more seriously businessmen took the call.

"I just wanted you to know I'm still working on that for ya," he began.

"I know you are. It takes *time.* I understand."

I was in a good mood and passing that spirit on to Joe. I was glad he had called me that morning.

He said, "You know, I've never been married," with a chuckle. His revelation just came out of nowhere.

I paused. "Okay." I needed to understand where he was going with it before I jumped to any conclusions.

He said, "I have a couple of kids though."

Talk about *confessions.* I paused again. One of the main skills of my work was being able to listen without judgment. You just allow the information to tumble forward. Then you deal with it cautiously.

"Okay. How old are they now?" I asked him.

"One is seventeen and on her way to college next year. The other is twelve. And both of them are real *sweethearts.*"

"I bet they are," I responded. "So, what's the problem?"

Since he brought it up, I figured he wanted to discuss it.

"They're both biracial, and I feel guilty about not marrying either one of their mothers," he revealed.

And the plot thickened. Joe had a lot of bones in the closet that he was still trying to deal with. But I couldn't do it all in just fifteen minutes.

"Would you like to set up another session?" I asked him. "That sounds deeper than the surface."

"I know, right? I would need an *hour* or more for that."

"At *least.* What's your schedule look like for Wednesday or Thursday?"

"I can figure out how to get an hour. What's best for you, morning, afternoon, or evening?"

"Let's knock it out in the morning," I told him. "You're available on Wednesday?"

"Yeah, I can make that happen."

"Around ten?"

"Let's do it. That's my coffee hour."

"Cream or black?" I joked to him.

"Ahhh, is that a *trick* question?" he asked with another chuckle.

"Depending on how you take it," I responded, grinning.

He said, "Well, both of them are not *white,* right? And they're not really *black* either. They're just various shades of brown."

He took it deeper than I thought he would.

"Okay, I follow that. So, which brown is it for you?" I asked him, curiously. "Light, dark, or medium?"

He laughed. "Ahhh . . . I like 'em all."

I figured he would say that. As a White man with money, he could afford to be versatile.

"You just won't marry any of them," I commented. I couldn't help myself. And I immediately felt bad about it.

"Yeah . . . that's what we'll need to talk about," he responded civilly. "But I didn't marry any *white* coffee either," he added.

I decided to change the subject to end on a good note. "So,

how are the conversations going on financing a minority entertainment project?"

He paused. "Well, let's just say that the group is very familiar with the popularity of African-American sports and entertainment. But . . . we might be better off pushing something that deals with education. That's where their heads are at right now," he informed me.

I nodded. Education was more about charity than business. It was rich White men preparing young minorities to work for them. But I rolled with the punch anyway. It was not the battle to fight that morning. I understood that my goal was a *process.*

"Okay, we'll talk about it when you're ready. And I'll be prepared for it," I told him. "So, we'll talk on Wednesday at ten."

"Will do."

Joe had a younger sister in her late thirties still living up in Massachusetts who he liked to bounce his ideas off of, particularly when he felt the difficult pressures of life. He knew there was no politics or positioning involved when he spoke to her. She was married with her own family and her own money, and she had nothing to gain from bullshitting her older brother. He knew he could always get a straight answer from her.

"Hey, Katherine, how's your day going?" he called and asked her. It was one of those mornings where he kicked back in his office with some heavy things on his mind.

"Hey, Joe, I'm fine. How's your day going?" his sister responded, cheerfully. That was a good thing. She was in a good mood as well. He could hear it in her voice.

Joe said, "I've had better days. But I'm healthy."

"Yeah, so what's on your mind? You're not calling me midmorning for nothing."

It was her *brother.* She knew Joe was not one for small talk. Every conversation would eventually lead where he wanted it to go. So, he cut through the chase.

"Have you ever wondered why I've never gotten married with kids?" he asked his sister.

"Hmmph," she grunted. "You mean with your *commitment* phobias? You've never wanted to give a woman that much *control* over your life, right? It's the whole ball and chain theory. But you're gonna have to *trust* someone. Or just keep *dating* your whole life if that's what your goal is."

Katherine wasn't particularly concerned about it. It was his life to live, not hers. She was very happy with her married life with kids, and she still managed to keep a full-time job from her home office, while dropping the kids off at school in the mornings.

"Those aren't exactly my plans," Joe responded.

"Well, what are your plans? You're forty-four years old now, Joe."

"I know that. I'm keeping score. That's why I'm asking you what you think about it this morning," he commented.

"So, does that mean you've had a recent change of *heart*?"

Joe smiled, setting back in his office chair. "Maybe. I'm thinking about it. I got a few things running through my mind."

"Well, is there a special *woman* who has you thinking about that?"

Joe paused and thought of his biracial daughters. "*Two* actually," he answered.

"Oh my God," Katherine groaned. "You're such a *diva*."

"It's not actually what you *think* though. I just need a little more time to work it all out," he told her.

"Joe, I don't know what you're talking about. You're not gonna work anything out with *two* women. That's *crazy*," his sister leveled with him.

Joe continued to smile while not telling his sister the details. He liked it that way.

"It'll all come out," he mumbled.

"Okay. Whatever. Next topic." Katherine was ready to move on from it. "Have you spoken to Mom and Dad lately?"

It was hardly an every-week phone call in their family. Sometimes they could go *months* without talking to each other, especially the three brothers. They all viewed life very differently.

Joe said, "I'll get around to it. You know that."

"What about Mike and Tommy?" his sister asked him about their brothers.

"Same deal. I spoke to Tommy a week ago."

"Was it a long one?"

Joe shook it off. "Not really." His estranged family was one of the main reasons for his disconnect in life. Outside of Katherine, Joe didn't really bother with them. And he surely didn't want to tell them about his fetish for Black women, let alone inform them about two biracial daughters out of wedlock. He had to warm up to even *consider* telling Katherine.

"What if I had to make a choice between two Black women?" he blurted.

"What?" Katherine responded dryly. Was he joking? Did she hear him correctly? "You said *two* Black women?"

"Yeah, what if that was my choice?"

He was prepared to ease his sister into the conversation, little by little.

"Are you *serious*?" she asked him. It wasn't particularly shocking, she just wanted to know if her brother was pulling her leg or not.

"I'm just saying *hypothetically*," Joe bullshitted, backing off a bit.

Katherine jumped right in on him. "There's no hypothetical to that. You're dating *two* different Black women?"

"I *used* to," he corrected her.

That made his sister even *more* confused. She stopped her work and said, "Okay, what's going on here?" The whole time she had been working while talking, but now her brother had her undivided attention.

She said, "If you *used* to date them, then what's the point? You're trying to go *back*? To *both* of them?"

He wasn't making much sense to her, and he still wasn't open to explaining it all. Not yet.

"Something like that," he told her.

"All right, I'm done with it. You're obviously talking in *pieces* right now, so you call me when you're ready to discuss all of it."

"Yeah, you're right. I'm not quite there yet," he admitted. "I'm working toward it though."

"Yeah, you've always been the loose cannon of the family," Katherine said with a chuckle.

"How do you feel everyone else will respond to it?" Joe asked her.

"So, is that what you're trying to do, bounce this off me first?"

"Well, yeah. You know you've always been my favorite, most honest and trustworthy family member. Who else am I gonna talk to about this?"

Katherine paused again. She said, "You really wanna get *serious* with that? Like, there were no regular *White* girls that you cared anything about?"

It was a great question. There had been regular White girls. But that was the problem. They were all *regular,* where Joe wanted something *extra,* he just didn't know how to commit to that extraness long-term.

"Yeah, I gotta . . . I gotta just work all of this out," he responded.

It wasn't just the race issue, it was the overall *perception* that he worried about. But it was what it was. He was attracted to the deep rootedness of Black history, and the history of his own family, who had sired a half dozen mixed-race slaves. Joe felt as if he was haunted by it and possessed to do it all over again by the ghost of his great-great-grandfather.

He even felt compelled to ask his sister about it.

"Have you ever felt, ah, attracted to Black men at all?"

"No," Katherine answered immediately. She was a married mother of three children with her White husband. She wouldn't have said yes even if it were true. It would have felt like disloyalty to her husband. And she admitted as much.

"I mean, how could you even *ask* me that? I'm not some single woman in my dating years. I'm not *you.* And I'm not in your position," she told her brother. In fact, he was starting to make her feel uncomfortable.

"What about when you were dating?" he questioned.

"Okay, that's it. I'm getting back to work."

Joe chuckled and said, "You can't even answer the *question*?"

"No, I can't. And I don't *want* to. Because it doesn't *mean* anything," she commented. "And you have to let the guilt *go*," she alluded. "We were not a part of *slavery*. Okay? We had nothing to do with that. But you've always been the one who was most *disturbed* by it. And that's not necessarily a *bad* thing, but I don't want all of that on my *conscience*. And I have a *right* to ignore it, because I didn't *add* to it."

"Yeah, but ignoring it *is* adding to it. You don't get that? There were millions of us who ignored it and let it go on for hundreds of years."

Katherine said, "This is not the time to have this discussion. I'm at *work* right now. So. If you don't mind, I'd like to get back to work, Joe."

"That's not gonna make it go away," he countered.

"Make *what* go away?" she asked him. "I'm not the one calling *you* up feeling guilty about anything. And if you want to go out and marry a Black woman or *two* of them, for that matter, because it makes you *feel* better about the situation, then go right ahead. It's your life. But don't think everyone's supposed to feel the same way you feel because we *don't*. And you're not gonna be able to force yourself on people that way."

"I'm not trying to."

"Yes, you are," she cut him off. "And it's not *fair*."

Joe frowned and said, "Nothing is fair in this world."

"Well, you do something about it then," she challenged him. "And dating two or three Black women is not it. Make yourself *useful* to them if you feel so guilty. Because I don't. I'm sorry, but I haven't done anything to them. Okay? Bye." And she hung up on him.

"Katherine?" Joe spoke into his office phone. "Katherine?" he repeated for dramatic effect. He realized that his sister had already hung up the line on him. So, he exhaled and sunk into his chair, feeling like a lonely man in a big world.

"What the fuck did I do to my life?" he asked himself. *I just made a big mess of it,* he thought. *Now I have to figure out what to do next.*

TYRELL HODGE

Reflection 21

JOE WASN'T THE ONLY ONE WHO NEEDED TO FIGURE THINGS OUT. Tyrell Hodge was off his rocker as well, while driving like a demon for PDS. And he was making good money doing it too, to the tune of twenty-five hundred dollars a week.

But it didn't matter to him. Tyrell wanted to be in the creative space of making movies, while no longer having the agreeable temperament or patience to make it happen. And as time wore on, with deal after deal falling apart on him, he continued to deteriorate into a very sour and unfulfilled man.

Nevertheless, he still had people in his corner who were willing to help him. For *free.*

"Look, just pull out something *old,* and let it go. Let *me* deal with it. Can you do that?" I told Tyrell on a late afternoon. He was out in the city of Atlanta driving hard and crazy as usual.

"Nobody wants anything *old,*" he argued. "They all want this kid shit now."

Although he wasn't landing anything big, he still talked enough about filmmaking and writing that he was constantly on his cell phone, even while driving some of his passengers, which was not good for the business. It made him appear very distracted. Nevertheless, he somehow got away with it, even after passenger complaints.

I said, "Tyrell, you really need to get out of your own way and let someone else pitch something for you."

"People pitch shit for me all the time," he barked. "And they come away with nothing. Or they come back and ask me to make a bunch of changes, which means they don't really like it."

"*Or* they could just need a few *adjustments*," I countered.

"Well, in that case, they can sign the deal and make the adjustments in the rewrites, where they pay for them," he snapped back. "I told you, I'm not a damn *rookie* out here. And I'm not gon' let them *treat me* like one."

At least he had a headset on where he could drive and talk with both hands on the wheel. So, he was perfectly able to make his turns when the airport exits popped up.

"I'ma call you back later. I'm heading into the airport now," he commented.

"You don't have anyone in the car, do you?" I asked him.

"Not yet," he lied as I found out later. The truth was, he had done a whole conversation with me while a professional Black woman sat in the back seat, minding her own business. But she definitely heard him. Tyrell was a loud and clear Chicago speaker.

I said, "All right, well, I still want you to be a part of this project that I'm pulling together."

I was just about to mention the name Charles Clay again, but I thought better of it. I didn't want to end the call with Tyrell on a bad note.

He said, "All right, we'll keep talking about it."

As soon as Tyrell hung up, the woman in the back seat was right on his case.

"Are you a film writer or something?"

He looked back and said, "Yeah. I used to be. But when you get old, they throw you away."

The attractive businesswoman in her mid-thirties smiled. "You don't look that old."

Tyrell grinned and said, "I'm not. But in the film and television writing business, once you hit *forty*, you're *old*. So, I'm trying to figure out how to be young again."

"You're only as old as you *feel*," she told him.

"Well, in that case, I feel like an *ox*. And I don't need none of that Viagra."

That wasn't the most professional thing for him to say as a driver, and the woman felt uncertain about it. However, Tyrell didn't say it with any flirtation or malice. He just said whatever the hell was on his mind. And those things were unscreened and uncensored. It was like taking a ride with Stephen King, Spike Lee, Dennis Rodman, or Howard Stern. You had no idea what they would say or where they would go with any given conversation.

The woman chuckled at Tyrell's response and said nothing. It was safer to take the Fifth with him. She was a professional woman in a committed relationship, and she had a plane to catch. So, her trip was what she bothered to focus on.

When they pulled up to the Delta terminal, Tyrell hopped out and grabbed her luggage from the trunk to roll over to her on the curb.

"Thank you. I'll give you a good tip," she lied. She just wanted a pleasant conclusion to their awkward conversation.

Tyrell nodded. "All right. Thank you." But he didn't care about her tip. What was an extra five dollars on a trip where he had already made thirty? Then again, if he had been more friendly and thoughtful with some of his riders, maybe he could have earned another two hundred dollars a week in tips alone, which would amount to another ten thousand a year.

It was simple math and logic. Be nice and make more money. But Tyrell considered that to be too much work. He'd rather just be himself, a raw and unpredictable man.

I'm not going out of character for an extra five dollars, he argued.

That same hardcore, Chicago disposition is what stopped him from securing many film and television deals that could have easily swung in his favor with more sugar and cream in his coffee. But Tyrell refused to be sugared down, as if it would kill him.

He jumped back to work behind the wheel of his silver Chevy Malibu and took off for his next pickup, feeling a bit horny.

"Damn, she looked good," he mumbled with a grin. He looked up into his rearview mirror to see if he still had a handsome look of his own. And he did. With a smooth brown mug of perfect symmetry, Tyrell had never been an unattractive man, he just had an unattractive attitude. Unless you were the kind of woman who liked his edge.

As a respected professional writer, Tyrell refused to realize that he didn't need to be that South Side Chicago kid protecting his lunch money anymore. He didn't have to fight the bullies in the schoolyard, and no one was coming to get him. But he couldn't seem to get his environmental need for toughness out of his system. And it was taking longer than normal for him to let his old neighborhood ways go.

Feeling the hard-on from the attractive woman he had dropped off at Delta, Tyrell was inspired to call up his lady friend at work.

"Hello," she answered softly.

"Hey, what you doin'?" he asked.

She paused. It was the middle of the day and she didn't get off work until five. "I'm working," she told him. But he knew that already.

"Yeah, I was just thinking about you, that's all."

"Okay."

Tyrell paused, disappointed. "That's all I get is an okay?"

"I mean, what do you want me to say? You know I'm at work."

"It would be beautiful if you could say something like, 'That's nice. I can't wait to see you later.' How 'bout that?"

She went silent, so silent that he thought something was wrong with his phone.

"Hello?"

"Yes."

"How come you didn't say nothing?"

"I told you, I don't have anything to say. I'm working."

Tyrell exhaled and said, "Look, I take the time out to call you like this in the middle of the day, because I'm thinking about you, and all you got to say is, *okay*?"

"Why are you thinking about me, Tyrell?" his lady questioned.

"Because I love you," he answered immediately. There was no hesitation about it. And he was not the kind of man to lie about his emotions. Everyone knew that. Tyrell was the last man on earth to tell you something he didn't believe in, and he was proud of his honesty. It was the same bold honesty that got him into trouble in business, where everyone else would lie to get what they wanted.

His lady friend responded, "You love the fact that I'm still *here*. That's all you love."

Tyrell paused to think about it. He said, "Any man would love a woman's who's *loyal*."

"Yeah, but you're not loyal to me," she countered calmly.

"Here you go with that shit again. I was just trying to get some, man. You can't keep turning me down all the time and think nothing's gonna happen. What's wrong with you?" he fumed. "That's *obvious*."

"What if I went out and got some?" she asked him.

Tyrell cringed and said, "For what? I give you everything you need. You know that. You're the one not giving me what *I* need."

She said, "I can't do this right now. I'm at work."

"You never wanna fuckin' *do this*!" he shouted. "That's the problem. Then you come home and lock yourself in the bathroom all the time. What's wrong with you?"

"Bye," she told him and hung up.

Tyrell took a few seconds to process it all before he went ballistic.

"This fuckin' woman! She's driving me *crazy*!" he yelled inside the car. "Just fuckin' *leave her* already! That's what she wants you to do. It's *over*! She just won't say the shit! But she's tellin' you it's over with her *actions.* Now she's fucking *torturin'* you!" he argued to himself.

"And I'm allowing the shit to happen by staying with her. Just fucking *leave*!" he ranted.

But he *couldn't* leave her. With all of the chaos in his life, she was the only calmness and stability he had left. No matter what, Tyrell could always count on her serenity, to the point where he felt he might *die* if he left her. Maybe he would wreck his car in a fatal accident on the same day that he left. Or get sick with no one there to take care of him. So, he was terrified.

With no kids and an ex-wife who couldn't handle him, he had been empty hearted for years before meeting her, and he didn't want to go back to the emptiness. So, he accepted everything she dished out to him.

And sure, he still had friends and family. But it wasn't the same as being cared for by a woman who knew him deeply and loved him. She just refused to allow him to consume her. And Tyrell could be an all-consuming man. There was no halfway with him. He wanted *all* of his woman. So, she held that one piece of her soul away from him. The piece that he needed the most. *Sex*, the human soul connection.

Whether women wanted to admit it or not, it was *true.* A man could be sucked into a woman's soul through her vagina. And the more she gave it to him, the deeper he could fall in. Especially for an all-consuming man like Tyrell. He had never had that before, that unconditional love and sex. Not from a woman that he really wanted. And never as often in a real relationship. That's what *she* did when he first met her. And he couldn't get those happy days out of his head.

Even his four-year marriage had been pretended. Tyrell had previously married a woman who wanted to be with a famous man. He was younger then with plenty of success and money. However, he and his ex-wife had taken more public pictures than they had private lovemaking. It was a sham of a marriage that he was happy to be done with.

But after his divorce, he seemed to be chasing women forever, while never finding what he wanted. Or being able to *get it* once he found it. Until he found *her*. Or did she find *him*? Tyrell was confused about that part now. All he knew was that their relationship had *changed*, as soon as she moved in with him and failed at what she wanted to do in life. Then he began to fail at being there for her, because she was no longer there for him. She had tapped out mentally, physically, and spiritually, but he was still holding on to her anyway, hoping for a miracle of revision, where they could go back to the beginning.

But now . . . the reality of their stale relationship hurt both of them, while they remembered how it *used* to be, and weren't able to get back to it. The same way Tyrell had not been able to return to his days of success as a screenwriter. And maybe he needed to succeed for *both* of them. But while he continued to fail, and she continued to deny him, Tyrell began to drive himself down a road of madness.

Who could not feel sorry for a man like that? And who could not feel sorry for his woman, who had no idea what she was getting herself into when she believed that she could achieve what she really wanted in life. And when she wasn't able to have it, how she envisioned it, it broke her. Now she was breaking Tyrell the same way, with rejection after rejection after rejection, the way life had rejected her.

But Tyrell sucked it up like he always did, while mad at the world, as he drove back around to the airport to pick up his next rider from the arrivals.

"Rodney Perkins?" he asked through his passenger-side window.

A short White man in gold-rimmed glasses nodded to him with luggage. "That's me."

Tyrell nodded back. "All right." He jumped out of the car and ran around to grab the man's luggage. He didn't need to do all that, but he had so much raw energy left over from his usual frustration with his lady that he felt a need to *use* some of it.

Once he had the luggage inside the trunk with Rodney sitting in the back seat, he went into his usual routine.

"So, where you flying in from, Rodney?"

"Chicago."

Tyrell perked up. "Oh, yeah? The North Side?"

The White man got excited. "Yeah. How'd you know?"

Because you're White, and you motherfuckers don't live on the South Side, Tyrell thought.

Then he smiled and said, "It was just a lucky guess of mine."

DESTINY FLOWERS
Reflection 22

I FIGURED MAYBE I COULD INTEREST TYRELL IN WRITING SOMETHING about the Bitcoin industry or network marketing. Both of those worlds bragged about the money they made while not being fully transparent with you. Or at least I didn't think so. There was always some *hook* to making your money by inviting other people in and getting them to keep investing in obscure products, whether you need these products or not.

So, in a new creative story, maybe someone becomes rich, while someone else gets frustrated after losing all of their money and becomes skeptical of the others in the group to the point where the situation becomes murderous. We could then create a wild goose chase of one individual's contempt, while tracking down the people who are responsible for the loss of their money. And we could call it . . . *The Network.*

Of course, Tyrell would add his gifts to my loose idea and make it more creative and complicated, but I could easily see Mrs. Melody and Dark & Moody both playing roles in the film, with Tyrell writing, Charles directing, and Joe helping us to produce it with the finances. Maybe I could play a cameo role in the film myself as a psychiatrist who evaluates the main character and calls her delusional.

And I really felt that Mrs. Melody could play the lead role.

She's interesting and extroverted enough, and she's *gorgeous* to White and Black people, like a Zoe Saldaña type. Then DM could produce the music with her gothic funk sound, which would fit perfectly for the soundtrack.

I had been bouncing different ideas around in my head for a couple of *weeks* until I came up with something solid. Then I was anxious to hear what Tyrell would think about it. Or better yet, maybe it would have been best to run the idea past Charles Clay first. I figured if Charles liked the idea, it would motivate Tyrell to write it faster than just me saying it—since he believed it was so hard for people to like the new things that he came up with.

As I continued to jot down notes at my desk during the gap periods of my workday, Destiny Flowers caught me on the phone again.

"Hello."

"Hey, Doctor, what you been up to?"

She was calling me from a different number, but I had figured out her voice and demeanor.

"Destiny?" I questioned.

"Yeeaahh, you know me now," she cheered.

I took a deep breath and exhaled before I responded negatively. I really had to catch myself before I became unprofessional with this woman.

"You know, I looked through my schedule and I still don't see where you booked a session. But yet, you keep calling me," I told her.

She said, "I'm gonna book one eventually. I just have to feel the process out."

"Well, where are you calling from?" I asked her casually.

"I'm at work."

"And you think it's a good thing to call me from your job? What if they track the number?"

I was just talking, since I had a few break minutes available.

"Track the number for what? You're not illegal," she commented. "I was just curious to see what you were working on."

I don't know what it was, but this crazy woman always seemed to know when to catch me and what to say. It's like she had a camera in my office to see me and listen to me.

"What makes you think I'm working on something?" I asked her.

"I can just *feel it.* I mean, you don't seem like a woman who's satisfied with just one job. You're the type who gets busy doing a lot of different things."

"Because I'm *serious* about getting things *done,*" I responded. "But that doesn't mean I'm unsatisfied."

She paused. "Are you *sure*? You just seem to be up to something."

This damn woman! I thought to myself. Does she have ESP or what? I started chuckling and came clean with her. "Okay, what if I *was* working on something? What does it matter to you?"

"Can I ask what it is?"

I paused. *Should I tell her?* I pondered. *Hell, it wouldn't hurt,* I argued. *She may have a different perspective on things. She's crazy enough, I know that much.* So, I did tell her.

"I'm pulling together a film idea with a few of my clients involved."

"Really? What's the film about?"

I had to stop and think about it. I hadn't come up with a logline or a clear synopsis for it yet. My ideas were still fresh.

"Well, it's like an ah . . . espionage business thriller, really."

"You mean like, *The Firm*? Or *Wall Street*? I love those kinds of movies," she responded excitedly. She was on point with her choices of film too. She said, "Did I tell you I do a little *acting* on the side? That's really why I moved here to Atlanta from Cleveland."

She had told me that before. But the woman rambled so much with no official session, that a lot of the things she spoke about failed to register. It wasn't as if I was obligated to remember. She still wasn't my client yet.

"I do remember you saying that," I admitted.

She said, "Do you have a cast yet? Is there a role for *me*? Or something I can audition for?"

Her questions were all rapid-fire.

"I don't even have a *script* yet. It's just a fresh idea," I answered.

Honestly, her erratic behavior fit right in for a thriller project.

"What kind of role would you want to play?" I quizzed.

She paused. "I would play the crazy woman."

I laughed out loud immediately. This woman continued to read my mind.

"What's so funny? You don't think I can do it?"

"Oh, I *know* you can do it," I told her. "I'm just . . . enjoying my day," I responded. I didn't want to say what I was really thinking.

"You think I really am crazy, don't you?" she asked.

I had to watch myself. "No . . . we all have our . . . eccentricities."

"Yeah, that's just another way of saying I'm crazy. I ain't stupid," she commented.

"Well, what do you even look like?" I asked, changing the subject. If she wanted to be cast in a movie, then I needed to know that.

She said, "I look better than *you.*"

I smiled. "Well, you should look better than me if you're young and you aspire to be an actress, a singer, and all of that. But I'm not bad looking. So, you must be a *dime,*" I teased her. I was curious to see how she would respond to that.

She said, "Oh, I am. You better *know it.*"

"Well, in a role like this, you would have to be a little more *humble,* too," I advised her.

"Humble for what? Crazy people ain't humble. Where you been at? I thought you 'sposed to be from New Jersey."

I didn't remember telling her that, but I rolled with it. After all, I did brag about being from Camden. I was *proud* of it.

I said, "Okay, I see your point. Maybe you could be *fabulous* and crazy."

"Yeah, that's what *I'm* talking about. Crazy and fabulous. I could do that *easily.*"

I could begin to see the film in my mind. Maybe she could be one of the people with money in the movie, without knowing how she got it all. We could have her in some of the most over-the-top outfits, hairstyles, jewelry, and everything. And when she falls . . . she falls *hard.* That would be her *Destiny.* Even her *name* fit the role. And we would put *Flowers* on her grave.

"I really got you *thinking* now, huh?" Destiny commented.

I grinned and nodded. "You really do. I think people would *love* your character."

All of a sudden, she went silent over the line.

"You're not fucking with me, are you? 'Cause I'm *serious.* And I don't like people playing games with my emotions," she stated.

This woman was really a piece of work.

I said, "Well . . . I really have to see what you look like. Because if you don't look the part . . ." I challenged her. I figured it would be a way to finally get her in my office.

"So, you wanna meet me?"

Bingo! I thought. "If you would have scheduled a *session,* like you said you did, I could have met you a while ago," I told her. This girl had been calling me on and off for *months.*

She responded with a pause, "You just want your money."

"Well, this is my *job,*" I reminded her.

"Making *movies* ain't your job," she argued.

"It is if I'm making one," I told her.

She piped down and thought about it.

"Well, where you wanna meet me?"

"In my office, like I meet everyone else."

She paused again. "Well, what if I'm not coming for a session?"

"Look, do you have a hundred dollars or what?" I snapped at her. "My *time* is my *money.* And it ain't like I charge a fortune. I discussed that with you before. Do they pay you for your job? Or are you volunteering?"

This woman was really working my *nerves.* Dealing with her was like jumping on a roller-coaster ride of temperament.

She said, "Of course they pay me. But I got a tight budget

right now, so I can't be spending like that. I'm trying to *make* money."

"Well, aren't we *all*," I told her. "What you think *I'm* trying to do?"

"Rob *me*," she commented.

I stopped and shook my head. A hundred dollars an hour was robbing her? *Please.* The woman needed some mental help in the worst way. I needed to charge her *three* hundred dollars with the way she acted.

"Naw, I'm just fuckin' with you," she stated.

I cringed. "You can say that over your *work* phone?" I asked her.

"Shit, I'm *grown.* I can say what I wanna say."

On second thought, I didn't know how this woman would act with the rest of the cast. Maybe it wasn't even safe to deal with her around other people. Her unprofessionalism could end up embarrassing me.

"Yeah, I really need to meet you," I repeated casually.

She said, "You will. It'll happen."

"Well, it needs to happen *before* I consider you for anything. I know that much."

She paused again. Then she said, "Well, look at you, making demands and such. You got some *nerve.*"

That made me pause. She had a way of sounding *older* at times, not necessarily in her voice but in her *tone* and *spirit,* as if I was younger than her, and I wasn't. She wasn't my mother or one of my aunts. So, I was ready for her this time.

"Sounds like you got a lot of different *people* swimming around in your head," I told her. "Maybe you *are* a good actress. But you'll need to stick to the *script,* too."

"I thought you said you don't have a script yet."

"We don't. But I'm talking about when we *get* one. You can't be improvising unless we tell you to."

"Wait, you're the director now? What if they *like* my improvising?"

She had a comment for everything. "I just wouldn't count on that happening," I told her.

"Well, if you don't have a script, then you don't know what I'm supposed to say anyway."

I was speechless. She had a point.

I said, "Okay, you got me there. I'll start working on it. But I still need to meet you."

I hadn't forgotten about that part.

She said, "I know. I'll get on your calendar."

I was about to ask her when. But what was the point? If she was serious, she would do what she said she would do. And if she wasn't . . . Oh, well. I had other things to prepare for.

CHARLES CLAY

Reflection 23

THE FIRST THING I HAD TO DO WAS GET BACK TO CHARLES CLAY on a couple of things, including my story idea for the film. He had called me in the morning with urgency, but we both had jam-packed schedules, so we agreed to meet up at a downtown Thai restaurant in the evening, a place that was low-key.

I arrived there before he did and grabbed a booth near the window, where I could look out on the sidewalk and into the street.

"Are you dining alone?" a young waitress asked me. I looked up into the deep brown eyes of a beautiful chocolate sister in her twenties. She looked like a model from the Carnival celebrations of Brazil. She was absolutely stunning!

I smiled and said, "No, I'm waiting on someone to join me."

She nodded. "Okay, I'll bring you another menu."

When she walked away, I looked around and noticed that all of their servers were wearing classy white tops with formfitting black pants, like a yin and yang symbol. They were of all races, White, Black, Latina, and Asian, as if the management had selected these girls deliberately. And they were all attractive.

"Interesting," I told myself.

This Thai restaurant had Asian décor with a lot of dark, contrasting film qualities to it. Hell, I even thought about using it as one of our filming locations. I wondered what Charles would think about it.

Charles walked in a few minutes later and instantly agreed with me, without me even asking him.

"Wow, this place is nice. It's dark and moody."

He actually said that. I smiled and thought about my young producer with her stirring music.

"Would you shoot a scene here?" I asked Charles curiously.

He took off his baseball cap and jacket as if he had been in hiding and was finally able to relax. The place was that low-key. I had chosen it well.

He looked around and said, "I don't know if they would want that much attention in here."

"I know, right," I agreed. I stood up to greet him with a hug. By the time we sat down together, our gorgeous Black waitress was back at the table. She looked Charles in his face and noticed him.

"Are you Charles Clay?" she asked calmly.

She was direct and very mellow. I liked her style. She wasn't about to be hysterical about it, but she was letting us know that she knew who he was, myself included, because she didn't whisper it.

Charles nodded and said, "Yeah, I'm him."

This young woman smiled with teeth so white it looked like someone shined a flashlight on them.

She said, "I love your movies. They're very intellectual."

You talk about a word sounding *sensuous*, when this young Black woman used the term *intellectual* instead of *cool*, or *clever*, or *dope*, or *lit*, or whatever else these kids liked to use, it immediately sounded as if she was flirting with him. And I was smart enough to know that. Intellectual sounded very *sexual*.

She suddenly struck me as a Spelman College girl, who *knew* better. So, I sat back, watched and listened, while holding my smile to myself.

Charles responded, "Yeah, I get that a lot. I'm just not into shooting films that depict us in the same way. So, I always try to change it up."

She nodded and said, "Well, you do a good job."

Maybe it was just *me*, but everything this girl said sounded sexual. You do a good *job*?

Anyway . . . maybe my mind was messed up and in the wrong place.

"Thank you," Charles responded to her. He wasn't fazed by it at all.

"Would you like to start with a drink or just water?" she asked us both.

"What would you suggest?" I baited her. I had to say something.

She finally paid attention to me again. "We have a lot of cool drinks on the menu. But I would probably suggest a Strawberry Mimosa. People really like that."

I nodded to her. A Strawberry Mimosa sounded good to me. "Okay, I'll have one."

"But is that what *you* like to drink?" Charles asked her specifically.

Her second smile was more contained, like a grin, with less teeth and more soft, brown lips.

"I actually like the Tokyo Iced Tea. It's like, sweeter than a Long Island, but it can still sneak up on you," she answered.

I nodded and thought, *Yeah, this girl is dangerous.* She was extraordinary, with her dark and exotic looks at a Thai restaurant, where she would learn more about foreign culture while attracting men of every age and nationality. Because I was certain that wealthy White men would salivate over her. Asian men, too. And Charles jumped right in her boat.

"All right, I'll take a Tokyo Iced Tea then," he told her.

That made her smile with the flashlight on her teeth again.

She said, "Okay, a Strawberry Mimosa and a Tokyo Iced Tea." When she walked away, Charles surely took a long, hard look at her firm young ass in those tight black pants she wore.

When he caught me watching him, the director came clean with it. "That's the other problem I need to talk to you about. I can't seem to control myself with these women."

I laughed and said, "You don't say." I couldn't even blame the man. He didn't ask for that extra attention, the young woman brought it to him, just because he made good movies.

I said, "Well, you can respond, *nicely*, just don't ask for any phone numbers or give out yours."

Of course, that was easier said than done, particularly in Atlanta where Black girls were traveling from all over the country to take part of the new "Black Hollywood" and "A-Town" music world that the popular Southern city had become. You literally had some of the prettiest Brown girls you'd ever see in your life in Atlanta, who were breaking their necks to be involved in movies and music. And when they failed, many of them ended up at the strip clubs.

Charles asked me, "Did you smell her?"

That question caught me off guard. I winced and said, "Well, she had perfume on, yeah." That was normal for a young and stylish woman. We all wore scents.

"And I could smell it a mile away," Charles told me.

That part *was* unusual. Guys typically had to be right up on a woman to smell anything. Maybe he had heightened senses.

I said, "To be honest with you, many guys have a fetish-for-women problem when they have power in an industry that women are attracted to. You even flirted with me the first time you were in my office," I reminded him. "And I *allowed* it. So, I was a culprit too—even though I'm old enough to be your *auntie*," I teased him.

He grinned and said, "Well, you're a sexy-ass *auntie*."

"See," I warned him, pointing my right index finger across the table. "You have to remind yourself to turn it *off*. You have to have an *off* and an *on* button. That's how you need to think about it."

"Well, maybe my off button is broken," he joked.

"And we'll have to fix it," I told him. "But while I have you here, I really wanted to run this screenplay idea past you on this film that I want to create," I commented, changing the subject. We could get back to his woman issue later. After all, I was giving him a *free* hour of consultation. So, we needed to trade professional expertise for a minute.

He said, "All right. Shoot."

Before I could open my mouth, the sexy, young Brown thing was back with our drinks in hand. She set them down in front of us on the table and asked, "Are you guys ready to order?"

Suddenly, I could smell the young woman as strongly as he did. And she smelled *great,* like a sweet floral mixed with a hint of peppermint. It was a clean and wholesome smell that made you open up your nostrils to sniff *more* of her. And if it made me react that way to it, I could only imagine what it did to Charles. He likely had this exotic young woman *naked* in his mind already.

He said, "We haven't even looked at our menus yet."

"Oh . . . well, take your time," she told him softly.

I looked across the table and couldn't stop my smile. I don't know what was wrong with me. I guess I was as bad as *he* was that evening. Suddenly, this young woman seemed overly sexual to me, and everything she said was below the belt.

Charles nodded to her and said, "Okay."

Then she looked over at me.

"I didn't look at it either," I told her.

"All right, I'll be back."

When she walked away again, Charles kept his eyes glued on me instead of on her ass.

"Did you see me turn it off?" he asked before sipping his drink.

I laughed out loud. "I sure did. That was good."

He said, "So, tell me about this screenplay idea you have," as he sipped on his Tokyo Iced Tea, which looked like a Dirty Lemonade.

I got excited and didn't bother to touch my Strawberry Mimosa.

"Okay, so, I wanted to do something that dealt with this whole Bitcoin, Forex, network marketing world. I mean, those people are just . . . it's really like a new *religion,* you know."

He laughed and choked on his drink. He said, "It really is. And they get mad at you for not understanding it."

"Oh, like you're the dumbest person in the *world* for not

jumping in," I added. "So, like, you have this one girl who *thinks* she wants to get involved, but she still doesn't understand it, so she ends up losing a lot of money that she really can't afford to lose. Like, maybe she's a senior in her last year of college, and she tries to flip her college loan money."

Charles started smiling from ear to ear and set his drink back on the table. "And she's *obnoxious,* the kind of young woman who thinks she *knows* everything."

"Yeah. So, when she gets her money taken, she's ready to bring the whole thing down."

"And then she meets this older White man who starts giving her clues on what to do and where to look for the bad guys."

"And bad *girls,*" I added. "Because they have, like, a whole crew of young women who are really making money from this thing."

"But it's really a cover-up for the older guys in the group that they're secretly dating."

"Older women, too," I added.

Charles nodded. "Yeah, we're in a new time now with boy toys *and* girl toys."

"A new playground for the rich," I added.

"Just when these kids thought they were doing something *new* and different."

"Yeah, it's all *rigged.*"

"So, what's the name of it?" he asked me.

"*The Network,*" I told him proudly. I loved the title.

But Charles frowned at it immediately. He said, "Eh, Facebook had *The Social Network* years ago. Remember that? Jesse Eisenberg became a star playing the lead role of Mark Zuckerberg."

"Oh, yeah," I moaned. "That's right."

"How 'bout we just call it *Trading*?" he suggested. "That's what they say they're doing, right?"

I nodded. "Yeah, they do."

"And they're trading way more than just *coins,*" he added with a chuckle.

I laughed. "I like that. That sounds like a great marketing slogan."

As I began to think about what Tyrell could do with the screenplay, I noticed a well-built man arguing with his girlfriend outside the window to my left, while pointing inside the restaurant. He seemed to be pointing directly at Charles, but Charles was still into our film discussion and didn't see it.

He said, "I really think you have something here. The Bitcoin, Forex world is international. We could really do some great things with that, with our locations and everything. Because those guys are always meeting at different places."

"Yeah, at fancy hotels and meeting rooms," I commented. "They have to validate . . ."

My comments trailed off as I watched this hulking, football player–looking guy barge into the restaurant with his beautiful girlfriend behind him and head straight for us.

Alarmed by it, I asked Charles, "Do you know these people?" right as they reached our table.

Charles finally turned and spotted them. "Oh, shit!" he stated, and ducked into the booth. But he had nowhere to go.

"Don't!" the girl told her enraged boyfriend. But it was too late for that.

He said, "I'ma fuck his ass *up*!"

He grabbed Charles in both hands and lifted him up into a savage headbutt before ramming him back into the booth.

"What the hell is *wrong* with you?" I shouted, and threw my untouched drink in his face.

He angled toward me while he continued to ram Charles into the booth. "No, what's wrong with *this* motherfucka?" he yelled. "He got a *problem* with thinking he can get away with shit."

This hulking guy was yanking and shoving Charles in the booth like a rag doll, and I was hesitant to put my hands on him because he didn't seem like the type who wouldn't hit a woman, and I didn't want to end up in the news in a bad way. So, I prayed that someone else in the restaurant would stop it.

"Security! SECURITY!" I yelled louder. Luckily, two older

Black men came to our rescue and broke it up. They were both big enough to stop it.

"Hey, what's going on, young brother? What's going on?" the two older gentlemen asked, while holding the enraged man back.

"This motherfucka think he can do whatever he *wants* just 'cause he makes *movies*!" the furious man shouted. But at least he had let Charles go.

By that time, Charles looked dazed and confused, while slumped over in the corner of the booth. I think he may have had a concussion from the first headbutt. And his face looked swollen.

I looked around the restaurant and came face-to-face with our pretty Brown server. She appeared embarrassed and shocked by it all with her hands covering her mouth, as everyone watched, including the management.

"What happened?" an older Asian woman asked me softly. I assumed she was either the manager or an owner of the restaurant. Maybe her husband owned it.

Before I answered her, I looked again at this beautiful girl who accompanied the angry young man. I assumed she was a young woman that Charles had gotten himself involved with. And obviously, his chickens had come home to roost.

I didn't want to discuss his business out in front of everyone. But I had to say something. He really *did* have a woman problem.

"I don't know. But I'll find out," I answered.

Before I knew it, the police and an ambulance were there. They started asking me questions for their report, while detaining the young man and his girlfriend for assault.

"Can you tell me what happened here?" a Black female officer asked me.

I swear to you, it didn't seem *real.* It felt like I was *dreaming.* Everything was moving fast, and people were talking at the same time, explaining what they saw and did, while the medics from the ambulance tended to Charles with an ice pack on his head.

Suddenly, all eyes were on me as the first witness of the incident.

I said, "This guy just . . . barged in here and grabbed him and headbutted him, while yelling about what he couldn't get away with." I was honestly saying *more* than what I wanted to defend Charles, but there was nothing I could do to change the story right in front of people who had heard and seen it all.

It was obvious that Charles had done *something* to this young lady that the man was not happy about. Yet, she didn't seem to be telling the whole story. So, I didn't know what to think.

Did Charles rape her? I questioned. I doubted it. She would have told us *that.* So, maybe she had *consented* to whatever happened between them, and Charles was too out of it to explain his side of the story. It was just a big *mess.*

I looked again at our pretty Brown server, who was shaking her head. I guess she still couldn't believe it. And if she had any intentions of hooking up with Charles herself, those ideas had been thrown to the curb and stepped on.

I remained with Charles Clay at the local hospital for the remainder of the evening. He hadn't been injured that badly. He had a lump on his head and a concussion. Other than that, he was fine, except for a damaged *ego.*

Charles didn't look manly in the situation at all. He had been caught off guard by it, but *still.* He didn't even try to put up a *fight.* At least I tossed a *drink* at the man.

Anyway . . . the police continued to ask him if he wanted to press charges, and Charles had not yet given them a solid answer.

"I just need a minute," he kept telling them.

I wondered how much of the incident he even remembered. When it was just me and him alone inside the emergency room, I asked him, "Did you know this guy?"

It was still unclear to me, but from how Charles reacted when he saw them, he *had* to know the guy.

While sitting on a gurney with an ice pack still held to his forehead, Charles answered, "I'd never *seen* him before, but I had a *feeling* when I saw him charging at me."

"Do you know the girl?" I asked. I hadn't gotten a chance to ask him anything earlier. There was too much going on.

He nodded slowly. I guess he did remember something. The concussion hadn't given him amnesia.

I leaned in and whispered. "Did you do something with her?"

He looked at me with the guiltiest eyes I had ever seen. He was a kid with his hand caught in the cookie jar. He didn't even have to answer me.

I nodded to him and exhaled. "Okay." What else could I say about it? The man had a problem with enticing women. It was official.

DARK & MOODY

Reflection 24

After hanging out and making music the first night with Mrs. Melody, Dark & Moody had a new crush that occupied her mind, and she was no longer excited about her current fling. So, she pushed her girlfriend Tammy away when the affectionate woman attempted to kiss her on the lips.

"I'm not in the mood right now," DM commented, while working on another track in her studio room. She didn't care for the hot pink, titty T-shirt her girlfriend wore with their names, *Tammy & Tasha*, printed across her chest in white cursive either.

Tammy paused, in deep contemplation, wearing a natural haircut like Amber Rose. She had the honey-brown complexion of Yara Shahidi and the brick-house body of Megan Thee Stallion. But it didn't matter. Tasha had her mind set on another woman.

"You know you've been on music *overdrive* lately. What's up with that?" Tammy asked her.

Dark & Moody thought of ignoring her, but that would have been too mean. Instead, she answered, "I'm just try'na get things done."

"You're talking about for this new artist you're working with, and this movie soundtrack thing?" Tammy questioned.

Initially, Tasha had spoken skeptically about the opportunity, while not liking Mrs. Melody or her subjective flow centering around sex. But that was before she had a chance to work with the artist, where her perception had quickly changed.

"Yeah," she answered. There was no sense in lying about it. Business was business, and whether DM liked the sex topic or not, Mrs. Melody was on her way up in the music industry.

"Well, I thought you said you didn't like her like that," Tammy reminded her.

While her agitated girlfriend hovered over the studio station, DM continued to work on her music and study the multicolored sound levels on her monitor. She even put her earphones on while listening to the volume of a new mix, while never answering Tammy's question.

After another minute of tense silence, Tammy pulled the left-side earphone cup away from Tasha's ear so the busy-minded producer could hear her.

"Hell-*lo-o-o*. Earth to Tasha," she hummed into the producer's left ear.

That was definitely a no-go. Dark & Moody looked up from her chair in anger as if she was ready to smack her. "What the fuck are you doing?" she snapped, grabbing her left-side earphone.

"I mean, you invited me over here just to ignore me? I'm *talking* to you."

"And I told you I'm fucking *working*. You always do that shit."

They engaged in a stare down while reading each other's demeanors.

"Well, maybe this was the wrong night for me to come over then," Tammy commented. She hoped DM would have a change of heart and soften her stance. But she didn't.

Instead, she responded, "Maybe it was."

That led to another awkward moment of silence.

"Then maybe I should leave," her girlfriend concluded, breaking it.

Tasha didn't want to respond to that. It would be Tammy's decision.

Her girlfriend nodded and said, "You're changing."

Dark & Moody exhaled, exhausted from the conversation already. She didn't feel like having it. "I change every day," she commented. *And I'm tired of changing,* she told herself. She wanted to be more consistent, she just didn't know *how* to be. Of late, her mind and emotions had been like a tornado, twisting and turning in unknown and violent directions.

"Well, you changing up on *me* ain't fair. I've been the same person for *you,*" Tammy whined.

She had been. That was true. But Tasha controlled the relationship, so it didn't matter. Life had always been unfair that way. Whoever controlled the relationship made the rules.

"It's just tonight," DM responded, going easy on her. She could feel the tension rising. No one liked being rejected. She said, "I'm just a little preoccupied while working on this, because it was unexpected. But now I'm in the middle of it, and I just wanna finish it."

It all made sense, so Tammy backed off and nodded, agreeing to a truce.

"Okay, well . . . you keep working . . . and I'ma go lie down in the room."

She softy rubbed Tasha's neck before leaving the studio. She walked across the hallway and into the larger master bedroom to relax on the bed and wait.

Dark & Moody took a deep breath and thought about it. It was good to have control over a situation. Her loose relationship with Tammy was one of the few where she had any control, as long as she kept the relationship *loose.*

As Dark & Moody had found the hard way, the more she committed, the less control she would have. Even with her music. Artists wanted her beats *more* whenever they were less available to them, or whenever she raised the prices on them. So, she learned to play the game of keep-away on purpose, while praying, scheming, and willing to sacrifice any and everything to control more.

You only live one time in this life, she told herself, while hammering out a new bass line, keyboard notes, and drums that reflected her emotions at the moment.

One time / one time / you live . . . one time / one time / yeeeaaahhh . . . One time / one time / you live . . . one time / one time / all riiight . . .

Mrs. Melody had even influenced the energy of her new beats, where the tempo swung more in tune with dance energy. And the rapper's coldhearted advice replayed in DM's head. *"You can be hardheaded and go your own way if you want, but then you'll end up complaining when you don't have the money to do the shit that you're really trying to do."*

So, she was finally willing to compromise some of her artistic beliefs.

Fuck it, I got hundreds of beats! Three or four commercial tracks won't kill me, she told herself while pounding away on her keyboards.

After midnight, Dark & Moody was good and satisfied with the three new tracks she had created, even if they didn't fit her typical gothic funk sound. In fact, she was so energized that her mood had changed from earlier, and she felt sexual again. So, she was glad her girlfriend was still there resting in her master bedroom. Tammy was butt naked in bed at that.

Tasha eyed the clothing that was purposefully dripped across the floor and grinned.

"Just like I like it," she mumbled. Instead of waking her up, Dark & Moody stripped out of her own clothes to join Tammy under the sheets, while pulling out a strap-on penis from her nightstand drawer.

Her girlfriend loved to be penetrated from the back, while soft, feminine fingers caressed her breasts, with soft lips that kissed up and down the back of her neck and spine. Soft fingertips on her nipples with kisses down her back, accompanied by the slow stroke of a big, hard penis gave Tammy the strongest orgasms. And Tasha knew exactly how to pull it off, along with seductive words to slip into Tammy's ears and consciousness.

"I'm sorry, baby. I didn't mean to be mean to you," she moaned as she slid the strap-on penis into position from the back and pushed it in.

"Mmmm," Tammy moaned as it entered her.

"Do you forgive me?" DM asked with a push of her hips.

"Mmm, hmmm. Yesss."

Tammy arched her head and neck backward as Dark & Moody's wet tongue and kisses began to tickle and electrify her soft, honey-brown skin.

"I'm *sor-ree,*" Tasha purred as she slowly worked her hips back and forth between Tammy's legs with the strap-on. It was just what the doctor ordered—the doctor of ecstasy.

But unknown to Tammy, as Dark & Moody continued to push, pull, kiss, lick, and whisper sexiness into her girlfriend's ear, she imagined it was Mrs. Melody there with her instead, which made the experience more delightful for her.

"You love me, baby?" she asked, imagining it was Melody there to answer her.

"You know I *dooo,*" her girlfriend moaned.

"You love how I make sweet music with you?"

"*Yesss,* I *dooo.*"

"You want me to pound it, baby?"

As she continued to tease Tammy with her slow stroke of the strap-on, Dark & Moody could see Melody clearly in her mind, still bent over and gyrating out in the hallway.

"*Yeeeaaahhh, pound it,*" Tammy moaned to her.

DM obliged and stroked her harder and faster from the back with the strap-on as her dark brown pelvis slapped against Tammy's smooth, honey-brown ass, until she was good and moist.

"You want it like *this*? Like *this*? Like *this*?"

"Oooh, *yesss, yesss, yesss!*"

Dark & Moody grabbed her girlfriend by the hips and pushed the strap-on penis as deeply as it could go inside her, until the young lady began to shake, explode, squirt, and whimper, while DM held her tightly from behind to let the convulsions all out.

"*Mmmmm,*" Tammy moaned as she continued to shake.

When she was all done, Tasha leaned forward and kissed her softly on the neck.

"Was it *good,* baby?" she whispered into Tammy's ear.

"Oh, *God, yes.*"

"Are you ready to eat me?" DM whispered again.

"You know I am," her girlfriend answered.

"And wet my titties?"

"Yeah."

"And make me cum?"

"Yes, girl, *yesss,*" Tammy moaned.

The honey-brown woman began to shake and shiver just thinking about it. All the while, Dark & Moody thought of Mrs. Melody, as if *she* was there saying it . . . and doing it. And Tammy had no idea.

MRS. MELODY

Reflection 25

SPEAKING OF THE SEXY DEMON NAMED MELODY, A SEXUAL ROMP with Dark & Moody was the last thing on her mind. She didn't go that way even if there was money involved. But she would definitely consider manipulating the situation if she needed to.

However, there was no need for it. Everything looked bright for Mrs. Melody. In fact, her future was *too* bright, to the point where it began to blind her perception of reality and the complicated negotiations of real life. Being offered a starring film role was too much for her to comprehend as well.

"So, let me get this straight. I would star as a college girl who gets involved in a Bitcoin trading group and loses all of her money, and then I flip out and try to bring the whole thing down?"

She regurgitated what I explained to her over the phone. But it had taken her nearly a *week* to get back to me on it. That's how busy she had become.

"Yes," I answered at my office. I had yet to follow up with Tyrell, Joe, and Tasha about the film. But I considered Melody as my lead domino. Even if she wasn't experienced or bankable enough as an actress for investors to allow her to play the role, in my mind, the lead character would still be based off her confident energy. At age twenty-three, Mrs. Melody had the right kind of personality, and she was definitely about to blow up. She had everything it took. I was only concerned about how fast it could all go to her head.

She said, "Wow, I need to get a fuckin' *manager*. Shit is coming at me real fast right now. I was just offered ten thousand dollars this weekend to jump on a feature with these three other girls out of Memphis, Dallas, and LA. The producer wants it to be like a *Set It Off* rap and video. You remember that movie with Queen Latifah and Jada Pinkett Smith, from back in the day?"

I grinned and said, "Of *course* I do. That's my era right there. Queen Latifah's my girl from upstate New Jersey. I even watch her *Equalizer* show on TV."

Melody said, "Yeah, well, I didn't even tell them *yes* yet. I wanna see if they're gonna take it up to *fifteen* thousand, because I got the best skills. *And* I look the best."

It was comments like those from her that made me nervous.

"Yeah, maybe you do need a manager now," I told her. "Because you don't want to come off as a greedy diva too early in your career."

She heard that and laughed. "A greedy diva? I like that. That sounds like a song idea. *I'm a greedy diva / I gotta have it . . .* Thank you. I'm gonna fuck with that."

I chuckled and shook my head. This girl was something else. I asked her, "Well, how are you and DM making out with the music ideas?"

"D-M?" she questioned.

"Oh, I meant Dark and Moody," I explained.

"Oh, she's cool. We making it work. But I told her she gotta stop thinking so hard and just let the beats *flow*."

"Well, I might want to put you on the line with someone else for a minute for this movie idea. He's a screenwriter, and I just want him to hear your energy and how quickly you process things."

"All right, just let me know. But I gotta take this call coming in," she told me.

"All right, I'll text you from my cell phone."

"Yeah, do that."

I was still smiling after I hung up with her. Melody had energy like a shot of morning coffee with espresso. I wondered what Tyrell, Charles, and Joe would think about her. And I wasn't worried about Charles's fetish for women when it came to Mrs. Melody. With the kind of guys that she dealt with in the music industry, she would read Charles a mile away. I was *sure* of it.

Nevertheless, the reckless egos and violent street psychology that were involved in the rap game were dangerous for *everyone*, including confident young women. So, I prayed for her.

Arrogance can get the best of anyone. In no shape or form was it smart for a young and attractive woman to find herself in between two grown men who didn't like each other. It was much safer to choose one and keep it moving no matter what. And there was no circumstance that would change that logic. When the conquest of a desirable young woman was at stake, a weak man could decide to become an emotional killer out of hurt and vengeance, and a strong man could decide to kill for respect and principle.

In a situation like that, a young and pretty woman could find herself between a rock and a hard place, where someone is going to die. But Mrs. Melody didn't care. Not as much as she needed to. She was too busy enjoying herself, while shopping for new clothes at the Lenox Square mall in Buckhead.

She got a call on her cell phone right before she stepped into the Fendi Roma shop. She looked down and read her iPhone screen with a call coming in from Gary. She hadn't heard back from him since she stood him up for BJ. At first, she thought of ignoring his call, but she got curious.

"Let me find out what he wants." She answered her phone instead of walking into the shop. "Hello."

"Hey, girl, I hadn't heard back from you. Everything all right?" Gary asked her civilly. It sounded *too* civil, but Melody rolled with it.

"Yeah, I just been running around, doing what I need to do."

"I heard you getting them feature deals now too. You comin' up in the world," he commented.

She smiled. "Yeah, a li'l bit. But it ain't like I'm Cardi B or nothin'. I ain't gettin' money like *that.* I got a long way to go."

"Well, you gotta start *somewhere.* Nobody starts at the top. Cardi B had to grind it out too."

"Yeah, I know, right." *But what's up with the small talk?* she pondered. She knew he wasn't calling her to shoot the breeze, especially after she stood him up. Gary wasn't the small-talk type of man. He was about the big picture. So, Mrs. Melody decided to cut to the chase.

"So, what's up? What's going on with you?" she asked him.

"Nothing. I was just checking in on you. You know, I hadn't heard back from you, so I wanted to see if you was all right."

"Yeah, I'm all right, just extra busy, that's all."

"That's a good thing," he told her. "It's better to be busy than doing nothing."

Melody glanced up the mall and noticed a guy who looked like one of Gary's crew members. That made her leery of the random conversation with him. After all, Buckhead was their area.

"Okay, well . . . I was just about to walk into this restaurant and get me something to eat," she lied, as she continued to look down the hall. She even started walking in the guy's direction to make sure he wasn't following her.

"Aw'ight, well, go eat your food. I ain't gon' hold you. I was just checking in."

"I appreciate that. Thank you," she told him.

As soon as she hung up the line, she asked herself, "Check in on me for *what?* You ain't my fuckin' *man.*"

Boldly, she continued to walk in the direction of the guy she thought was spying on her. But when she got close enough, she realized that it wasn't Gary's friend.

Okay. That's not him, she thought to herself, nervously. *Good thing I don't have my gun in my bag,* she added. She didn't know what she would have done if someone *had* been spying on her.

As she walked back to the Fendi shop on edge, she thought about calling BJ about it, but she decided against it.

"Nah, that's too complicated to explain," she told herself. *He don't need to know all that.*

She was right. It was unwise to tell a man about a recent fling unless she absolutely *had* to. And that was not the case. She had not been back with Gary since she started dating BJ. So, what was the point? She was just a little jittery about Gary's untimely phone call.

"Yeah, I need to watch myself with these guys," she mumbled as she finally walked into the Fendi Roma shop.

"How are you? Are you looking for something in particular?" a well-dressed saleswoman asked her inside.

"I'm not looking for anything in particular. But what do you think would look good on me?" Mrs. Melody asked.

The older White woman looked at her curvaceous body and cream-colored skin and grinned. "I know just the thing. Follow me." She led the rap phenom to the back of the store. "This just came in last week," she stated.

When they arrived at a wooden cabinet rack at the back, the woman pulled out a lime-green Fendi sweatsuit on a hanger. The Fendi brand name flowed down both sides of the pant legs and the arms of the jacket in red and dark blue, and was also embedded large across the back. Even the sleeves featured the Fendi brand name. And to Mrs. Melody, it was love at first sight.

"Oh, shit! Let me try that on," she gushed.

"Of course."

The saleswoman led her to the dressing room so she could squeeze into material that was meant to hug the body with comfort.

Mrs. Melody walked in, stripped out of her blue jeans, pulled on the Fendi sweatsuit, and walked out to look at herself in the mirror, and everyone in the store stopped to stare at her.

"Oh, the fit is *too* perfect," the saleswoman commented. Melody's ass looked like sculpture. Even the store manager stopped and stared. He was a White, high-class gay man, the type of man who didn't flaunt it. He didn't need to. He looked good, had money, and hung out in all the right places.

He stepped to Mrs. Melody immediately and asked her, "Have you ever modeled before?"

"Not professionally," she answered him. "But I always look good in my clothes, so I *could* do it."

The well-groomed man in his late thirties nodded and thought quickly. "Do you mind if we take some pictures of you in the sweatsuit? I have friends in the fashion industry I would like to send them to."

Melody got excited and said, "Sure, as long as you share them with me." She was used to taking pictures and wanted to brag about it. How often does a high-end retail store ask to take pictures of you in their clothes?

The manager said, "Definitely," and pulled out his updated iPhone to hand over to one of his assistants to take the pictures, while customers watched and marveled. Some of them were even put off by it. Imagine an upper-class White woman watching some biracial urban girl taking pictures in clothes that she didn't even *buy* yet. Could she even *afford* to buy them?

Nevertheless, the distinguished man was able to do it because he was more than just a manager. He was also a talent scout, who had been empowered to make such moves when he felt someone was worthy. He knew nothing about Mrs. Melody's rap career, her ego, her confidence, or any of that. He just knew she *rocked* that sweatsuit like no other girl he had seen in it. And her acceptable look had a lot to do with it. Like it or not, he already understood what the decision-makers would want to see. And Melody had the look that *sold* internationally.

After they had taken a dozen pictures of her, she pulled out her purse and credit cards from her carry bag and said, "All right, wrap it up."

The girl was not playing, and she knew how to move. You don't walk into a high-end store, put on some new clothes, excite the manager, take pictures, and then turn around and not buy the clothes. It would have come off as a complete waste of time. Whether she thought their interest was real or not was out of the question. As the urban saying goes, *nobody got time for that.* Either you were *game* or you were *not.* And Mrs. Melody was *game.*

So, by the time she walked out of the store, with her name and contact information left with the manager, everyone was curious to know who she was, even the jealous White woman in her forties.

"Was she a video vixen or something?" the blonde suburban housewife asked rhetorically. She stopped just short of calling Mrs. Melody a *stripper.* But it didn't matter. The biracial urban girl could garner the type of public attention that the blonde woman still *dreamed* about, and it had never happened for her in her own youth. So, she went ahead and got married . . . twenty years ago.

Back inside the mall with a new bounce in her step, another call popped up on Melody's cell phone while still watching her surroundings for spies. She looked down at her screen and saw that it was Dark & Moody, aka Tasha Samuels.

Melody answered her call in a great mood. "Hey, girl. What's up?"

"I'm still waiting for you to record this second song when you're ready," DM reminded her. "Did you hear the mix on the first one?"

"*Did I?* That shit is *pounding,*" Melody responded excitedly.

Dark & Moody laughed, tickled by her use of words.

"It really *does,* right? Did you hear the new heat I sent you?"

"Not only did I *hear it,* I played it in my car, and people were like, 'What the fuck is *that*?' You are really stepping your game up now. I *told you.*"

"Yeah, you did. So, I'm just waiting on you to finish up this next shit."

As Mrs. Melody approached the mall exit, she asked, "Have you talked to Dr. Victoria about her movie idea? I was just talking to her like, an hour ago."

"Naw, I haven't talked to her about it. I just been busy working on these new beats. But what she say? Does she have a solid idea yet?"

"Yeah, I'll let her tell it to you. But it sounds like a *thriller,* where you're guessing a lot. And she wants me to play a college girl in the mix of it."

"A *college* girl?"

"Yeah, a college girl who loses her money in a Bitcoin trading scam."

"Whaaattt?" Dark & Moody squealed. "I can *see* that. Those people are always talking about money that you can't *spend.* You're just supposed to invest it and let it ride."

"Yeah, while *they* use it. Just like the banks do. But at least the banks let you take your money out," Mrs. Melody stated, while walking out the mall doors with her Fendi bag in one hand and her cell phone in the other.

Just as she reached the curb to the parking lot, she tripped over her feet and stumbled forward right as a car was passing by in front of her.

"Shit!" she panicked. She caught her balance right in time to save herself from a ridiculous, headfirst accident as her Fendi bag slung forward and grazed the car.

"What happened?" Tasha asked her, alarmed.

Melody stood up straight and tossed her left hand over her heart with the Fendi bag.

"I damn near tripped into a fuckin' *car* out in the parking lot. Is God try'na tell me something?"

Dark & Moody paused. She said, "I *hope* not. That sounds like some *Final Destination*-type shit. Remember them movies, where random shit happened to people?"

"Girl, don't bring that shit up to me," Melody snapped with her heart still racing. "I got a lot of shit I still wanna *do* out here."

"Me and you *both,*" DM told her. "So, watch how you *walk* out there."

"Yeah, watch how I do *everything,*" Melody responded. She became nervous to even walk to her car, and she did so while watching everything that moved.

"I'ma call you back later," she told Tasha. "I'm a little *shook* right now. I just need to make it to my car."

"Aw'ight, well, text me when you get inside."

"Cool. I'll do that."

Mrs. Melody hung up the line and made it cautiously to her electric-blue Volkswagen Jetta. It had been her used, get-around car for three years. She had just been thinking about upgrading it to a BMW or a Mercedes. But she hadn't done it yet.

She climbed into the driver's seat behind the wheel and tossed her Fendi bag in the passenger side. Honestly, she couldn't believe how shaken she had become after her accidental stumble. The fear felt unnatural for her.

She took a deep breath and asked, "God . . . am I moving too fast? Are you really trying to tell me something?"

Like any other young and ambitious woman, she wanted it *all*, but not if she would lose her *life* trying to get it. That was the fear a lot of young hopefuls had. How much of themselves did they need to barter to succeed?

It was similar to Dark & Moody's ideas of human sacrifice, an extreme that Mrs. Melody was *definitely* not thinking about. So, she relaxed in her car and exhaled again.

"God . . . I just wanna make it back home *safely*. That's all I ask."

JOSEPH DRAKE

Reflection 26

THE WHOLE MOVIE IDEA WAS EXTRA FOR ME, BUT I WAS STILL COMmitted to doing it. However, there would be no movie without the financing. So, after I spoke to Mrs. Melody about my ideas for her role, I needed to check back in with Joe about the money, and he seemed to be going through his own tangent.

"Hey, Joe, how are you this week?" I called and asked him. After our last few conversations, he had given me his cell phone number. And I must admit, had I not been trying to entice him to find funding for my film and entertainment project, I probably wouldn't have used it, because it wasn't about business. But sometimes you had to go *off* the record to get more *on* the record. The real dealmakers out there know exactly what I mean.

He said, "I'm actually heading out of town right now to meet up with one of my daughters." He sounded all excited about it, and I could hear the airport traffic in the background.

I paused. "Really?" We had spoken about his daughters in more detail, but he didn't say he was planning a trip out of town to see them. "Did you have this planned?" I asked him.

"Nope. Not at all. I just woke up a couple of days ago and decided I would go ahead and just *do it.* And I booked an open ticket."

I didn't mean to be rude, and he didn't sound like he was in a business state of mind. So, there was no sense in me going there.

I had to talk about what was important to him and scratch my financing agenda for later.

I said, "Do they know you're coming? You know, the mother and daughter?"

"Nope. Not yet. I'll call and tell them when I get there."

He sounded damn-near delusional, as if he was laughing at it all. But it wasn't a game.

I said, "You're just gonna pop up in their city? What if they're not even there?"

"No, they'll be there. I mean, I spoke to them and all. They just don't know that I'm coming yet."

I paused again. I was trying to follow his logic. "And you think that's a good thing, to just pop up on them like that?"

I don't know if I was being a "reverse racist" or whatever, but that kind of thing struck me as incredibly *White* and *privileged.* I guess he thought they were going to give him a holiday for showing up out of the blue, like he's Superman flying in to save them from an earthquake.

I couldn't imagine Charles, Tyrell, or any other brother being that presumptuous. I mean, what was this man *thinking*?

I said, "I don't know if that's a good idea, but it sounds like you're already on your way."

"Yeah, I am. And I'm feeling really *good* about it."

"Are you gonna try and rekindle something with the mother?"

At that point, I was just curious. There wasn't anything else I could do about it. Like he said, he was already at the airport.

"Ahhh . . . I don't know yet," he answered.

I began to wonder if he was still a businessman, because he surely wasn't acting like one with his personal life. Maybe his "go for it" rationale is what had landed him in the compromised situation in the first place.

I said, "Would you make any *business* decisions last minute like this, without planning anything?" If he did, then I was ready to ask him for a million dollars to start the preproduction on our movie. I didn't know what the final cost would be, but a million dollars sounded like a great start.

Joe answered my question immediately. "Aw, hell no. Of *course* not. No deal would ever get done like this."

Well, duhhh! Then what the hell are you doing? I wanted to ask him, but I held my tongue for a more professional response.

I said, "Exactly. So, why are you doing this?"

He said, "She's a *woman.* They're more emotional. Logic never worked with her."

I didn't know if I should have felt *offended* or what when he said that. But I didn't. I just rolled with the punches as if I were back on the job.

"And what is *your* logic? What exactly are you trying to do now? Are you trying to climb back into their lives?" I asked.

"Well, that's what I'm gonna try and *see.* It's better late than never, right?"

I started wondering why he hadn't told me. I was still a psychologist, and he had paid me for our last two hours of conversation. But if I hadn't called him on his cell phone for an update on my film ideas and our need for capital, I would have never known he was heading out of town to surprise his baby momma and daughter.

"Were you planning to tell me about this *after* the fact?" I asked him. I figured if his visit had gone haywire, he definitely would have told me about it later. Or would he?

He saw my point and chuckled. He said, "I didn't want you to talk me out of it. So, once the idea came to mind, I figured I would just go with it and let the pieces fall where they may."

"Even if they fall all over the place?" I joked.

He continued to chuckle, as if he was taking it all lightly.

I said, "Well, at least you find this all to be *humorous.*" He reminded me of stereotypical White guys who liked to play pranks in high school and college. Everything was a damn *joke.* But this was grown-ass-man time now.

"Trust me, even after our talks about it, I've been all over the place with this thing," he told me. "It's like I'm riding a wild buffalo. And with that being the case, I figured it'd be better to jump on the damn thing and see where it takes me instead of being afraid of it. And again, neither one of us can predict what's gonna happen. We have no idea."

He had a point about that. I could speculate all I wanted, but I didn't really know these women. All I knew is what he told me about them, and it wasn't enough.

"Okay, so, I'm assuming you're visiting the older girl who's a senior in high school now."

"Yup, you got that right."

"And that's the *older* and more difficult mother," I reflected from our previous conversations about them.

"Yeah. She was the first love," he answered.

That made me pause again. He had never told me *that* before.

"She was your *first* love?" I repeated, making sure I heard him correctly.

"Well, not my first *love*, but the first one I got *pregnant*, so to speak," he corrected himself.

I didn't like the sound of that. It sounded so insensitive. And that insensitivity about pregnancy came from a lot of men. That's why I made certain to never get pregnant out of wedlock. But it was what it was, and that's how guys spoke about it. They always made it sound as if it were an accident.

Then again . . . just because a man wanted some . . . *pussy*, didn't mean he wanted a baby with it.

"Well, good luck with that," I told him. I didn't know what else to say. "I guess I'll hear about it when you get back," I concluded.

"Well, what were you calling me about?" he asked. "I got a few more minutes before the plane boards."

At that point, my whole conversation about the movie idea and financing would sound selfish and off base. But he did ask me.

"Well . . ." I hesitated. "I was just calling to check up on you," I lied. I couldn't bring myself to say it.

"Okay. Thanks," he responded. "And how's that movie idea coming?"

I hesitated again. But he was giving me a wide-open door.

"Well, I came up with some real cool ideas for it, in the business sector actually."

"Oh, yeah? Like a *Wall Street* kind of thing? What kind of business ideas?"

He was really trying to pull it out of me after I had backed down from it.

"Well . . . what do you think about the Bitcoin industry?" I asked him.

He paused and chuckled again. He said, "I don't, actually."

"Why not?" With Joe being a legitimate businessman, I was really interested in what he would have to say about it.

He said, "When you're successful in *real* business, you don't have time to think about the speculative. It's kind of like getting your hair done at a new shop that may or may not do a good job. And it's like, if you already love your barber or hairdresser, then what's the point of trying someone else? Unless you're just *bored*. But . . . we don't get *bored* with making real money. You know what I mean?

"But on the other hand, if you're like, a celebrity who hasn't been paid well from your last movie or album or whatever, and you want to ramp up your income in the meantime, then you might try something like Bitcoin or Forex in the cryptocurrency game," he explained. "But if you're making millions of dollars every year in real estate, then good luck with moving those guys into cryptocurrency. You get it?

"The key words are *real* and *estate*," he concluded.

I laughed. Joe was still a real businessman all right. He made his point perfectly clear. I was only moving into Bitcoin trading if everything else I made money on failed. So, I told him the rest of my movie idea, and he listened to it all and had this to say.

"I see where you're going with that. But you have two ways to consider it. Number one, it could come across like you're picking on the cryptocurrency traders, and if the business continues to hold steady and become legitimate, you'll have egg on your face. *But* . . . if it all falls apart in the next few years, then you could come out like Nostradamus," he told me.

"Either way, you don't want it to be *too* obvious that you're talking about Bitcoin."

"But do you think it's a good movie idea overall?" I asked him.

"Well, it depends on how you execute it to make it relatable to the largest group of people. So, it really depends on the writing."

I nodded. "Okay." That brought me right back to Tyrell Hodge and his quirkiness.

Joe added, "I like the title though. That *Trading* title could relate to a lot of different things. It reminds me of Dan Aykroyd and Eddie Murphy years ago in *Trading Places*. That was a business-type of movie too, before *Wall Street*."

"Oh, yeah, you're right," I remembered. "That was a good movie. And they were *on* Wall Street."

"And they made it highly relatable with two huge comedy stars," he reminded me.

That made me nervous about Mrs. Melody again. Would Joe believe that she was bankable? Who would vouch for her?

"Yup, that's my boarding call," he told me. I could hear the announcements in the background.

I said, "One more question before you go."

"All right. Shoot."

"What do you think about biracial women in movies?" I was thinking about Melody again.

Joe said, "Halle Berry. Dorothy Dandridge. Irene Cara. Zoe Saldaña. Lisa Bonet. Zendaya. My two daughters," he added with a laugh. "Need I say *more?*"

His point was well taken. Obviously, he had already been thinking about biracial women. So, I smiled and felt stronger about Mrs. Melody.

"Have a safe flight," I told him.

"Thanks. I will."

Joe was being quite audacious to travel back up to Boston to surprise his older daughter and her mother with a visit. Actually, they lived outside Boston in a suburb called Milton. Milton was an area where some of the better educated and gainfully employed Black people moved when they could afford it. It was right outside the Boston areas of Dorchester, Mattapan, and Hyde Park, where even more Black people lived.

Joe arrived at Boston's Logan International Airport right at rush hour at a quarter to five PM. He still had plenty of friends and family in the area, but he wasn't there to see any of them. He had a one-track mind to deal with his pressing and personal mission. So, he called the mother immediately upon landing and walking out of the bridge from the airplane.

"Hello?" she answered.

"Are you just about ready to get off of work?" Joe asked her.

Inside her office, Carole Ogurah, a milk-chocolate Black woman with silky smooth skin, deep-set eyes, and a royal-blue business suit looked down at her Android cell phone to see who it was. She had answered the phone too quickly without looking.

"Joe?" she asked, confused.

"Yeah, it's me."

"Calling me *twice* in one week? What's going on?" she asked him. He hadn't called her like that in *years*.

"Yeah, I know, right?" Joe responded with a chuckle, luggage in hand. "But our baby girl is heading off to *college* soon. Time to step my game up."

Carole looked at her cell phone again and scowled. Joe had always been on time with his child support payments. But that part was easy with an account already set up for yearly deposits and monthly disbursements. But him actually being *involved* with their daughter was something he hadn't done.

She asked him, "Is there something you're trying to tell me?" with no accent. Her Jamaican and Nigerian accents only came out when she spoke to her parents or used them on purpose for business. She was now a life insurance saleswoman at the top of her game, who specialized in minority families. So, she used every cultural advantage at her disposal to pull them in, including the strategic use of her Jamaican and Nigerian accents. But now she was dealing with an enthusiastic White man with a guilt disease.

"Yeah, I'm at the airport," Joe answered. "I wanna have a sit-down dinner with you guys."

Carole cringed. "What? You flew into *Boston*?" A touch of her Jamaican-Nigerian attitude jumped out.

"Yeah, I got inspired," he told her. He was really drinking the comeback dad Kool-Aid.

She said, "You can't just *pop up* and demand a dinner, just because you called and spoke to her this week."

Joe headed for the airport exit and said, "You think she'll turn it down? Does she have a big homework assignment to finish tonight? She likes *seafood*, right? Or would she rather eat Jamaican or Nigerian food? It doesn't matter to me. Whatever she wants, she gets."

"I mean, what's going on?" Carole pressed him. "What's the *urgency* now? You knew she'd be going to college for the past *three years*. Why get all concerned about it *now*? Did you doubt that she would be ready to go?"

It had been a recurring theme between them, the battle over intellect. Was it a Black thing or a woman thing that he continued to doubt her establishment? Or maybe it was a little bit of *both*.

"I didn't imply that at all," Joe argued. "But you continue to think that way. That's a problem that *you* have."

Carole shook her head and said, "Okay. I'm not going to argue about it. I'll ask my daughter and see what she says."

That immediately made him feel nervous. Did he really want to leave the success of his trip to Boston in the hands of a temperamental seventeen-year-old . . . ?

"I'll call her," he suggested. He figured he'd talk her into it if he needed to.

To his surprise, Carole didn't argue. "Okay. Call her."

Joe didn't like the sound of that either. It felt like a setup. Did she know something that he didn't? Did his daughter secretly hate his guts? She didn't really speak to him that way. Then again, there wasn't much passion in her conversations with him either. She spoke to him as if she were having a conversation with a guidance counselor, with a bunch of "okays" and "all rights." So, he figured he would have to find out more for himself.

"What time are you trying to do this?" Carole asked him.

He shrugged as he walked out of the airport and into the taxi pickup area. "Ahhh, around eight or eight thirty. That gives me time to check into my hotel room and freshen up."

Freshen up for what? Carole thought over the line. She hadn't even *seen* the man in years. Nor had his daughter. Outside of the money he provided, they had no expectations of him.

"All right, well, go ahead and call her and see what she says," she repeated of their daughter.

Joe paused and forced the question. "She doesn't ahhh . . . secretly *hate me* or anything, does she?" he asked with an awkward chuckle.

Carole paused as well. "I don't know. She's seventeen now, so she has her own opinions on things."

Joe took a deep breath and stopped himself from calling a taxi. He wanted to speak to his daughter without a driver being all in his business while he spoke on the phone.

"All right. I'll call her right now," he agreed, while waiting outside the airport.

He hung up the line with the mother and took a deep breath before calling the daughter as planned. It took three rings before she answered.

"Hello?"

"Hey, Ayana. It's your dad," Joe said with confidence. He wasn't going to let a seventeen-year-old scare him. He had just spoken to her a few days ago. But he had not asked her and her mother out to *dinner* like he was about to do now. That part changed things.

"Oh, hi," she responded calmly. Sure enough, she was at work on her high school assignments at the kitchen table, where there was more natural light and space than in her bedroom. As with most biracial girls with a White parent, she was light-skinned with a wild grade of light brown hair that she allowed to grow into long and neat dreads. Upon first look, she wasn't particularly striking, but she did have a pair of kaleidoscope hazel eyes, the kind that looked like they changed colors depending on the lighting.

Carole said they came from her Jamaican side of the family, where she had "Cooley" grandparents with East Indian blood, combined with the blue-eyed genetics of Joe. It was an exotic eye color shared by many biracial children, and an element of Ayana that stood out, along with her Nigerian surname—Ogurah.

"Did I catch you doing homework?" Joe asked her.

She chuckled. That was a good thing. "Yeah, you kind of did," she told him.

"Are you gonna be hungry tonight?" he asked.

Her easy smile turned into a frown. It was an obvious question.

"At some point, I assume I will," she answered.

"Good. How 'bout we get some seafood? Or would you rather have Jamaican? It doesn't matter to me."

Ayana stopped what she was doing and focused completely on him. "Are you *here*?"

Joe continued to chuckle as if it was all a game. "Yeah, I am. I just got in at the airport?"

"Are you here on *business*?"

She figured there had to be a *reason* for it, and it wasn't for her or her mother.

Joe said, "Actually, I came here to see you guys. You and your mother."

Ayana paused, perplexed by it. "Did you tell my mother that?"

"Yeah, I just got off the phone with her."

Ayana looked confused as hell. "Did she know that you were coming?"

"Nope. Not until I got here."

His logic wasn't adding up for anyone but himself.

His daughter asked, "And what did my mother *say*?"

"She said to call and ask *you*?"

"Call and ask me what?"

"If you wanted to meet up for dinner tonight."

It all seemed awkward and forced. She didn't really have any feeling toward the man. He was pretty much a gene donor who paid monthly for her life expenses. She didn't even ask about him anymore.

"Ummm . . . wow." Ayana didn't know what to tell him.

"Look, it's just *food,* right? Let's just get something to eat," Joe pressed her.

"Yeah, but . . . did my mother tell you she has a *boyfriend*?"

Joe paused. "Okay . . . I didn't ask her about that."

"Yeah, well, he kind of . . . *lives* with us," his daughter revealed to him.

Finally, Joe got the point. Him flying up there to Boston, unannounced, to meet up with his estranged daughter and her mother was ridiculous. But he wouldn't allow anyone to tell him differently. It was his little secret, like his whole relationship with them had been.

He said, "Okay, well . . . what does that have to do with us going out to a dinner? We're just sitting down to eat."

That's what he said, but deep down inside his *feelings* were hurt. How could Carole have a man living with them in a house that *he* helped her to pay for? He didn't like that idea at all!

If you want a man, then marry him and move into his house. Why let him freeload off yours? Joe thought to himself, disturbed by it.

Ayana said, "I mean, this is just kind of . . . *weird.*"

Joe snapped, "What's so *weird* about it? We're just having a *dinner*? What's the big deal?"

He was ready to blow his top at the airport. He had been paying out of pocket for child support and other gifts for years, and now he couldn't ask them out for a basic *dinner.* It sounded incredibly unappreciative. The next thing he knew, he started thinking about his wealthy White partners in his hedge fund and venture capital enterprises.

Shit! Maybe those guys are onto something! he pondered.

He said, "You know, I had no idea that me asking you guys out to dinner would be such an issue. I mean, I may not have been around you all these years, but I don't consider myself to be a *stranger*, either."

Particularly after sending your mother more than a million dollars over seventeen years, he reflected. But he surely didn't want to blurt that out to his daughter.

She said, "Well, it's just . . . we would need more preparation for that. But you just got here *today*? I mean, it would be better if we went out *tomorrow*. That would at least give us a day to think about it."

Joe was incensed. *What is there to think about? It's a fucking dinner!* He couldn't see what the issue was. Nevertheless, he realized that he needed to be more *patient*. His decision to visit them had been very sudden.

"Okay. Tomorrow then," he responded, compromising.

"Yeah," his daughter told him.

Joe calmed down and took another breath. "How's everything else going?"

"Fine. Everything's good," Ayana answered casually.

"Well, that's good."

"Yup."

That was the norm of their usual conversations. Nothing was really being said or asked. So, when Joe finally hung up the line with her, he felt like a lonely man on the moon again.

"Shit!" he fumed with his luggage still in hand at the airport. "This is just what I get for waiting so long. I should have done this *years* ago."

Then he started thinking about his younger daughter and *her* mother.

"Yeah," he mumbled to himself as he nodded and eyed the taxis. "I need to call them in advance."

TYRELL HODGE

Reflection 27

With three down and two to go, I didn't want to talk to Tyrell about my film ideas over the phone again. He was too argumentative and difficult to deal with over the phone. And with all of his driving, I rarely felt like he was giving me his full attention. So, I needed to talk to him face-to-face, where I could calm his ass down, even if I had to *pay him* for his time. And if he blew me off in a face-to-face meeting . . . then *fuck it.* I would have to find a new talented writer.

I caught the temperamental Chicago man on the line and made my pitch. "Tyrell, let me treat you to a late lunch and give you a hundred dollars to talk to me about my film ideas."

He paused immediately. I knew I had to front-load my pitch with the money, otherwise it would take too long with the back-and-forth. Tyrell was the kind of man who forced you to put everything out front. There was no stringing him along. You had to put it all on the line with a total commitment to him. That's why he lost out on so many business opportunities. Most people weren't willing to meet him at 100 percent. But I was.

He said, "Let me get this straight. You're gonna pay for my lunch *and* give me a hundred dollars?"

"Yes," I confirmed to him. "I'm that serious."

He chuckled and said, "Aw'ight. What time you wanna meet?"

"Three o'clock. At the Midtown Cafeteria at Georgia Tech."

"Oh, yeah, it's easy to park around there."

"I know. That's why I chose it."

"Cool. I'll see you at three."

I hung up and smiled at how easy it was. You have to commit to Tyrell the whole way. And if you commit to him, he'll commit to you. He was that easy. What made it *hard* was when someone failed to take him seriously. And in the business of paying writers, people were forever bullshitting. So, he complained about it. Plain and simple.

I walked into the Midtown Cafeteria on time, looking and smelling good. I had a full-package plan ready just for Tyrell. I knew just how to deal with him.

I found a booth table near the front entrance to catch him as soon as he walked in.

When he walked in shortly after me, I made sure to stand and greet him with a hug so he could take in my fashion and smell my perfume.

"Thanks for meeting me today," I told him.

"Yeah, you paying for lunch and a hundred dollars. I can't turn that down."

Like a real Chicago man, Tyrell was incredibly physical. You could tell he was used to being around hardened men. Even his hug felt as if he could shove me through a glass window.

"Have you ever learned how to be *gentle*?" I joked as we sat across from each other.

"Yeah, I know how to be gentle . . . when I *need* to be," he said, taking off his black Chicago White Sox baseball cap and setting it on the far end of our table.

"So, you don't need to be gentle with me, huh?" I teased.

"Oh, my bad. My hug was too rough for you?" He had a fresh haircut and a shave that made him look ten years younger than his mid-forties.

I shook my head and grinned. "Seems like everything you do is rough?"

"If you like it that way," he flirted.

I gave him a knowing eye. "Cut it out," I told him.

"With a razor blade or scissors?" he asked me. He was that sharp mentally, and it was hard for many people to keep up with him. But I understood it. Genius was simply *different*. It didn't do what you wanted it to do. It was out of your control. So, you simply had to deal with it or not. And most people chose not to.

"Anyway . . ." I began. "So, someone came up with the title *Trading* for my new project. What do you think about that title?"

"Trading what?" he asked me.

I shrugged. "You tell me."

I wanted to hear what he would *do* with it.

He said, "It reminds me of *Trading Places* with Eddie Murphy. Or trading hearts . . . Trading bodies . . . Trading souls . . . Trading dispositions . . . Trading economics . . . Trading cultures . . . Trading gods. You could do *a lot* with that. It depends on what angle you wanna take with it."

I smiled and said, "Bitcoin people talk about trading too."

Tyrell frowned immediately. "Aw, them motherfuckas are crazy. You're buying *coins* that you can't cash in. What the hell is that? That's like putting your money in a vending machine and nothin' come out that motherfucker. Then you start shaking it and banging it."

He grabbed an imaginary vending machine with both hands and shook it. "If this motherfucka don't give me back my money."

I chuckled at it. The man was extremely passionate and visual. Now you'll get to see *why* I respected him.

"So, a college girl loses her money in this trading group. But you can't necessarily make it about Bitcoin," I told him. "You don't wanna make it seem like we're calling them out."

I was keeping in mind what Joseph Drake had told me.

Tyrell nodded. "And then this girl goes crazy trying to get her money back. When people told her ass not to do that shit. But she thought she *knew* something. Yeah, that's easy. A young big-headed bitch. Excuse my French," he apologized.

I grinned and waved it off. "We're grown. I heard it all before. So, how complicated could you make it?" I asked him. We couldn't keep it *that* easy. Or could we?

Tyrell thought about it. He smiled and said, "You know, that *Angel Heart* shit was *deep*. You remember Lisa Bonet got in all kinds of trouble for that movie? They kicked her off *The Cosby Show* for that. I guess Bill wanted some," he joked, and laughed.

I didn't touch that joke at all. Like I said, Tyrell was more than most people could take.

"What does *Angel Heart* have to do with what I'm talking about?" I asked him seriously. I needed to redirect him. He was falling off track from discussing my ideas.

He said, "In this day and age, you notice how much these kids talk about the Illuminati and blood sacrifices and all that shit? That shit *been* around. But these kids talk about it in pop culture now like it's all new.

"Well, what if this trading idea is deeper than money? And we give these kids what they keep talking about?" he commented.

"So . . . you wanna make it a *demonic* group?" I asked him. I wasn't thinking about that angle. I frowned and shook my head. "That sounds too *dark*," I complained.

Tyrell said, "Money is the root of all evil, right? So, it's *all* dark and demonic. That's why these kids are always talking that shit. They're already dark. Listen to the music they like. It's *dark* pop music," he stated.

I smiled. "Or gothic *funk*," I added.

Tyrell was intrigued by it. "Yeah, I like that. That funky, spooky shit."

Of course, I was thinking all about Dark & Moody again. She was my next conversation.

I said, "I have someone who does that."

"And we can use that shit for the soundtrack."

He was reading my mind. That's why I loved him.

He said, "But let's take it even deeper. These people don't know who they're *fucking* with. And while they're out here *trading* and deceiving people, they stole some shit from her *father* years ago. And she infiltrated them to get it back. So, she's really been huntin' these motherfuckas down.

"And it ain't about the money. It's their *souls* that she's after," Tyrell explained to me. "And like *The Usual Suspects*—one of my favorite movies—they find out that she's the daughter of the devil. But by that time, it's too late. She's already *slaughterin'* these motherfuckas.

"So, it'd be best for us to *fake it* like it's about Bitcoin anyway, knowing that's it's much *deeper* than that," he told me. "The Bitcoin angle would only be a *front.*"

I cringed. "But they would still *complain* about it. Then they would say we think they're demonic."

Tyrell sat back against the booth and frowned. "Real art takes that chance. And if you don't want to offend anybody, you end up creating vanilla shit," he argued. "But we'll figure it all out. And whoever plays this college girl role gotta be *bad.* A girl that everybody wanna fuck," he added with his typical rawness.

I smiled again. I said, "I got someone like that too. And I want you to meet her before you start writing it."

"Who's paying me for the writing?" he asked immediately.

I shook my head. Tyrell was always about his *money.*

"Money is the root of all *evil,* Tyrell," I reminded him sarcastically.

"And I'm one *evil* motherfucka," he countered.

I smiled and chuckled. "I'm still working on that part," I told him.

He said, "And this girl you're talking about. Are you sure you wanna introduce me to her? Because, if she's all that, then I might wanna fuck her too. You know I ain't getting none at home right now."

I started laughing. Tyrell was outrageous. But he was actually *safer* to me than Charles Clay was, because he was so straightforward and *honest*—to a *fault.* If any girl chose to fuck him, she would know *exactly* what it was about, his pure, unadulterated *hunger,* and nothing else.

I grinned and said, "She wouldn't touch you with a ten-foot *pole.*"

He frowned and said, "Why not? I ain't a bad-looking guy. I still got my *swagger.*"

I continued to smile. There was nothing wrong with Tyrell's looks. And I was *certain* that he had plenty of women in his prime. That's why his lady wouldn't fuck him now. She was still in anger mode over the women he could still pull—if he wanted to.

I said, "Because you're too *obvious.* And she would know she's not getting anything from it. Unless she just wants to see how you *fuck.*"

The man had turned *me* into a potty mouth to match *his* rawness. So, I was embarrassed when a young Asian girl walked up on us as our server and overheard me. Tyrell and I had been talking all that time, and she had just made her way over to us.

"Oh, I'm sorry," I told her. She was grinning and covering her face with both hands.

"Yeah, bring us out some water to cool things off. I can make women *hot* like that, you know," Tyrell teased. That made the girl squeeze her hands to her face even harder.

"Okay," she told us, and walked back away.

"You think her panties are wet now because of your mouth?" Tyrell asked me.

"Stop it," I told him with a glare. "That's perverted."

He frowned and said, "That's not *perverted.* She's a *college* girl."

"*Exactly,*" I told him. "She's too *young* for you to be making those comments about her."

He smirked and said, "Yet, you want me to write about a college girl for your *movie.* What, she don't fuck nobody in the film? She's trading *kisses* and Valentine's Day candy?" he asked me.

He had a point. I was busted. So, I took a deep breath and sighed.

"Anyway . . . now I forgot what we were talking about," I told him.

"We were talking about me fucking your college girl, the one you want me to meet for your movie," he reminded me.

I said, "No, we were talking about you *not* fucking her."

"Well, there's a whole lot of *fuckin'* and *not* fuckin' that we're talking about at this table, huh? No wonder our Asian girl walked away," he joked. "You need to be *ashamed* of yourself. And you call yourself a *psychologist*?" He shook his head. "I don't know about you sometimes."

I grinned and kept right on grinning. I genuinely *liked* being around Tyrell when I could get him to stop being so angry. I said, "So, getting back to the movie . . . you would make it like a Jordan *Peele* kind of thing?"

He stared across the table at me and said, "No. I would make it like a Tyrell *Hodge* kind of thing. Because I was doing this shit *before* him. He just got a chance to do it *bigger*. And I'm proud of him for it, but I'm not taking shorts to *nobody*. And I liked the original *Candyman* better," he griped.

I laughed. I liked the original *Candyman* myself and didn't care much for the revision. I guess we *agreed* on that.

I said, "But you're not gonna write *anything* without the money first?"

He looked at me and sighed. "Maybe . . . if my lady finally decided to give me some . . . I might feel inspired enough to do something without the money."

I eyed him across the table and continued to grin. He had me thinking all kinds of things that I didn't want to admit.

"So . . . *sex* is that important to you? It's worth *more* than money? Really?"

Tyrell was perfectly calm about it, the calmest he had ever been while I was around him.

He said, "Sex is how we all got here. And down here in Atlanta, what they call the *new* 'Black Hollywood,' we got millionaire rappers and athletes from all over the country and the *world*, who go to these strip clubs and throw money in the air to make it rain for the *illusion* of sex. Imagine that."

"But that's only one-dollar bills," I argued. "That ain't *real* money."

Tyrell frowned. "That ain't *real* money?" he repeated. "Can them strippers pick it up and spend it? What the hell are you talking about? They ain't throwing up *fake* money."

"I mean, it's not like *significant* income," I explained. "Especially if you're talking about *millionaires* doing it."

Tyrell said, "Money is money. And people blow a whole lot of it for *sex*. But you don't see anybody in here making it rain over this *food*."

He tossed his hands in the air with imaginary money and said, "Damn this macaroni and cheese is banging! Who made this spaghetti? And the barbecue sauce on this chicken is the *shit*! Bring the chef out here, I got something for him."

I laughed again. The man was hilarious.

I said, "So, if your woman broke down and gave you some, you would be inspired enough to write something for me for *free*?" I had to get him back on topic.

Tyrell said, "For *free*? Naw, I didn't say *that*. You're eventually gonna have to pay me. You just won't have to pay as much up front," he explained.

I took a deep breath and exhaled. I couldn't believe what I was about to say and where I was about to go with it. But the *truth* was the *truth*.

I said, "Well, does it have to come from *her*?"

He nodded rather quickly, as if he had already been thinking about it. "I mean, I've invested a *lot* in her," he stated. "A lot of *time*, emotions, ideas, *energy*, frustrations. We ain't *new*. So, it *means* more from her.

"But I can still go out and get some random *ass*, right now. That's *nothin'* to me," he boasted. "The hard part is getting the woman you *want* to submit. Otherwise, why would any man choose to be in a committed relationship? Especially for guys who got it like that. You could just have a rotating-fucking-door of women," he concluded.

"But why do you ask?" he questioned.

That was the hard part for *me*. Where was my mind going?

I said, "Well . . . if you just *needed* some, then . . . I'm still a *woman*," I hinted.

Tyrell saw my point and started laughing. He said, "So, you

would give me some just for your movie?" That was the elephant in the room. It all sounded *crazy*. But I had to clarify it.

"Not just for my *movie*," I told him. "But . . . I like you. I really do," I admitted with a slow nod. I said, "There's a lot of *fake* people out here in this world. But there's nothing fake about *you*. You *are* who you *are*. And I appreciate that."

There was silence in the restaurant. Tyrell looked at me with moistness in his eyes that he *refused* to succumb to, as he nodded back to me . . . diligently.

"You have no idea how that makes me *feel* just hearing that validation of my manhood," he told me. "It's almost like . . . we can't be *men* anymore. So, I gotta *apologize* for how I was *raised*. And how my *dick* still gets *hard* when I want a *woman*. So, I appreciate you for saying that. And I *thank you*. Because it *sounds* like you understand me. And that means *a lot*."

Then he smiled at me. "So . . . we gon' work on this movie of yours," he told me, right as our server made it back to the table with the water.

The Asian college girl sat our glasses of water on the table and asked us, "Are you ready to order?"

Tyrell looked at her and smiled with confidence. "Yeah, we ready." And he made his order.

CHARLES CLAY

Reflection 28

BEFORE GETTING BACK TO DARK & MOODY WITH AN UPDATE ON her role in creating the soundtrack music, I needed to check in on Charles. I had left him alone for a minute while he healed his head and his ego. I figured he needed a bit of time and space to think about things.

"Hey, Charles, how's it going?" I asked him when he picked up. "I hadn't heard back from you. I wanted to make sure you were all right."

"Yeah, that was an embarrassing night," he responded. "Now the girl's trying to *sue me*?"

"What? Really?" That caught me off guard.

He said, "Yeah, she served the paperwork right after the incident. And my attorney contacted me about it."

I paused. I still didn't know enough about the situation and hadn't gotten a chance to ask him more detailed questions about it. But I *needed* to.

"On what grounds?" I asked him.

"Sexual misconduct," he answered. "She claims she hasn't been able to work or focus on getting jobs, while going through psychological counseling and all of that. She also claims her relationship has suffered with her fiancé."

I was still hesitant to ask, but I *had* to. "Well, what happened?"

"Of course, I can't talk about it now. We have lawyers involved," he told me. "And unfortunately, it also puts the breaks on some of the new film projects I had on the table until we get this all worked out."

Shit! I thought. *Do you believe this?*

"Well, do people know about it?" I asked him.

"Yeah, the first thing she wants to do is take it *public.* So, we're trying to get out in front of that, so it doesn't negatively affect my career," he answered.

"But if you're already putting some of your projects on hold, then it's already affecting your career," I commented. *Including the film I've been planning with you,* I thought.

"Not necessarily. It would only be a *minor* delay if any," he assured me.

"*If* it gets handled correctly, right?" I assumed.

I wasn't even thinking about the *victim* or the *truth* of the matter. Obviously, Charles had done *something* with her. Was it all consensual? Either way, they both had a story to tell.

He said, "I've been thinking that I needed a break anyway. I've been going really *hard* for the past few years. Maybe I need some time off to reevaluate things."

He was right, of course. He was just saying it at the wrong time *for me.* Which was selfish on my part.

I took a deep breath and stated the obvious. "So, I guess I can't count on you to direct my film idea anytime soon, huh?"

"When were you realistically trying to get it done?" he asked me. "It wasn't gonna happen *this year.* You don't even have a screenplay."

Instead of spilling the beans too early about my deal with Tyrell Hodge, I told Charles, "I'm working on that right now."

"Exactly. So, that's not gonna be ready for a few *months,* at *least,*" he predicted.

He didn't believe in Tyrell's writing skills like I did. So, I bit my tongue and didn't say anything. I figured it was best to hand a screenplay over to him once we had a first draft to read.

Charles was probably right about the time period. Tyrell was pretty busy making money driving PDS, and I didn't have the budget to pay him yet. Nevertheless, instead of me sweating it all, I moved on. I had other calls to make and other preparations, including building an outside production team. I was initially going to lean on Charles and his team, but maybe it was good for me *not* to do that. I didn't want to give one person too much influence over my efforts anyway, particularly with the potential of Charles and Tyrell knocking heads. Maybe it would be best for me to have a neutral mediator between them.

I took in all the information he presented to me and sighed. "Okay, well . . . if there's anything you need to talk to me about on a professional level, I'm still a psychologist and it would *all* be confidential," I reminded Charles. I didn't want him to forget what my profession was, and I was still able to help him in what he was going through.

He said, "I know. But right now, I just need time to pull back and reflect on everything, and allow the lawyers to do their job."

I nodded. "Okay." There wasn't much more to say about it, at least on my part. But Charles's production partner was a whole other story.

Jacqueline Clark already had issues with Charles's ego and careless sexual appetite. Now his uncontrollable vice threatened to sabotage *her* career, reputation, and income after she had jumped through a dozen circus hoops to set up multiple film deals for them to execute without setbacks. But Charles had now presented her with a full load of embarrassing drama to overcome.

Jackie called him shortly after we hung up and asked him another heavyweight question. "Who is DeAndra Kittles?"

Charles froze before he asked her, "Why?"

"Because she just filed a *second* sexual misconduct suit against you. Now *who* is she?"

Charles's heart nearly jumped through his chest. He was busted again and at a loss for words.

That was consensual! he fumed to himself.

In anger, he blurted, "This is *ludicrous*! You know what this is, don't you? It's the *Me Too* movement," he accused. "Once one person starts it, others jump on the bandwagon to get *paid.* And it's just *sad.*"

"No, what's *sad* is *your* dumb ass!" Jackie snapped at him. "And you *still* refuse to take responsibility for your *actions.* I thought you told me you were gonna get *help*? What happened to the psychologist you were seeing from New Jersey? Did you fuck her too?

"I am *sick of you*!" she shouted. "Call the fucking *lawyers*! You're gonna have to pay *me* too for this shit! So, put me on that long, damned *list* you're building!" And she hung up on him.

Charles felt as if he had been hit by a tidal wave. He had no idea *what* to think. He even thought about calling Jackie back to try and save himself. But instead, he took her advice and called their lawyers. He was curious to know what they had on him.

"Hey Jeffrey, this is Charles. What's going on? Jackie told me to give you a call."

There was a pregnant pause over the line before the attorney responded to him. He said, "Charles . . . I need you to come into the office."

Charles chuckled nervously. "Is it that bad?"

"Yes, it is," Jeffrey confirmed. "This young lady claims you handcuffed her to the bed."

Charles froze again. *But she asked me to!* he yelled in his own mind. Instead of voicing it, he asked his attorney, "Have you ever seen the movie *Fifty Shades of Grey*?"

There was another awkward pause. "This is not the *movies,* Charles. You make them, but you're not *in* one," the attorney told him. He said, "This is your real *life.* And you need to come down here so we can figure this out. ASAP! And don't talk to *anyone* until you talk to me."

Charles nodded, slowly. "Okay." There was no more to be said. He had to gather himself together and head to his attorney's offices downtown.

Yet . . . he found that he couldn't move. He just sat there at his desk in his office, staring into empty space, as if he had gazed into the eyes of the Greek Gorgon Medusa, and he had turned into stone.

DESTINY FLOWERS

Reflection 29

LIKE CLOCKWORK, WHILE IN THE MIDDLE OF MAKING MY MOVES and more phone calls, this crazy woman Destiny Flowers caught me right in between my appointments. But I was ready for her.

As soon as I heard her voice on the line, I told her, "Excuse me, Destiny, but I *still* haven't seen where you've made an effort to sign onto my schedule, *or* to finally meet up with me. So, if you don't *mind*, I'd like you to stop wasting my time with these random, noncommittal phone calls of yours."

I expected her to bullshit me again with what she *planned* to do, while I planned to ignore it all and move on with my day after hanging up on her. But she immediately threw a curveball.

"It looked to me like you fell *hard* for somebody," she commented. "I guess you *do* like guys."

I stopped my rant and said, "What? What are you talking about?"

She was digging into my personal life again.

She said, "I'm talking about your lunch date. It looked like you were enjoying yourself. *Sounded* like it too."

I winced and thought about it. She had to be talking about *Tyrell*, because he was the only lunch date I had—if you really want to call it that. But it was *business* more than *personal*. Was she in the restaurant with us that day?

"Well, how come you didn't come over and say hi?" I asked,

leading her where I wanted the conversation to go. If she had been stalking me at the Midtown Cafeteria, I wanted her to give me the evidence.

She said, "I didn't want to break up y'all *talk*. It looked like you were really going at it."

"And you say you were close enough to *hear us*?" I questioned.

"I wasn't *that* close. But y'all were *loud*, talking about *fuckin'* and carrying on," she told me.

Now I *knew* she was there. But she didn't know all of the facts.

"Well, if you're gonna *eavesdrop*, then you at least need to get your information right."

Meanwhile, I began to think of *where* she could have been sitting. I was so knee-deep in my conversation with Tyrell that I couldn't remember anyone else around us but our Asian server.

"Did you have the same Asian girl serving you?" I asked.

"Yup," she answered easily. "And whatever y'all said had that poor girl *blushing*. Poor, little thing."

I forgot about the stalking for a minute and laughed. "You must have ordered *a lot* at your table then, because it took a while for that girl to make her way over to us, even for our water."

"It wasn't *my* table that slowed her up. She had a whole table of college girls who did that," she responded. "You didn't hear them talking all loud and laughing?"

Honestly, I really hadn't. To my recollection it had been a quiet day.

On cue, Destiny said, "It's funny how you don't hear nothing else when you're with somebody you really like. You can end up putting all your focus on *them*. So, you must really like him, huh?" she asked me.

I paused again. That was none of her damn *business*. So, I avoided answering the question.

"We were there for *business* and for *business* only," I told her with emphasis.

"Not with you smelling all *good* like that, you wasn't," she commented.

I frowned. "You were close enough to *smell me*?"

That sounded a bit extra. She had me on alert again. *Did this woman walk past me or something?* I asked myself. I even started thinking about who was in the bathroom with me.

"How do you know how I *smelled*?" I asked her.

"*Duuuhhh,* because I could *smell you.*"

"You were sitting that *close*?"

"No. I walked right past you when I came in. But you were so busy hugging the man, you didn't even notice me."

I snapped and said, "I don't even know what you *look* like. How am I gonna *notice* you?"

She ignored my rant and said, "If this lunch date was all about *business,* why you try to come in there looking and smelling all good?"

"Because I have an *image* to upkeep," I argued. "I *always* look and smell good."

"Well, what you think his *woman* would say about that?" she asked me.

"How do you even know he *has* a woman?" I asked back.

"Every grown man has a *woman.* They may not be on good terms all the time, but he *definitely* has one."

"Oh, so, now you know him like that? Really? Well, tell me something I *don't* know about him. Since you *know* so much."

This woman knew how to get under my skin like she was a damn *relative* or something.

She said, "I know he don't like *your* ass. He likes *younger* women," she blurted.

"How do *you* know what he likes?"

"*All* men like younger women. And you pushin' *fifty* now. So, he don't like your old ass," she insisted. "He would fuck that li'l Asian girl *ten times* before he even *looked* at you."

I don't know how or why, but that shit actually hurt my *feelings.* So, I snapped and said "Fuck you! You don't know what he *likes.*"

"How do you know what I know?"

"Because you don't *know him.* You just saw me out there with somebody, and now you're *assuming* shit."

She said, "I'm not assuming *nothin'.* I *do* know. *You* don't fucking know. But I know *everything* you do. *And* the people you deal with. That's why they're getting all fucked up now. Because you don't know what you're *doin'*. Try'na call yourself a psychologist. Girl, *please.*"

I hated when this woman did that shit! That *old,* condescending tone of hers made me feel like a *child.* But I was *older* than her. So, I had to remind myself to act my age.

I said real calmly, "You obviously have some mental problems. So, once you finally schedule some time to come in and *see me,* we can handle that and get to the bottom of this. But until then, I need to let you go and be *crazy* somewhere else. Because I have things *to do.*"

Before I could hang up on her, she caught me on it. "Don't you hang up on me," she warned. "I ain't done talking to you yet."

"Well, I'm done talking to *you.*"

"You don't *need* to talk. *I'll* do the talking."

"About what? Because you obviously don't have anything to *say.* You just call up to aggravate me," I barked at her.

"I'm just try'na warn you not to crave people's significant others," she told me.

"What does it matter to *you?* You're not involved in it," I argued.

"How do *you* know? You don't know me like that."

"I sure don't."

"So, don't question what I'm involved in."

I shook my head and was through with it. "Okay. I have to go now," I told her. I don't know why I wasted so much time with this woman anyway.

She said, "No, I'm still talking."

"And you're not talking about anything I want to *hear.*"

"I know you don't. But you gon' hear it anyway," she insisted. "Now, what's going on with your movie? Do I still have a part?"

I stopped and thought about it. "I still haven't met you to determine that."

"But I thought we already *agreed* to it."

"I agreed to *meet you* first," I reminded her. "And that still hasn't happened."

"Oh, it'll happen. *Trust me*," she commented.

"Yeah, I heard *that* before. So, I won't hold my breath, waiting around for *you*."

"You shouldn't do that anyway. You're not *underwater*."

Those were the kind of random comments she made as an obviously broken woman. And I bet she got a kick out of every call she made to me.

"Did you have a difficult childhood?" I asked her.

"We *all* did. You're a *Black* woman, right? We don't get to escape nothing," she answered. "We get the worst of *everything*. You don't know that by now? How old are you again?"

I shook my head and wondered how long she planned to keep me on the phone with her usual nonsense, so I looked at the time.

"Okay, I really need to . . ."

"I know, I know. You gotta make your next *session*, right? It's at the top of the hour."

She already knew the drill. "Thank you," I told her.

"You just remember what I *said*," she reminded me.

I shook it off and sighed. I couldn't honestly take this woman seriously. But she continued to say things that made me *think*. So, when I finally hung up the line with her, she left me with too much to regurgitate. But one thing really stuck out in my mind. She said she knew *everything* that I did. *And* the people I deal with.

How . . . ?

DARK & MOODY

Reflection 30

I couldn't spend all day thinking about Destiny Flowers. I had a packed afternoon schedule to deal with before trying to catch up with Dark & Moody. I hadn't spoken to her in a bit while following up with everyone else. And to be honest, I was falling behind in my own profession and losing focus on my other clients. This film goal of mine was beginning to affect my real career. Even one of my regulars noticed it.

"You, ummm . . . ain't been the same person over the last few months, Dr. Victoria."

That was what Tamarra Baldwin told me a couple of hours later in my office. She was an older sister in her seventies with beautiful silver hair from Savannah. She was dealing with depression and loneliness after her husband of forty-five years had recently passed away. I really felt sorry for her, so I offered her a half-price discount, but she wouldn't take it. She insisted on paying my regular rate.

"Don't feel sorry for me. You still got a *job* to do. And I don't have no *use* for this money now no way. So, I'm glad to give it to you to for helping me. Otherwise, I'd be hanging out at the casinos and game rooms with it," she joked.

She had a great spirit, and I was glad that I could help her.

"How do you think I've changed?" I asked. She was right, I just wanted to hear the specifics from her.

"Well, you used to be a lot more *calm* and *patient* when I first walked in your office. But lately, you seem more annoyed and hurried, like, people are bothering you and wasting your time," she explained.

I smiled. She was dead-on. I said, "You got that right. I've been under a lot of *stress* lately. But it's of my own doing. Sometimes you take on more than you need to."

She said, "I know that feeling. I used to do that in my younger years too. And I got myself in a whole lot of trouble that way," she added with a laugh. "But when you're *young*, you do it anyway, 'cause you got a whole lot of *energy* to use up."

"Don't I know it," I told her. "Well, you're on point with that. I've been try'na work on a new movie, and it's been pulling me in a bunch of different directions."

Tamarra looked intrigued. "Oh, yeah? A *movie*? What about?"

That was a much longer conversation that I was *not* about to have with her. So, I gave her an abbreviated version. "It's about a good girl chasing after bad guys who did her wrong. But what they don't know is that she's actually *badder* than they are," I told her, based on Tyrell's vision.

Tamarra's eyes lit up with excitement. "That sounds *good*. Sounds like one of those movies that got a lot of *twists* and *turns* in it."

"Exactly!" I told her, grinning. "I'm gonna be talking to a girl who creates the perfect music for it tonight. We're gonna use her music for the soundtrack," I added.

The older sister increased her excitement. "Do you have any roles for an older woman? I could be the mysterious older lady who warns everybody." She even squinted her eyes and held up a wicked finger.

"I'd be *careful* about that girl if I were *you*," she quoted.

We both laughed and enjoyed her audition. Movies were a universal language in America.

"That was *good*," I told her. "But I'll let you know. We just started working on the screenplay."

"Yeah, you do that. And I'm *serious*. That would give me something to be excited about."

I had to watch myself with that and not promise her anything. The last thing in this world I wanted to do was make a promise I couldn't keep to a woman who suffered from depression.

I said, "We'll keep talking about it. I can assure you of that. Unless I change my mind about doing it."

"Well, you just let me know," she responded.

After I dodged that bullet at the end of my day, I was prepared to drive over to Dark & Moody's studio to see what she was working with. She was in the southwest Atlanta area near Clark University and Spelman and Morehouse College. And that was not that far from my office.

So, I headed over to her apartment complex, thinking about her music, while listening to it again. She actually sent me a track called "Dracula" for fun that featured loud pipe organs. It sounded just like an old-school horror movie with funky drums behind it.

I smiled and chuckled. "This girl is crazy."

When I arrived in the parking lot of her complex, it was just beginning to get dark, and there was a group of college students standing out in front of her building, smoking weed.

I looked and mumbled, "Yeah, this is the university area, all right," as I climbed out of the car. These guys and girls had no shame to their game either. They kept right on smoking with their pants hanging down and their crazy hairstyles as I walked right up on them.

"How you doing?" one the guys spoke as the rest of them nodded or ignored me.

"I'm not doing as good as you," I commented slyly.

A few of them caught my sarcasm and chuckled through the smoke as I walked past them toward the building. At least these buildings were new and well lit; otherwise, I probably wouldn't have wanted to walk through there. I would have called Tasha down to come get me instead.

When I walked up the wooden stairs of the complex and knocked on her third-floor door, as soon as she answered it, I immediately told her about my experience.

"I think I'm a little *high* from the contact down there in the parking lot," I joked.

She laughed and said, "Yeah, they all live on the first floor."

"And no one complains about it?"

She paused and thought it over as she let me in. "Actually, most of the people in this building are *young*. But if they did that up the street, the tenants *would* complain about it. That's where the older people and families are."

"I see," I told her. "So, they set these apartments up strategically."

"It looks that way. I guess so."

As soon as I walked into her apartment, I could tell that she was a neat freak. Everything was clean and in proper order. The place had a mellow aroma of incense and fresh air. And it wasn't dark at all in her place. She even had tall plants spaced around the living room. I wasn't expecting all of that. So, I was pleasantly surprised.

I looked around at everything and nodded. Tasha had a little bit of money and knew how to spend it on the right things. "Nice," I told her.

She smiled, pleased by my compliment. "Thank you. I try."

"You're doing more than *trying*," I told her.

"Let me show you my studio. It's in my smaller bedroom."

She led me up the hallway to her studio bedroom on the left, where I walked inside a well-thought-out setup. She had her equipment rack against the large left-side wall for her oversized monitor, laptop computer, keyboards, left and right speakers, and a subwoofer on the floor.

I nodded and smiled. "This doesn't look like the setup of a woman talking about *sacrificing* people," I hinted. I wanted to see how she would respond to me.

"What, you thought my place would look all chaotic?" she responded.

I nodded again. "Yeah." And I left it at that. I wanted her to explain herself.

She said, "Naw, I like *order*. I don't like stuff all over the place. That's not how I get down."

Upon further review of her studio, I noticed a large brown dildo to the right of her keyboard. I pointed to it. "This is yours?"

She looked and was immediately embarrassed by it. "Oh, shit! That's my girlfriend's," she answered, and grabbed it to take it away.

"On your *keyboard*?" I questioned.

"Ummm, I'll explain," she told me with a laugh, while taking it out of the room. When she returned, she said, "I was using it as inspiration for a new track I was working on."

I eyed her skeptically as she continued to grin. I said, "And what is this track gonna be called? 'Kinky'?"

She laughed again. "No, but I like that. I might just call it that now."

"Let me hear it," I told her.

"I'm not finished with it yet."

"Let me hear what you got so far."

She shrugged. "All right. I'll let you hear it. I usually start with the bass line and the drums anyway. That sets the mood most of the time. Or, if I have specific notes I wanna play, then I'll start with the keyboard."

She pressed play on her laptop for the track that she had been working on, and a deep, thick thump began to play that was more up-tempo than what I was used to hearing from her. It was the kind of beat that made your head nod immediately.

"Oh, shit," I responded with my neck rocking.

"Yeah, that's an influence from your girl, Mrs. Melody," she commented.

"Oh, yeah? You mean, you *listened* to her?" I considered that a challenge for *both* of them.

Tasha grinned. "It just kind of happened that way. So, I did a *few* tracks like that now."

"And how's the music making out between the two of you?"

"I mean, she finished one song, but we haven't gotten around to finishing a second one yet. She's been a little busy with her *guy* friends," she commented.

I detected a little wrath and resentment in her, something I wanted to delve deeper into.

"Did she promise to work on other songs with you?"

"Of course she did. But like I said, she got extra busy."

"Well, that's a *good* thing, right? That means she's putting in the work, so she'll be more successful with the music that you make for her," I suggested.

"I guess. But you like this beat then, huh?" she asked, referring to the "Kinky" track.

I nodded. "Do you still produce your gothic funk? I wouldn't put this song in that same category."

"Oh, yeah, definitely. I do that in my *sleep*. That's easy," she boasted.

"Good, because we have a title and a story for the movie I'm working on now. It's called *Trading*."

"*Trading*? Trading what?"

"Everything," I told her. "It's an ambiguous title on purpose. But ultimately, it's about a college girl who breaks down a social business group after they take the grant money that she invests."

I left my explanation at that to see what she would think about it.

"So, it's like a *business* movie?"

I smiled. "It gets a lot *deeper* than that. Like, what if she's a lot *more* than they think she is? And what if she wants *more* than just her money back? That's where your music comes into play. It's more than just about *business*. It might be about *blood* and *sacrifices*," I teased her.

She stared at me and smirked. "Really? I thought you told me to stop thinking about stuff like that."

"Yeah, but it's a topic that your generation is familiar with. So, we go with what's current and add characters of all ages to it." I even had my client Tamarra Baldwin in mind.

"If you say so," Dark & Moody responded. "It sounds interesting though. I can *definitely* add music to it."

"I know you can. And I'll see if Mrs. Melody can play the college girl role."

When I said that, Tasha stared with new intent. "You're trying to cast her as like, the *star*? She told me you talked to her about it. But she didn't go into any great detail. She wanted *you* to explain it."

"You don't think she can do it?" I questioned. I was still curious.

"I mean . . . nobody really knows her like that for *acting*."

"And nobody knows your *music* for *soundtracks*," I countered.

"Yeah, but the music is secondary. You're talking about having her in a *lead* role. Did you tell her that? I think she believes the college girl role is just a regular part."

I nodded. "Yeah, I didn't go into much detail when I told her. She seemed distracted and busy, just like you said. But she didn't back down from it."

Tasha stopped and thought about it all. Then she shrugged. "Okay. That's pretty *big* if they let her do it. I would be happy for her."

"So, you would want her to succeed?" I quizzed.

Tasha answered immediately. "Yeah, why wouldn't I?" She didn't seem to be involved in anything extra with Melody. Or at least she wasn't letting that on to me. So, I backed off it.

"What else is going on with you, outside of your girlfriend with the big dildo?" I teased.

She started laughing again, feeling embarrassed, I'm sure.

"Are you sure that's not *your* dildo?" I pressed her.

"No, it's not," she assured me.

I said, "You don't have to be embarrassed by it. I understand. A girl gotta *do* what a girl gotta *do*."

"Yeah, well, you need to tell that to my *friend*."

"You don't use them at all?" I asked her. I was on a roll, so I decided to keep going with it.

She said, "Do you?"

"Girl, at my age that thing might *break* something," I answered.

She got a real kick out of that and laughed harder.

"You are out of your element right now," she told me.

I was. But I was allowed to have a little bit of fun in life. There wasn't anything wrong with that. And I wasn't back at the office.

"Do you have a husband, or a guy friend?" Tasha asked me. She had never asked me that before. I guess I had instigated it.

I paused. "I've never had a *husband*, and I don't have a guy friend right now," I told her.

"When's the last time you had a *friend*, if you don't mind me asking?"

It was a rather personal question, but I had started it by teasing her about the dildo. However, I couldn't even *remember* my last friend.

"You mean *intimately*?" I clarified, while stalling.

"Yeah, you know, I've always felt like . . . *intellectual* women don't necessarily get off sexually the way everyone else does," she commented. "It's like . . . you find other things to do that takes the place of sex. I know I do. I'd rather make *music* a lot of times. Sex can be too much of a mental and emotional hassle."

As she continued to speak, I reflected on my past flings and couldn't come up with any. That was ridiculous in itself! I wasn't a nonsexual woman, so how come I couldn't recall anything?

I smiled it off and said, "Well, I *do* have someone I have my eye on."

I figured that was better than me saying nothing.

"Is he *smart* or just a garden tool?"

"Oh, he's definitely *smart. Very*. I can't even see myself going for the garden tool, unless he's smart as well."

"Well, most of them *are*, at least when it comes to knowing women," DM commented. "But I've found that some of your smarter *career* guys may not be that great with women. You know, they focus more of their energies on their *careers* and the women just come along with that."

I thought, *Where is all of this psychoanalyzing on sex and relationships coming from?* Had I sparked all that with my comments about her dildo?

I said, "Very few people can have it *all* in this life. Even those you think who *do* can have all kinds of other *issues* that you may not know about." Charles Clay came to mind as I spoke, so did Joseph Drake. And Tyrell had his own personal issues to deal with.

"You'd be *surprised* about what people have going on behind closed doors," I told her.

She grinned and said, "It wouldn't surprise *you* though, would it? You've probably seen and heard it *all* by now."

"Not all of it *yet*," I told her. "But I'm getting there."

CHARLES CLAY

Reflection 31

CHARLES SAT IN FRONT OF A WIDE, DARK WOODEN AND HIGH-quality desk with the brand name of ATTORNEY JEFFREY ALEXANDER printed in gold across a nameplate. The powerful attorney kept it there as a reminder of how far he had come in his thirty-five-year career. Over that time, he had mastered his trade by preparing his clients for every scenario.

He was an honest, older White man in his sixties, who loved his profession and honored it by being fair to anyone he represented, regardless of their race, class, or creed. He believed that everyone deserved strong representation under the law. But that didn't mean he was cheap. And there was nothing about him that wasn't the best, including his impeccable suits, ties, shirts, shoes, and haircuts, with a beautiful grade of salt-and-pepper hair to match his clean-shaven face.

Jeffrey *looked* like a powerful lawyer, and his look alone spoke volumes inside and outside of the courtroom for his clients. He nodded and prepared himself to speak as soon as Charles got comfortable in the dark leather chair across from his desk.

"Charles, you've gotten yourself in a real *pickle* here. I wish Jackie would've told me earlier the kind of things that you were getting yourself involved in, because I would have *warned* you. This era is not the climate to get away with outlandish behavior with women. It's just not being *tolerated* anymore," he stated. "And you don't have the money to fight the cases like some of these other guys."

Charles looked across the attorney's desk at a pile of paperwork that he hoped and prayed was not about *him*. But those prayers were not answered with any comfort when he nervously asked about it.

"That pile of paperwork there is not about *me*, is it?" he asked with an awkward chuckle.

Jeffrey eyed him calmly for a minute before he answered. "Charles, I'm afraid it is. They've been building a case against you for the past *two years*. So, they've been very diligent, strategic, and *patient*. That's the new world that we live in. And the more success you have the stronger they'll build their case."

Upon hearing that, Charles's heart began to race a hundred miles a minute, like it had been doing off and on ever since he first spoke to Jeffrey. It was as if the lawyer had given his heart a hyper-speed button through the information he shared.

Jeffrey sighed and continued. "They added plenty of details here, Charles. With handcuffs, forced showers, knives, loaded handguns, urination, feces, kidnapping and abandonment, you *name it*. So, I'm thinking we may be able to explain some of this where, in your line of work, people tend to be very *creative* at telling stories. That's about the only way I can see getting you out of some of these depositions and lewd reenactments in court."

He said, "I hate to say it, but the singer R. Kelly comes to mind when I'm reading some of this stuff. And that's not a name you want to be *associated* with when it comes to dealing with women right now."

"But those are things that some of these women *fantasized* about," Charles blurted in his defense.

"It doesn't matter," Jeffrey told him. "If they can make the courtroom believe they were *your* fantasies and not theirs, you're looking at a very expensive, uphill battle. And quite frankly, these are the kind of cases that wealthier men are advised to settle out of court. And they'll spend whatever dollar they need to get it done."

"Well, if I don't have the money to fight them or pay them off, what's my next option?" Charles pleaded.

Jeffrey paused and took a deep breath. He exhaled and said, "Your film career is going to take a hit, but you now have to assassinate the characters of every accuser. And you have *seven* of them. *Five* of them are represented by the same attorney. But with you having to cast and direct actors who come to you with *confidence* in your judgment and guidance, who's gonna trust you after this?"

Charles understood his dilemma and slowly shook his head. "So, I lose either way . . . unless I can find the money to fight it."

Jeffrey said, "The problem with that is, you've also pissed off the only woman who could help you. *Jacqueline.* She's pretty convinced that you're gonna ruin her career as well. So, she wants nothing else to do with you."

"How can she help me then?" Charles asked.

"Well . . . if you could convince her *otherwise,* Jackie *has* the people who have the money. But then you would be in serious debt to *her.* And I'm talking *millions.* But if we're able to stop this train before the rumor mill gets out of hand, you can save your film career with better judgment in the future."

Charles could see the writing on the wall. He would have to do everything Jackie said for at least five years and ten million dollars' worth of film income, with no room for hiccups.

"That's gonna be a headache," he predicted glumly.

"And you gave that headache to yourself," Jeffrey told him. "So, you either deal with someone who can possibly get you out of this, or your film career is ready to drop off a *steep cliff.* And I can't guarantee that you won't do any *time* over this."

When Charles heard that, his heart started to race again.

"How is that?" he asked.

"In *civil* court, you can pay your way out of it. But in *criminal* court . . . that's a whole other ballgame."

"So, these women just wanna be *paid* or else? What is that?" Charles complained.

"It's called *America.* And you put yourself in harm's way with your *actions,*" the attorney told him. "No one did this to you. You did this to *yourself.* And there's repercussions that have to be *paid* now."

Charles sat there in silence and brooded. He thought of calling Jackie immediately and pouring his heart out to her to save him. And he *hated it.* He had landed himself right into a position of helpless need. The same helpless need and desire that he held over actors and actresses. How ironic was that?

Suddenly, he could feel the indomitable pressure that *actors* felt. There was no way around it. Jackie and her legion of unknown financiers would have him by the *balls, literally.*

"Shit!" Charles cursed himself inside the room.

"That's how ninety-nine and a *half* percent of the people in this world think about their lives as well, Charles," Jeffrey told him. "Not even the *one* percent in power get to do whatever they want, because they have *wives, children, family* members, and other authority figures who hold positions of *weight* in their lives that they must account for.

"That's the way this world must *be,* Charles. There's always checks and balances," Jeffrey explained. "Otherwise, we'd have absolute *power,* and absolute power would want to rule *absolutely.* Which we can't have. So, these humbling lessons of life continue to be learned for *all* of us."

Charles remained silent as Jeffrey continued to lecture him.

"Just think. Tom Brady had it *all* and could have retired as the greatest quarterback of all time to enjoy his international model wife and his beautiful children. Instead, he forced himself to come back for a *third* year with the Bucs, and he lost his marriage and had a miserable season where everyone *knows* it's the end," the attorney commented.

At that point, Charles had heard enough. He understood his lesson already. And he had been brought back down to earth with scorched wings.

"I get it," he commented. "I'll call her this evening."

* * *

During the time that Charles had alone to think, his mind worked itself into paranoia. Of course, he hated having to prostitute his professional services in film for the immediate money he needed, but that was the situation he had found himself in. So, he began to think hypothetically about everything.

What if Jackie set this whole thing up just to get control over my directing? Charles asked himself in the silence of his office. He was certain his business partner knew at least *three* of the women he was now in trouble with. Jackie was there when he first met them. *So . . . what if she reached out to a few of them to join in on the bandwagon?*

It was a far-fetched idea, but that's what a skeptical mind can do, particularly with fear and time on our hands. So, by the time Charles called his film partner that evening, he was in full-fledged doubt and was skeptical about everything.

"Jeffrey told me everything that's going on at his office today," he began with Jackie. "And he's basically saying that I should try and settle these cases out of court and pay off the debt by accepting new film projects with you."

There was no sense in sugarcoating anything with small talk. Charles's career was in trouble and time was of the essence to stop the rumor mill from spinning with his name attached. He needed to make fast decisions on what to do.

Fortunately, Jeffrey had already discussed the case with Jackie, step by step, and in great detail. She even paid him for the full hour that they conversed about it. So, she already knew what needed to be done and was perfectly calm. She just needed to hear what *Charles* had to say.

"And how do *you* feel about that?" she asked him.

"I mean . . . what are we talking about, as far as the *numbers* are concerned?" he questioned. If he was going to be on the hook for money, he wanted to know *how much.*

Jackie was all business and no emotions. "We're looking at five to six films and ten million dollars. Anything over that, and you get to keep."

Charles did his math. "That's nearly two million dollars, *per film.*"

"One-point-six-seven to be exact," she corrected him.

He paused. "That's like three times *more* than what we've *been* doing."

"And? I told you where I'm trying to take it," she explained to him. "We've been doing small films for far too long anyway."

"So, if you plan to make *that* kind of money, then what are the films taking in, fifteen to *twenty* million?"

"Or *more,*" Jackie answered calmly. She was just waiting for him to doubt or question the process, because he was already skating on thin ice. He had no wiggle room left to argue.

"And what if these films don't make that kind of money? I wouldn't make *anything* off of them," he calculated.

"Yeah, but you would still be a *free* man with a *film* career," she reminded him.

"And you would be *six* to *eight* million dollars *richer* off *my* sweat and toil," he pouted.

"Not if you do what you're supposed to do. Just do a good job on every film, stay on your best behavior, promote the hell out of each project, and make sure we hit our *mark.* Then you *will* get paid, while establishing yourself on that next level."

It all sounded *good* on her side of the table, but it amounted to three to four years of professional *slavery* on Charles's end. Or at least that's how *he* thought of it.

He said, "And you really think I'm supposed to *agree* to this?"

That caught Jackie off guard, but she remained calm over the phone.

"Charles, you are about *five* minutes away from *pissing* your film career down the drain. Now, I had to think *hard* and *long* to even *consider* trying to do something like this with you. Because in that *same* time span of three to four years, your ass could end up out here with your greedy dick in somebody's *mouth, ass, ear, nose,* or *whatever,* and the payout would be *much higher* and *more* damaging than this one.

"So, look at it from *my* perspective," she told him. "*I'm* the one who would be on the *hook* for the money, not *you.* Because *I'm* the one who's going out here to *get it.*"

"Yeah, but *I'm* the one who has to make it all *back,*" he argued.

"Well, what do you want to do, Charles? Because I could just walk away from this crazy shit right now and be *done* with it," Jackie countered. "*You* got yourself in this shit, not *me.* But yet, *I'm* trying to help you to get out of it, and all you're thinking about is *you.* Which is *typical.*

"Matter of fact, you can find someone else to produce your shit with, because I'm *tired* of this," she told him. "I told you before, I'm *not* one of your little *fluzzies* or *jump-offs,* where you can talk that bullshit to me and *think* you're gonna get away with it. I've told you that *one* too many times.

"So, *fuck you,* and the white horse that you rode in on!" she spat. "Have a good time in court with your little *groupies,* and may God bless your life!"

When she hung up the line, Charles held the phone to his ear in disbelief. It was a moment of *truth,* where he realized he had screwed himself again, but it hadn't quite hit him yet.

"Okay . . ." he mumbled, while still holding the phone in suspense. "Just call her back," he told himself calmly. "I never said I wasn't going to do it."

He called Jacqueline back, but that didn't mean she was going to answer him, even after calling her four times. So, he called her a fifth time and left her a message.

"Jacqueline, this is Charles. I'll do it," he told her in his phone message. "The price is just a little bit *steep,* that's all. So, it *shocked* me. But Jeffrey warned me that I should expect that from you. Business is business. And I thank you again for helping me out in this way.

"And I won't let you *down,*" he added. "Maybe this is all for the *best* to discipline myself in my personal life, while reaching for higher goals in my career. You've always talked about that anyway. So, maybe it's now time for that to happen. Whether I like it or not . . .

"And I really don' have at *choice* at this point," he continued. "So, call me back. I agree to your terms."

He hung up the phone and waited in silence for a return call. At the same time, he doubted it would happen. Jacqueline sounded really *firm* in her statements. And she was right, she *had* put up with him. But she had run out of time for his nonsense. Realizing as much, Charles thought of making a few other phone calls to people who could bail him out with a few projects on the side.

Feeling optimistic, he made his first call to another producer.

"Hey, Charles Clay. What's going on with you, man? I haven't talked to you in a *while*," the chipper producer answered.

"Yeah, we've been rather busy pulling new projects together, Bailey. You know the usual grind," Charles responded to him.

"Yeah, what are you working on?" Bailey asked.

"Actually, we may have a *gap* in the schedule, so . . . I'm calling to see what you have lined up to shoot that we may be able to help out on," Charles pitched.

Bailey paused. "Oh, yeah? Well, let me think on something like that. I mean, we already have a packed schedule of our own. But Jackie pretty much told me a while ago that you guys were aiming for bigger projects now."

Charles paused himself. He didn't want to say the wrong thing and get himself into *more* trouble on the business side. He had to be cautious.

"Well, what level are you shooting on?" he asked.

"I mean, we got a bunch of *two-hundred*-thousand-dollar films we're shooting now in high definition to fill out content for these smaller streaming networks that keep popping up," Bailey answered. "I got a couple of small contracts with some of these guys. But with them, it's all about *volume* and not these *Titanic* or *Avatar* type films, you know.

"If you can't compete on that Marvel Comics level, then don't even try it," he commented. "So, I told Jackie a few months back that our goal is to keep the direction budgets at forty thousand or *less.* So, we're basically breaking in new people, and professional *friends* who are doing us *favors,*" he added with a chuckle.

Neither of those scenarios fit what Charles needed at the moment. There was no way in *hell* he was touching a forty-thousand-dollar project when he needed a few *million.*

Wow! Bailey's talking about shooting projects for two hundred thousand, while Jackie's talking about earning two million, Charles thought.

The numbers and expectations were so far apart that Charles chuckled at it.

"Yeah, I can imagine what she said to that," he commented.

"So, you're breaking out on your *own* now? You're not working with Jackie anymore?" Bailey questioned him.

"Oh, no, I didn't say that. I just didn't know she had talked to you already, that's all."

Bailey chuckled over the line himself. "Yeah, she probably wouldn't wanna tell you that. She had designs on you shooting those multimillion-dollar budgets for *your* pockets *and* hers," he joked.

"You already know it," Charles agreed. "But these contracts that you get for these smaller streaming networks, are they like, two million, for like, five to eight projects?"

He was trying to figure out where he could pitch for his price point.

Bailey cut his ideas down to size. "Oh, no, they don't cut checks like *that.* They'll give you more like, *five* hundred thousand to shoot, like, three or four films. And they don't give you all the money *up front* either."

Charles nodded. "I see."

Bailey cut to the chase and said, "What, you need money right now? You sound like you *huntin'* for it," he joked.

Charles had to be careful with his answer again. Black Hollywood was a very small industry, and hunting for last-minute money was not something to have a reputation for.

"No, I'm just seeing how it all *works,* that's all. I have a few people coming up under me now, who could *use* those opportunities," he lied.

"Oh, okay. Well, in *that* case, send me their reels and we'll see what we can come up with together. I like that kind of *teamwork*," Bailey suggested.

"Yeah, I'll pull that together and get back in touch with you," Charles lied again.

"Yeah, you do that. And nice talking to you, man."

"Same here."

The compromised director hung up the line and took a deep breath. "Yeah, that was pretty *dangerous*," he warned himself. He had to watch *who* he decided to call and *what* he decided to say to them. And it wouldn't be an easy task, because Jackie made most of their calls and did most of their talking, particularly in regards to *money*. So, Charles felt like an inexperienced shopper in a grocery store, trying desperately to figure out what he could afford to buy.

He even pulled up his online bank account on his cell phone, where he had just over three hundred thousand dollars in his account. That's where he liked to *keep it*, which sounded good for a regular American citizen, but for a popular filmmaker who was now in trouble with *seven* money-hungry accusers, his healthy savings could disappear in a matter of *weeks*.

I just have to figure this all out and see where I can pull money from, he mused. So, he started thinking about selling the studio loft that he lived and held his office in.

TYRELL HODGE

Reflection 32

WHILE ONE MAN SCRAMBLED TO SAVE HIS CAREER, ANOTHER ONE wrote furiously to resuscitate his own. That was Tyrell Hodge, who was busy at work on the *Trading* film screenplay that had unwittingly inspired him. He had taken the undeveloped story and made it his own in a matter of *hours*. In fact, he had been searching for something new that could arouse him, something with the right presentation and message. And now he had found it.

Obviously, the presentation of intimacy had moved Tyrell, while proving how seriously the project was being taken. As cliche as it may seem, the gift of a woman's love and treasure could *always* inspire a man, since the Garden of Eden. It was only a matter of what a man chose to *do* with that inspiration, and how he chose to acquire it.

Like many professional artists, Tyrell had used inspiration as a source of energy that he could return to whenever he needed it. It was like a battery, recharging his creative engine. But sometimes the battery needed recharging as well—from a jump. And those jumps were external, coming from other people who held their own storage of energy, transferred from one human to another in various forms, including sex.

That was one of the many dilemmas Tyrell had found himself

in, where the transferrable energies and boosted confidence of sex was no longer available to him from the person he loved. And there was nothing he could do about it without successful negotiations and forgiveness from *her,* who was uninterested in those vital conversations, which locked them both into a stalemate.

Yet, Tyrell refused to walk away, believing that he could somehow fix their real-life story, which had been broken now for years. Nor did he realize that Neanderthals lacked the tools to fix it. And he could never be compassionate enough, giving enough, understanding enough, selfless enough, or dependable enough to *heal* the spirit of a broken woman who needed to heal . . . *herself.*

Enthused with her energy, Tyrell could drive to the edge of the world and back, only for her to tell him that he had forgot to bring her donuts on the way. There was always *something* that made her world incomplete. That made her glass half-empty. That made the rain fall and muddy up her flowers instead of watering them.

That was the source of energy that he found himself involved in, an abyss of insatiable *need.* And his own personal failures intensified the issue, where two souls learned to wallow in misery together, while expecting sunshine from a tomorrow that never came. Which became frustrating for *both* of them.

So, you *felt sorry* for the man, the way he wanted *her* to feel sorry for him. But she never did. Not anymore. Because she was still searching for her *own* energy, until *he* became broken and transfixed with knocking on her door, and knocking on her door, and knocking on her door . . . that she would not open.

And then . . . a new door swung open for him, and he wrote . . . *furiously.* The way he used to write years ago, with joy, and passion, and purpose, and a goal that he *knew* was attainable.

Tyrell needed to return his *confidence,* where there was no longer randomness or a mystery to his executions. Because he *knew* that he could finish the job that he had been given to complete with *excellence.* And he would be rewarded for it, the way *she* used to reward him.

But now she was different. And Tyrell refused to acknowledge how different she was, where he no longer inspired *her.* Or excited *her.* Or appealed to *her.* Where her confidence in him had been depleted. Yet, he continued knocking on her door that she *refused* to answer, while she called him *selfish.* So, what was *she?*

Nevertheless, she acknowledged his efforts, while wondering if she could ever find another man who would work as hard as he did . . . even in his *failures.*

But the point was, she was tired of the failures, *hers and* his. Failures that neither one of them could control. Or, maybe he *could* have controlled them, by listening more to *her.* Maybe he *could* have controlled them, by being more patient with *her.* Maybe he *could* have controlled them, by consulting more with those who knew better than *he* did. Maybe he *could* have controlled them, if he had only learned to *adapt* to the new ways of the world instead of harboring his old-school days of Chicago.

Maybe Tyrell could have controlled his failures . . . if he wasn't so damned *hardheaded*!

In fact, maybe she could have controlled more of her *own* life, if she had not given so much of herself to *him* . . . as if *he* had given nothing to her and had not continued to give.

Giving is what a man is *supposed* to do for a woman, especially if he claims to love her. And when she felt that he did, she gave the love back to him, *willingly.* But that was before the heartbreak occurred, with the constant failures and cheating, until their happy days were over, while he continued desperately to chase the memories.

Oblivious to all the years of their damaging head games, Tyrell continued to write this new screenplay with determination, knowing that he still had the skills, and he lost all track of time with no driving, until she came home and found him there at the kitchen table with his laptop out, typing. And she stopped and stared at him.

"What are you doing?"

She had these *eyes,* the kind that saw everything, straight, steady, large, and piercing. And they worked well with her face, a golden-brown softness of symmetric lips, nose, and a chin that all looked perfect, set within her wild dark hair that looked like a fire burning outward from a tree. Her hair represented the explosiveness of her personality without speaking.

Tyrell said proudly, "I'm working on something."

She looked down at his computer on the table and knew that already, while standing there like a picture, frozen in a magazine. She was that stylish, from her colorful boots to her fitted blue jeans, and her short, white jacket, topped with a baby-blue leather Coach bag over her right shoulder.

Tyrell just wanted to impress her, like he used to be able to do. But she was no longer impressed. She had seen and heard it all before. So, she turned and walked away . . . and said *nothing.* And it *crushed him,* but he went on to talk about it anyway, like she knew he would.

"Yeah, I'm working on this new screenplay called *Trading.* I had a meeting with this psychologist the other day who gave me the idea."

When she heard that, she stopped and turned to face him from the staircase.

"Who?"

"This psychologist I know."

"From where?"

He immediately read her probing and doubtful body language.

"Oh, it's nothing like *that.* I met her at a networking event years ago, and I went to see her a few times in her office for my *mind,* you know. Then we just stayed in touch with one another as I needed information for my writing or whatever," he explained. "You know, she deals with a lot of different people who have different kinds of issues and stories."

"And she's talking to you about a *movie* now?"

"Yeah, people always talk to me about movies. I'm a *screenwriter.*"

She nodded. "Okay," she said, and went back to walking up the stairs.

"You wanna hear about it?" he yelled behind her.

She ignored him and kept stepping. Ignoring him had become her new modus operandi. But all Tyrell could think about was how she used to talk his ears off with her own stories and ideas. Stories and ideas that he rarely used, but now he was interested in someone else's.

It was a common woman's struggle of being with a man every day, as they learned to take her for granted. And he was now being *punished* for it. Until he found the common sense to *leave*, which he struggled to realize.

So, as his lady disappeared inside the bedroom upstairs, Tyrell forced himself to write and write and write until he couldn't focus anymore. *Why?* Because he still wanted *her*, and all of her *womanness.* Her *magnetism.* Her *cheerfulness.* Her zestful *spirit.* And her *imagination.* Things that she no longer bothered to share with *him.* But her qualities were still there for other people who hadn't pissed her off the way *he* had.

The reality of human relationships is that every one of them has three stories, *his* story, *her* story, and the *truth.* And the *truth* was always a combination of the first two, but never in an exact percentage. Humans have never been that *perfect* to create exactness. It was always a hodgepodge with a little bit of this, and a little bit of that. But in their case, it was *a lot* of this and *a lot* of that.

Nevertheless, Tyrell figured they still had a connection, because they were still *there* together. Why else would she *stay*? That was the pregnant question in the room. What kept her around him? Was it simple *comfort*? The comfort of knowing every move a man is going to make and knowing exactly how to counter him? Or maybe it was just the *money* that Tyrell continued to fork over to pay the bills.

After finishing all that he was inspired to write on the screenplay, Tyrell reached the top of the staircase and paused. "Please don't tell me no tonight," he mumbled to himself in the hallway.

He was afraid to even enter their bedroom, knowing that he had spent countless nights on the sofa downstairs to avoid her rejections . . . and his anger. Yet . . . maybe this time she would say *yes.* So, he held on for a miracle without prayers, which was fruitless.

Nevertheless, he forced himself to walk into the room again, where she watched television in bed, while checking messages on her cell phone.

"Who's that?" he asked about her messages.

It was close to eleven o'clock at night. By then, she was in her nightclothes with a wrap over her head to protect and cover her hair.

She winced and asked him, "Who are you talking about?"

"On your phone? Who's sending you messages?"

It wasn't even a question he wanted to ask her. He just wanted to start a conversation.

She frowned and snapped, "Whoever the fuck it is. Why does it matter?"

He stopped and stared at her. "Damn, you ain't gotta respond like *that.* It's just a simple question," he pouted.

"Whatever," she responded, knowing better. She knew good and well what he was there for, and she was ready for it. Ready to send his ass away again.

"How was your day today?" he asked her.

She shrugged. "Telemarketing is telemarketing. What do you want me to say?"

He shrugged back at her and sat at the foot of the bed near her feet.

"Just tell me if something happened that was interesting."

"Not as interesting as your psychologist," she commented.

Tyrell grinned and shook his head. "I *told you,* there's nothing going on with her. And you need to stop doing that," he complained. "Every woman I talk to is not an object of affection. And she's an *older* woman," he added, as if that would make a difference.

"Is she attracted to you?" she asked him.

Tyrell chuckled, full of himself. "Well, I'm still a handsome guy. But nah, this is *business.*"

She nodded, unconcerned. "Okay."

Pressed for a conversation, Tyrell was ready to pull any question out of a hat, just to get her talking again.

"You're not *tired* are you?"

Wrong question. He was giving her easy answers based on the relationship insecurities that she had given him.

"Of course I'm tired," she responded. "I'm *always* fucking tired!"

Well, stop fucking working then! he wanted to shout at her. But he *couldn't,* because it would start a whole new argument filled with negativity. And if she stopped working, not only would he be paying the mortgage and utilities, he would also be forced to buy her fancy clothes, while paying for her cell phone and hair appointments. So, he kept his mouth *shut.*

Instead, he said, "You're too tired to *relax* with me tonight?"

She cringed. "*Relax* with you? Doing what?"

From an outside view, it was comical, not in the silly sitcom way of network television, but more like the dramatic comedies of Shakespeare, because she *meant* every part of her bitterness. And there was nothing funny about it. It was thought-provoking. And *sad.* It was sad that she could take an intellectual and powerful man and break him down like child's play. Until he found the common sense to *leave,* which he struggled to do.

"Just fall back, *relax,* and unwind with me," he stated civilly.

Maybe he should have brought two glasses of wine to nail home his point. Instead, he began to massage her feet only for her to pull them away from him.

"Don't do that! I'm already relaxing. I'm watching TV."

Tyrell stopped and stared at her again, while she returned to eyeing more messages on her cell phone, which covered her face and eyes from his view.

At that moment, he felt an urge to snatch her phone away and scream into her face, *What the fuck is wrong with you, woman?! I'm still here for you!*

But he didn't. He *knew* better. That would only get him another few months of punishment. *If* . . . she didn't leave him for good. So, he shook his head and stood back up from the bed.

"I try to do everything I *can* for you, and it just doesn't seem to fuckin' *matter*," he ranted.

"You only do shit so you can have your *way*," she countered.

"Well, what do *you* do shit for?" he barked back. "Don't act like you don't *count* the shit that *you do*! That's why you're so *bitter* now. You want a fuckin' *response*! You're not doing shit from *the heart*! You got *motives* too! So don't give me that shit!"

Whenever Tyrell got irate, she would settle down and give him the silent treatment. Anything else would be dangerous for her, and she was smart enough to understand that. An angry Chicago man was not to be trusted. So, she had to pick her spots and not go overboard.

Tyrell knew it as well. "Okay, now you gon' get all *quiet* on me, right?"

She looked away and didn't answer him. Instead, she counted numbers in her head. *One, two, three, four, five, six, seven, eight, nine, ten, eleven* . . . until he left the room again—like she knew that he would. Because he had been checkmated.

Instead of heading downstairs for a beer to watch TV and crash on the sofa as usual, Tyrell was still pumped with enough energy to drive that night. But it wasn't *good* energy. It was *violent* and *reckless*. And he drove that way. Until his riders began to complain about it.

"Ummm, I'm not really in a *rush* tonight, if you don't *mind*," a tactful mother told him on her way home from work after midnight.

"Oh, my bad. You get to cruising out here and thinking about shit on your mind and forget what *speed* you're doing," Tyrell commented. "Especially when nobody's out here like this."

Sometimes honesty was *not* the best policy. That's why suspected criminals were given the right to take the Fifth Amendment and not incriminate themselves like Tyrell would often do. But *genius* wanted to express itself, *foolishly*, as several riders filed reports on their PDS apps of his "dangerous" driving—even though he was excellent at the wheel.

The point was, it was more important to satisfy your clients in every way, while they were still in your car, and not allow any personal issues, driving skills, or *opinions* taint the job. And for riders who were comfortable with moving *slow,* seventy miles an hour is *too fast.* Period!

By the time Tyrell returned home in the wee hours of the night—too exhausted to bother his woman for sex—he had gone over his rider complaint limit with a reprimanding email waiting in his inbox from PDS.

He briefly eyed the complaint on his cell phone but was too worn out to deal with it. So, he shook it off and grumbled, "I'll read that shit in the morning."

And he crashed on the sofa with another beer for another unsatisfied and sexless night of rough and unsettled sleep.

JOSEPH DRAKE
Reflection 33

THINGS HADN'T GONE MUCH BETTER FOR JOE UP IN BOSTON WITH his daughter and her mother. He met up with Carole and Ayana Ogurah in Hyde Park, where they felt more comfortable at a Caribbean restaurant filled with people who knew them.

The three of them sat down awkwardly after sharing cordial hugs. But imagine never sitting down with your father until you're a young woman ready to head off for college, and you have to deal with the fact that he's *White*. Of course, Ayana knew that already, but she never had to deal with it up close and face-to-face until then, so it felt very different.

It was one thing to talk to the man a few times a year over the telephone, but it was another to sit down with him over jerk chicken and oxtail. So, Ayana was trying to determine how *cool* or *uncool* he was in person.

On Joe's part, he was excited to have such an exotically attractive daughter. Biracial children held that societal reality. They were *different*. But Joe also felt a slight irritation about her mother having a live-in boyfriend at a home that *he* helped to make the down payment on.

"This is really unexpected," Carole noted with a grin.

"Yeah, it *is*," Joe responded.

An easy flow of eyes bounced over to their table from the other customers in the small restaurant.

"And you say that *nothing* in particular sparked this visit?" Carole asked Joe.

Joe eyed his daughter as he began to slice into his jerk chicken with a cutting knife. He said, "I just wanted to see you guys."

"Why?" Ayana asked him instantly. He had barely answered her mother's question before she was all over it.

They looked each other in the eyes, with his blues to her hazels. The tan sports jacket he wore with a light blue dress shirt made Joe's eyes seem even bluer.

"Is there a problem with me seeing you?" he asked his daughter. "You don't seem to have a problem with talking to me over the phone."

Ayana shrugged. "I was just asking."

He felt maybe he had come off a little too strong with her. So, he added something to his answer. "I just felt deep in my spirit that it was *time.*"

Ayana eyed him and repeated, "*Deep* in your *spirit?*"

Joe nodded and took a bite of his food. "Yeah."

Carole continued to grin across the table to the right of him, while eating her serving of oxtail. She was amused by it all. She already knew how her daughter would respond to it. And it was a curious situation.

"Do you ever talk about me?" Ayana asked her father.

Joe swallowed his food and glanced at her mother before he answered.

"I didn't *used* to."

"But you do now?"

"I just started recently," he admitted.

"Why?" she asked him again. "Your *spirit* told you to do it?"

There was a hint of sarcasm in her delivery. She was a cunning smart-ass, but Joe had to deal with it. She was asking him legitimate questions.

He shrugged and said, "I guess you can say that. Yeah."

"Do you talk about my mom?"

Joe paused. "Occasionally."

"Do you talk about her *favorably* or *unfavorably?*"

"That's *enough*, Ayana," Carole finally spoke up. Her daughter was going overboard.

"No, I can handle it," Joe responded. He said, "I *always* speak favorably about your mother. Now, she definitely can be a little *headstrong*, but that's one of the things that attracted me to her."

Ayana nodded, taking it all in. She was barely eating. "Did you like her *skin*?"

Carole exhaled through her nose with food in her mouth.

Joe eyed her and said, "Of course."

Carole's deep brown skin was still as smooth as leather. Even Ayana smiled at that.

"You ever think about getting back with her?"

"Ayana," Carole warned through her food with piercing eyes.

Her daughter grinned. "I'm just asking him *questions*, Mom."

Joe took a gulp of his Jamaican ginger beer and sat it back on the table in front of them.

He answered, "I don't think getting back with her is possible." Then he looked into Carole's deep brown eyes.

She sighed and didn't respond to it, while continuing to eat her food.

"Ayana tells me you have a new boyfriend," he commented.

"He's not *new*," Carole responded flatly.

"I didn't say he was new," Ayana stated, defending herself.

"You said he *lived* with you guys," Joe responded to his daughter. "But did he live with you *before*? I mean, that *had* to be new."

Carole didn't like where the conversation was going.

"I don't think that's any of your business," she commented.

Joe eyed her and held his tongue. Or at least he *attempted* to. That's when Ayana looked away and finally stuffed her mouth with her food.

"Well . . ." Joe started, and stopped.

Carole was just *waiting* for the argument. He couldn't tell her who could live in her house just because he helped her on the down payment. It was still *her house*, and they were *not* a couple.

She even instigated the argument. "You have something you wanna say?"

Joe ate more of his food and shook his head. "It's your house," he mumbled.

Ayana eyed both of them and dropped her head to continue eating.

"I know it is," Carole blurted. She was ready for the argument. When Joe failed to give her one, she added, "We have a *daughter* together. But we don't have a relationship outside of that."

Joe swallowed his bite of food and eyed her again. Realizing he was in a predominantly Black Caribbean restaurant in Hyde Park, he made sure to keep his cool.

"You don't have to be so cavalier about it. I mean, I *did* help you to buy that house," he commented with a measured and even tone.

Ayana eyed them both, like a tennis match.

"And I *thanked you* for it," Carole reminded him. "But that doesn't mean you get a *say*."

"What if you burnt it to the ground?" he questioned disparagingly.

"Then my *insurance* would pay to rebuild it," Carole answered curtly.

Joe nodded. "Sounds like you got it all mapped out."

Ayana eyed him and grinned. Her father could be a smart-ass too.

Carole caught her daughter's grin but didn't comment on it as their table went silent. Joe felt as if someone had turned the heat up in the room, but he managed to ignore it.

"So . . . how's your food, Dad?" Ayana teased him.

Joe eyed her and smirked. Despite her continued sarcasm, he loved the fact that she called him *Dad*. She was agreeing to a *truce* and sending him a message on it.

He said, "You, ah . . . have a great sense of *humor*."

She chuckled and admitted it. "Yeah, I've been *told* that. I guess I get it from *someone*," she hinted.

Joe grinned and said, "Yeah, I guess you do." And he felt *great* about it. It was a small victory for him that his daughter had joined his team of sarcastic barbs. He then joked and said,

"Maybe you'll become a staff writer for *Saturday Night Live* after college."

Ayana winced and didn't catch the joke. "*Saturday Night Live?*" she questioned, confused.

"A lot of Harvard grads became writers for the New York City variety show on Saturday nights," her mother filled in. She and Joe had spoken about it years ago.

"But I'm not even going to Harvard," Ayana responded. "It's too close to home. I'm applying for U. of Penn."

Somehow, Joe had not previously asked her what university she wanted to attend. Imagine that. But he was glad to hear her talk about the University of Pennsylvania.

"That's a great Ivy League business school," he commented excitedly. "As long as you don't follow after the *Trumps,*" he added.

"Oh, *never* that," she told him. "John *Legend,* maybe."

"Or Elon Musk," Joe suggested.

"Yeah, the CEO of Twitter and Tesla. He has a very cool *name,* too," his daughter gushed.

"*You* have a very cool name," Joe told her. "Ayana Ogurah. It sounds *important.* And international."

Carole grinned across the table, agreeing through her smile.

Ayana smiled back and said, "If I added *Drake* at the end, it would sound even *more* important. Ayana Ogurah *Drake.*"

Carole frowned and said, "It would sound like you're *married.*"

Ayana ignored her mother and asked her father, "Would you even let me *use it?*"

"Of course," Joe responded without thinking.

Carole eyed him and didn't know how to respond. Was he telling their daughter the *truth?* Or was it a spur-of-the-moment lie from a question that had obviously caught him off guard?

"That name has a lot of bad *history* on it," Carole commented to her daughter. She had discussed that topic with Joe before as well.

Ayana eyed her mother and asked, "Would you have taken it if you two had gotten married?"

Great question! Joe thought. He looked at Carole and waited for her answer.

"In that case, I guess I would've *had* to," her mother answered. "But it didn't happen," she added quickly.

Their table went silent again.

"Hey, Carole? Every'ting *irie*," an older Jamaican man greeted her.

She turned and eyed the man with a long, gray beard and a colorful Jamaican hat.

"Hey, Bernard? Yeah, mon, every'ting *irie*," she greeted him back in their Caribbean tongue.

He walked closer to their table and immediately eyed the White man sitting with them.

"Who's 'dat?"

"My daughter's father," Carole answered, drama free.

Bernard eyed Ayana and back to Joe. "Ohhh, I see. The *eyes*, they never *lie*."

"They sure don't," Carole agreed with him.

"Are you still with *Yusef*?" he asked her openly. There was no shame in his old-school game. Bernard liked Yusef.

Carole answered, "Yeah, mon. I'm just having *food* with my daughter's *father*," in a full Jamaican accent.

Bernard nodded furiously. "All right. Good. Okay. Nice to meet you, sir," he finally said, extending his aged brown hand to Joe.

Joe took his hand and shook it. "Nice to meet you."

It was a good natural break of their awkward silence at the table. But then Ayana brought the awkwardness back up again.

"So . . . if you could do it all over again, would you have asked my mom to marry you?" she asked her father.

Carole exhaled and shook her head, but the loaded question was already asked.

Joe exhaled as well. He had been through tons of regrets since then, regrets that all added to his feelings of loneliness and unsatisfaction.

He said, "With all things considered, I believe that would have been the *best* thing for me to do. And you could have had a couple of brothers or sisters who look like you."

Carole heard that and didn't comment. What was the point? It was all aimless hypotheses.

Ayana nodded to her father and said, "Interesting."

The hypothesis had brought their energies back down again. However, Joe was determined to end their dinner on a good note.

"But that doesn't mean we can't all start something *new*," he commented. He even reached out and squeezed his daughter's right hand.

Carole saw that and exhaled again. She didn't know how she felt about *any* of it. The sudden surprise of Joe's visit had taken her out of her normal comfort zone of ignoring him. But was his presence there a good disturbance or a bad one? She had yet to know. She only wondered how *consistent* he could be in his new efforts with their daughter.

That first mother-and-daughter meeting took so much out of Joseph that he felt too *drained* to follow through on his late drive up to Hartford, Connecticut. He needed a minute to recharge, and he had already allotted himself a *week* off from work, while telling his staff he'd check back in with them—unless his personal mission ended earlier than he expected it to.

And after his excursion in Boston, he booked a hotel room that was closer to Interstate 90 for his drive to Connecticut in the morning. And he crashed *hard* on the king-sized bed.

I wish I could go back and do it all over again, he told himself. *More courage would have helped me to make the right decision years ago.*

MRS. MELODY

Reflection 34

A LACK OF COURAGE WAS NOT THE CASE WITH MRS. MELODY. SHE possibly had *too* much courage and not enough discernment. So, after her little scare at the Lenox Square mall, she went right back to her overconfident norm at a recording studio with BJ.

"Ain't nobody rockin' the party / like I rock it / ain't nobody droppin' this beat / like I drop it / ain't nobody stoppin' my flow / you can't stop it / and if you ever bet against me / you out of pocket . . ."

BOOM, BOOM, BOOM . . . / Boom, Boom / BOOM, BOOM, BOOM . . . / Boom, Boom / BOOM, BOOM, BOOM . . . / Boom, Boom / BOOM, BOOM, BOOM . . .

BJ smiled and nodded in the engineer's room with several of his crew members, all iced out in the expensive hip-hop jewelry and clothes of excess income, while swinging to the infectious track production as Melody laid her lyrics inside a small, dark recording booth in front of them.

"Man, this beat is a *monster*!" BJ commented.

"Who produced it again?" one of his friends asked.

"Um, Dark and Groovy, or something like that."

"Dark and *Moody*," the engineer corrected him.

"Yeah, she on her way over here now," BJ added.

"A *girl* made this beat?" the same friend asked him.

"Yeah, Melody know her," BJ filled in.

"Aw'ight, well, I need to get *me* a few beats when she pops through."

BJ nodded to him. "Do that. I hear she got a lot of beats."

As soon as Mrs. Melody walked out of the booth, looking fabulous as usual, and joined them inside the engineer's room, they all raved on Dark & Moody's track production.

"Yo, I hear you got a *girl* producer who did this beat," the same friend commented.

Melody smiled and said, "*Woman* producer," correcting him.

"Yeah, you know what I meant. She coming over here tonight?"

Mrs. Melody looked down at her cell phone that read 10:07 PM.

"Any minute now," she stated. "She told me around ten."

"How much she charge for beats?"

Melody grinned. "How much can you *afford*?" She and Tasha had spoken on the subject before. A higher price created a higher respect, especially from the so-called ballers. So, she was calling the man out.

Like clockwork, the late-twenties Black man dug into his deep right pocket and pulled out a wad of hundred-dollar bills.

"What, you got hundreds on the outside and singles in the middle?" Melody joked to him.

"You *wish*."

BJ laughed and said, "We'll see what she says when she gets here."

As soon as he finished his comment, the outside buzzer went off.

"She's here," the engineer informed them all. He buzzed the producer in.

Dark & Moody walked in, dressed very ladylike on purpose in all black, accented with red, suede heels. She didn't want these guys thinking about anything but business. Mrs. Melody had already prepped her on them.

"It's the woman of the hour," the engineer responded.

Tasha looked around skeptically and grinned. "What, y'all were in here talking about me?"

"Yeah, just a li'l bit," BJ told her. "They all couldn't believe you did this *beat.*"

She grinned and said, "I got *more,* too."

"How much you selling 'em for?" the eager friend asked on cue. He still had his wad of money in hand.

Dark & Moody eyed his cash and said, "Now, that's real *business.* I like you already."

They all laughed in the room. She was making an immediate impact on them.

"That's my *girl,*" Mrs. Melody bragged.

The man with the money in hand smirked.

"I thought you just called her a *woman* a few minutes ago."

"I did. But she still my *girl,*" Melody joked.

Tasha chuckled and felt *great* about it. Her relationship with Mrs. Melody was flourishing right before her eyes. All she had to do was be a little bit *patient.*

As was her norm, a new message popped up on Mrs. Melody's cell phone. She looked and ignored it, but the damage was already done. Since she was already in studio with BJ, Dark & Moody assumed someone else was sending her a message. Another eager man.

When BJ received a message on his cell phone seconds later, Tasha glanced at him as well and felt uneasy about it. Especially when he read the message and frowned. Whatever he had read, he didn't bother to share it with the rest of the group either.

"It looks like this gon' be a good end of the year," he commented, smiling.

Dark & Moody was impressed with his ability to mask his emotions so effortlessly, but that also made her leery. A man possessing such meticulous poker skills could be dangerous. But Mrs. Melody paid no attention to it.

"It's fifteen thousand a beat, right?" she asked Tasha.

Tasha grinned, allowing Melody to work her magic.

"Is that what she charged *you?*" the man with money in hand asked.

"You're not *me.* You don't get no discount," Melody told him.

"But you gon' get your money back if you make it a *hit.* You need me to write for you?" she joked.

They all laughed again.

"Aw, you on a *roll* tonight," the money man responded. "But for fifteen *thousand,* I need *two* beats." He looked right at Tasha when he said it.

DM grinned and remained cautious. She didn't want to ruin their good vibes with the wrong response. "You haven't even heard them yet," she responded civilly. Her crafty reply allowed her to stall on his price question a bit longer.

"Yeah, bang his head off with that *new* shit. He can't handle your *old* shit," Mrs. Melody hinted.

That made the money man even more curious. "What's your old shit?" he asked.

They *all* wanted to know.

Dark & Moody smiled and eyed Mrs. Melody. "I thought you told me you're not into my gothic funk."

"Yeah, but *they* might be," Melody responded. "You know I like that up-tempo shit for the strip clubs. But *guys* . . . they be on that dark trap music shit, and yours is even *darker* than that. The way you play the *keys* and shit."

"Yeah, let us hear it," the engineer asked her.

BJ watched and listened to it all while mentally distracted. He was thinking about speaking to Mrs. Melody *alone* about the disturbing text he had received. So, once Dark & Moody took a zip drive out of her bag to load her tracks into the soundboard, BJ tapped Melody on her shoulder to leave the room with him.

Still alert to it all, Dark & Moody watched them walk out into the empty hallway.

"What's up?" Mrs. Melody asked BJ, concerned.

BJ slid his cell phone screen into her face and showed her the text he had received. It was a picture of her with Gary at a hotel bar.

"You know him?" BJ asked her.

Mrs. Melody sighed, understanding that she had just been pulled into some nonsense. So, she showed him *her* cell phone message.

BJ looked and read it. **Do your boy BJ know about us?**

When he looked up into her face, she said, "Now, why would he text me that shit and then text you a picture if he wasn't try'na *start* some shit. I mean, that's so *obvious.*"

BJ paused, understanding that she was telling him the truth. Nevertheless, he was now curious. "Was you with him though?"

Melody paused. "What do you want me to say?" she asked him. "Do you want me to *lie*? Or you want me to tell the *truth*?" And she waited for the verdict.

"When did you take this picture?"

"Like, three months ago?"

He stopped and thought about it. "That's when you first started dealing with *me.*"

"Exactly."

BJ thought more about it. "Are you sure this wasn't more *recent* than that?"

She nodded. "I'm sure."

At that moment, Dark & Moody popped out in the hallway, looking for the restroom.

"Is there a bathroom this way?" she asked, pointing to the other side of them.

BJ pointed in the opposite direction. "It's that way."

Mrs. Melody smiled, knowing better. She knew Tasha was checking in on them. It was women's intuition at work.

"Are they digging your beats?" she asked her protective producer and friend.

"More than I imagined," Tasha commented. Then she eyed BJ. "You okay?"

"Yeah, I'm good."

She nodded to him with steady eyes. "That's good to know."

When she headed to the restrooms away from them, BJ turned and smiled at Melody. "She's your bodyguard too?" he asked in a low tone.

Melody grinned. "If she *needs* to be. Just don't give her a *reason.*"

"Well, you don't give *me* a reason," he countered.

"I'm not. But somebody else was," she alluded.

BJ shook his head. "I never liked that guy. He always seemed like the jealous type."

Mrs. Melody shrugged. "It is what it is. And some people *hate* when you move on. And *obviously*, he didn't know that we were together today."

BJ nodded, understanding it all. "Yeah, so now, he try'na ruin you."

"That's what jealous people *do* when you 'bout to blow up. They try to bring you back down."

BJ grabbed her by the hips. "But you ain't going back down," he told her. "You goin' all the way *up*."

"And nothing can stop me," she stated with swagger.

Tasha walked back out from the restroom and eyed them both again.

"Aw'ight, y'all," she said with a grin as she reentered the engineer's room. She wanted both of them to know that she was *there*.

BJ grinned back and figured as much.

"Yeah, I think I like her. She got your back," he commented to Melody.

Mrs. Melody continued to smile, all up into his smooth brown face.

"That's why she's my *girl*," she responded, and kissed him on the lips. All the while, she was *pissed* at Gary for trying so hard to play her.

That motherfucka needs to get his! she thought to herself. *I don't appreciate that petty shit he just tried to do!*

And she had plans of giving him a piece of her mind for it.

CHARLES CLAY

Reflection 35

Nervously, I called to check in on Charles Clay as soon as I got into my office, and I was glad that I did. I didn't know the extent of his updated situation, nor was he at liberty to tell me everything, but he did tell me some things.

"I'm in discussions now to sell off some of my properties and things to beef up my finances just in case this suit doesn't go as planned," he told me.

That sounded *serious.* I said, "*Really?* It's that bad?"

"Yes. I'm afraid it is," he answered.

"Well, how are you dealing with it mentally and emotionally?"

He paused. "Honestly . . . some days I'm feeling optimistic about my chances, and some days not. It's like a hot-and-cold-water faucet," he added with a chuckle.

That fit the manic-depressive world of the entertainment and sports industries that many African-American stars made their money in. The waves of success and failure could fluctuate from high peaks to low crashes. And it was smart to figure out how to ride the calmer waters in the middle.

"So, what have you been doing to keep yourself occupied?" I asked him. The last thing in the world he needed to do was get involved with a new young woman. I hoped he wasn't doing that.

He said, "Actually, I've been reading a lot of screenplays in my office that I hadn't been able to catch up on. And it's therapeutic in a way, to read about issues that other people are going through, even if they're all *fictional*."

"Well, as they say, the best fiction is based on the *facts*," I commented.

"Yeah, really. So, how's your film idea going? Have you found a writer yet?" he asked, changing the subject with fresh energy. I could hear it in his voice. But before I could answer him, he added, "You're not still thinking about Tyrell Hodge are you?"

That question stopped me in my tracks. "What's so wrong with Tyrell's writing?" I pleaded. "I mean, I understand the personality issue. But once he writes the screenplay, he's out of our way, right?"

I was trying my best to play devil's advocate and talk straight business, but Charles didn't give me a fight that morning.

"Yeah, maybe you're right. He could come up with something presentable."

"Sure, he could," I agreed. "He could come up with something *great*."

After that, we hit a note of silence, where I could tell that Charles was preoccupied with his thoughts.

"Again, if you need to clear your mind with everything that's going on, you can trust in me. I'm still a professional," I reminded him.

He chuckled again. "Yeah, I know. You're a *good* professional. And I thank you for checking back in on me."

"Oh, yeah, not a problem. I thank *you* for taking the time out to talk to me."

Once I said that, I immediately felt guilty. What if I had never called Charles to meet up and discuss my film idea at the Thai restaurant? Would he still be in the deep trouble that he was in? It seemed like his troubles snowballed after that one shocking incident while out with me.

Then again, if Charles had it coming to him, he had it coming to him. It was only a matter of *time* before the water broke. However, I missed the flirtatious and pompous Charles Clay that I first met in my office. The troubled and humbled version seemed lifeless.

"Okay, well . . . I'll let you get back to your reading," I told him. There was no sense in me holding him on the line in silence. I had other calls to make and work to do.

"All right," he told me. "Thanks again."

TYRELL HODGE

Reflection 36

SPEAKING OF TYRELL, HE WAS MY NEXT PHONE CALL THAT MORNING. I didn't want to wear him out or anything, but I had to make sure he had gotten started on the screenplay. Hopefully, he had, but I wouldn't know unless I asked him.

He answered his cell phone on the first ring and said, "Hey. You caught me bright and early, huh?"

The man was a shot of *coffee*, I swear. I began to smile, bright and early, just like he said.

"Yeah, I just wanted to check in with you before my day got started, and I don't have any early appointments this morning."

"Naw. Good for you. You can eat a long breakfast then," he joked.

"What about you?" I asked him. "Did I catch you in between your rides this morning?"

I assumed that he was out driving again, but he surprised me.

"Actually, I'm home working on that screenplay of yours."

My heart jumped a beat. "Really? You're not playing with me, are you?"

He paused. "When have I been known to play?"

"True, true. I hear that. So, how long have you been working on it?"

"All this *week* actually. Those PDS guys I was driving for cut me off the app. So, I don't have nothing else to do *but* write."

I frowned. That didn't sound good. "They cut you off the app? For what?"

"Driving too fast. But usually, they let you back on after a week. So, I just gotta wait it out. But that ended up being a good thing for you though. Now I can finish this screenplay before I drive again. At least the first draft of it."

I was still stuck on him being cut off from his driving.

"So, what, did they just *suspend you* or something?"

"Yeah. That's what they do. Like you're in fuckin' high school."

What about your money? I wanted to ask him. I didn't have it to pay him for the screenplay writing yet. Well, I did, but . . .

"Don't worry about that money, yet. I got money saved," he commented, cutting off my thoughts. "But you gon' have to get it to me soon though. I give you about two weeks."

I winced and repeated, *"Two weeks?"*

He laughed. "Naw, I'm just fuckin' with you."

"I thought you just said you're not *playful*," I reminded him.

"I'm *not*, but I got fuckin' *jokes*. How you gon' be a writer without jokes?"

"You could be a *serious* writer," I countered.

"With all serious characters? And nobody makes you laugh? Good luck with that shit," he commented. "Especially if you're writing for *Black* people."

He had a point. "Okay, I can agree with that," I told him. "We *do* love to laugh. You got me laughing right now."

He paused and got serious again. "Yeah, my lady used to laugh, too. Now she just laughs at other people's shit."

I hated to say it, but it just came to mind. "Have you ever thought about moving on from it? I mean, she just sounds like . . . she's not into you anymore."

The truth was the truth. She don't laugh. She don't smile. She don't fuck. She don't get excited. I mean, what was the *use*?

Tyrell sighed and said, "Yeah, I'm still thinking I'm writing a fuckin' *screenplay*, where there's a happy ending with a hammock on the beach for us. I just . . . I can't give it up, man."

Mmmph! I was *speechless*! When a hardcore man can simplify romance that easily . . . it's something *special.* He just couldn't simplify it in his real *life.* His lady friend wouldn't cooperate.

I said, "Wow. I wish I could *be* her for you." I actually said that to him. I was that envious. This woman obviously had him *hooked.* So, how special was *she*? And she didn't even *get it.*

He chuckled and said, "Yeah, I wish you could jump in her mind, too. So you can tell me what's going on in there. But it's just real life, man. I can't control her. And she can't control me. But we keep *trying.*"

I didn't follow his logic on that. I said, "I don't think *she's* trying. That sounds more like your *ego* talking. When a woman is scorned, she's *scorned.* And that's what it sounds like. She's not the person you think she *is* anymore. Or, at least not with *you.* That person is gone."

"And I can never get her back?" he asked me.

He sounded so innocent. He was like a *child,* wanting Santa Claus to be real for Christmas. But there was no Santa Claus. And he was not coming down Tyrell's chimney.

I exhaled and didn't expect to have that kind of conversation so early in the morning with him. We were supposed to be talking about the screenplay he was working on for me. And we had gotten off on a tangent.

I said, "I don't wanna . . . be the bearer of bad news. So, yeah. Anything can happen. She could come back to you." And I left it at that. Only for him to laugh at himself.

"I'm a damn *fool,* right? A *fool* for *love,*" he emphasized. "And that shit gets to *all* of us. That's why she's so bitter with me now. She used to *love me.* And I let her down. So, now she's punishing me for it."

"Okay, you're *allowing* her to do that," I snapped at him. I was getting tired of all the sappy shit. I mean, *be a man* already! I said, "When you finally have the *courage* to move on, that's when you'll see what she's really about. But right now, it's like you're blinded by your own *willpower.* But she is *not* a screenplay. You can't change her in the editing. She's *real.* She is not a character in your head. And you can't seem to accept that."

Silence.

Silence.

Silence.

And more silence.

"So, what do I do?" he finally asked me.

Run, motherfucka, run! I wanted to tell him. *And come to me!* But I didn't. Instead, I told him. "Keep writing that screenplay we're working on." And I chuckled, selfishly.

Tyrell laughed and kept on laughing. He said, "It's like . . . it's *weird,* man, but you understand me. And I used to get in trouble with girls like you."

"You mean, *women*?" I corrected him.

He said, "Naw. I mean, *girls.* 'Cause when y'all grow up and turn into *women,* that's when y'all fuck it up and start *thinking* too much. But when you're still a *girl,* you just *do the shit.* That's what I need her to do now. Just *do the shit* and stop fuckin' *thinking* about it."

I shook my head. He was really *hopeless.*

I said, "Yeah, well . . . she's not a *girl* anymore, Tyrell. She's a grown woman now. And she's *gonna* think about it. That's what stops her from *doing it.* She doesn't *want* to."

"Well, *fuck her* then," he snapped back. "If that's how she feels about it. *Fuck her!*"

I didn't expect that from him. He was having an outright *tantrum.*

"You don't mean that," I told him.

"But *she* does, right? That's what you're telling me. To move on from her."

"That doesn't mean you have to be *angry* though."

"*She's* fucking angry!" he shouted at me.

"And how has that worked out for *her*? You think she's still in her right *mind*?"

"Naw. She's *crazy,*" he commented. "We *both* crazy. But did *I* make her crazy? Or was she crazy before me, and I just brought it out of her?"

I paused to calm our discourse down. I said, "We all have our own psychosis, every last one of us. And you *both* are showing yours." I looked at the clock in my office, and it was time for my first session. I said, "But I have to go now. Let's talk again later."

"Aw'ight. Let me get back to this screenplay."

I hung up the phone and was convinced. Tyrell was a piece of *work.* And so was Charles, who was dealing with his issues. And Mrs. Melody with hers, while I continued to listen to Dark & Moody's music and think about Joseph Drake's White guilt and privilege.

None of us could really control *anything.* But like Tyrell had said, we were all *trying* to, while believing that we could.

DESTINY FLOWERS

Reflection 37

I MADE IT THROUGH THE DAY WITH A LOT ON MY MIND, AND BEFORE I knew, it was after seven o'clock and dark out. For the life of me, I couldn't remember a *thing* I had done all day. After talking to Tyrell that morning, everything went *blank*. It was like I had a spell of amnesia. So, I packed up my things and was ready to head home that evening in a state of confusion.

When the phone rang before I could leave the office, I already knew who it was. I calmly placed my bag down on the desk and answered it. I didn't even have to look at the number.

"Destiny Flowers?" I assumed.

At first, she paused. Then she said. "So, you know who it is now?"

I sat back in my desk chair and said, "You've been calling me like this for *months* now. Whenever I have a damn *break*, you call me."

"Because I know your fuckin' *schedule*, dumbass," she told me. "But I'm *tired* of playing games with you now. I want my *mind* back."

I grimaced and said, "Excuse me?"

"You fuckin' heard me. I want my *mind* back."

I looked at the phone in my hand and didn't know how to respond to her. This woman was really *crazy*.

"Ahhh . . . what exactly are you talking about?"

She said, "Look, I let you borrow my shit, and I want it *back.*"

"You want *what* back? I haven't even *met you,*" I told her.

"Oh, you gon' meet me. Soon enough. You might meet me *tonight,*" she responded. "And you gon' give me my *shit* back."

"I have *not* taken anything from—"

"Like I said, I let you *borrow* my shit, and your time is *up,*" she stated, cutting me off. She said, "You dun' fucked shit all up, runnin' your damn *mouth,* like you *know* something. And you *don't.* Your ass was just born yesterday. But you think you *know* something," she told me.

"Okay, I'm gonna have to let you go now."

I started to hang the phone up right as she warned me.

"Don't you do that," she told me. "You gon' *listen* to me. 'Cause I've been listening to *your dumb ass* for a *while* now. And you ain't that *smart.* Try'na fuck up somebody relationship. I see what you doin'."

I paused and thought about it. "Who *are* you?" I asked her.

"No, the question is, who the fuck are *you? Dumbass!*"

"You're gonna stop *insulting* me," I warned her back.

"Or what? You gon' whip my *ass?* 'Cause you from *Camden, New Jersey?* Girl, *please,*" she responded. "You don't know where I'm from. I just *told you* I was from Cleveland. But you don't really *know.* 'Cause you never *met me,* right?

"Well, I'm from a *way* darker place than you. But you gon' find out," she told me. "*Dumbass!*" she insulted me again.

I was *stunned.* I just held the phone to my ear and listened to her. I had no idea where she was going with all, or what she going to say next.

She said, "You dun' fucked up everything I was trying to do. Thinking you so damn *smart.* So, we gon' have to *fix things* now."

"And what was that that you were trying to do?" I asked her to humor myself. I couldn't let her get the best of me. I had an *ego* too.

She said, "Oh, so, you gon' be a *smart-ass* again. Okay. Watch this. Watch what I do for your ass. Since you *know* so much." And she hung up on me.

I continued to stare at the phone and didn't know what to think. She had hit me with a mental hurricane.

"Yeah, she's definitely crazy," I mumbled to myself. I shook it off. Stood back up. Grabbed my things. And I headed out of the office for home.

JOSEPH DRAKE

Reflection 38

BACK UP IN THE NORTHEAST AREA OF MASSACHUSETTS, JOE shook off the regretful feelings he had after meeting with Carole Ogurah and his daughter Ayana, and he drove a white rental SUV on Interstate 90 West toward Hartford. Hartford, Connecticut, was less than a two-hour drive from Boston, and he had already made his reservation at a downtown Hartford hotel. So, he changed his mind about staying in Boston for a second night, and he headed on his way to meet up with the second mother and daughter in Hartford.

He figured the second meeting would be much less difficult. So, he had called and made plans for an early evening dinner at a steakhouse with no drama involved.

Joe even found a Caribbean music channel on the radio for his drive, and he sang along with the classic feel-good song "Life (Is What You Make It)" by Frighty & Colonel Mite.

"Liiife / life is what you make it . . ."

Joe was enjoying the good spirits of the song so much that he didn't panic when he spotted an eighteen-wheeler truck that was swerving slightly in front of him. With several lanes available, he moved farther to the left and attempted to pass, right as the eighteen-wheeler swerved fully into his left lane.

"SHIT!" Joe yelled, pulling the wheel of the SUV harder to

the left. But it was already too late. With an eighteen-wheeler truck and cargo, there was nowhere for the SUV to escape an accident. But Joe *tried,* as he sped through the median and into a grass area off the road, where the SUV smashed into a massive tree.

BOOMM!

On impact, Joe's head and neck jerked forward like a rag doll, as the airbag engaged from the steering wheel and pushed him back into the driver's seat. But again, it was too late. Even with his seat belt on, the brutal impact of the tree had already done fatal damage to his spine. Joe didn't even have a chance to *blink* before he died behind the wheel.

MRS. MELODY

Reflection 39

"WHY WOULD YOU FUCKIN' DO THAT SHIT?" MRS. MELODY snapped into her cell phone at Gary. She considered his antics *childish*, and he was a grown-ass man!

Gary didn't even deny it. He said, "I'm just letting you *know* that there's reper-*cussions* out here to how you move. And you gettin' a li'l cocky now. But everybody can be *touched* out here. So, you need to think about that the next time you try to play a motherfucka! 'Cause I play for *keeps*."

Melody had driven her car and parked in a barren area of Atlanta, where she climbed out to be as loud as she wanted to be on her cell phone. She carried another expensive handbag with her gun inside. And she remained incensed. A jealous grown man was the *worst*!

"So, you admit it then?" she questioned him. Gary's blunt honesty had caught her off guard. She expected to have to bend the truth out of him.

He said, "Ain't no shame to my game. And that toy-ass *punk* you got over there and sayin' shit."

Melody calmed down and thought about it. She was not only intensifying the issue for herself, she was also pulling BJ further into it. So, she thought better about her anger.

She said, "You know what? You're right. I need to get my head in order. So, you got me on that one. Now he don't fuckin' trust me," she lied. She knew that was what Gary wanted to hear. Jealous people *loved* negative stories. So, she gave him one.

Gary said, "You did that shit to yourself. Atlanta is small. We *all* know each other out here. In fact, I could have people watching you right now," he warned her.

Right as he said it, Mrs. Melody angled to her left and spotted a Black man dressed in all dark clothes, lurking. Paranoid, she immediately panicked and reached inside her bag for her gun.

"Why you got people following me?" she asked Gary, with her heart racing. "That shit is so *petty*!"

She had her fingers on the trigger of the gun while it was still inside her bag. But the prowling man in dark clothes continued to approach her, as if she had a can of Mace in her bag, instead of a loaded gun.

Gary told her, "I'm not saying I got people following you. I'm just saying you never know who's *watching*."

With Gary still on the phone with her, Mrs. Melody pulled her gun out to address the man who was steadily approaching.

"I got *more* than *Mace* in here, mother-*fucka*!" she barked at him with her gun out.

The man finally stopped and looked. He was hesitant at first, but then he spoke to her defiantly.

"Don't pull it out if you not gon' *use it*," he warned her. He shoved both of his hands into his dark hoodie jacket, as if daring her for a shoot-out.

Over the phone, Gary asked her, "What's going on?" He sounded confused.

Melody said, "You *know* what's going on? You got you're fuckin' *goon* out here *following* me. And I got a *gun* for his ass!"

When the lurking man made a move toward her, Mrs. Melody lost her mind and started shooting in his direction.

POP! POP! POP!

"What the fuck?" Gary blurted over the line.

More prepared than she was at gunplay, the man at the scene dropped to the ground and immediately pulled out his own gun to fire back with better aim.

BOP! BOP! BOP! BOP!

A bullet caught Mrs. Melody in her abdomen and another in her left shoulder.

"Unnnhhh," she moaned, crashing back into the driver's-side door of her car, while dropping the gun.

Not liking how his potential robbery had gone sour, the man quickly jumped to his feet and took off running, leaving the sexy rap artist alone to bleed against her car.

"The fuck is going on?" Gary continued to ask over the phone.

With blood leaking fast, Melody ignored him and pulled the car door open with her right hand and good shoulder to climb behind the wheel. She pressed the automatic start button to ignite the engine. Only then did she remember to call 9-1-1. Gary had distracted her from the thought while he was still on the line.

"Yo, what's going on?" he asked her urgently.

Mrs. Melody cut him off the line and called 9-1-1. But by the time they answered, she was losing consciousness.

"Did someone call nine-one-one?" a female operator asked.

"Yeah," Melody mumbled. And that was it.

"Are you okay . . . ? Caller . . . ? Caller . . . ? Melody Anderson . . . ? Are you still there . . . ? Caller . . . ?"

CHARLES CLAY

Reflection 40

CHARLES'S PRODUCTION PARTNER, JACQUELINE CLARK, WAS ON another call at her home office with a film affiliate they had recently produced a project with.

"So, what does he need the money for? He doesn't seem to have bad spending habits. I don't see Charles flaunting and whatnot," the affiliate commented.

While she was on speakerphone to free her hands for her computer, it was a difficult question for Jackie to answer. She didn't want to put Charles's business out there, but his desperate phone calls for new projects had quickly become troublesome for *both* of them. And everyone was calling *her* about it, even after normal work hours.

"I don't know. I'll need to talk to him and see," Jackie lied. She knew exactly what Charles needed the money for. The rumors were already beginning to swirl concerning his sexual conduct with aspiring actresses.

Right on cue, the film affiliate asked Jackie, "He's not in some kind of trouble with the actors, is he? People been asking about his relationships on and off the set."

Jackie sighed, feeling the weight of the impending drama. Whether she had cut Charles off or not, she was still in the middle of his life and career. No one even knew that she had stopped doing business with him yet. Their breakup was still fresh, and she was not ready to tell anyone why. She was still trying to figure it all out while keeping herself busy.

She said, "I'm gonna talk to him tonight. But people are *always* talking about rumors on the set. You know that."

"Yeah, that's why I didn't pay it any mind when I first heard it. But if he's calling around for new projects to earn fast money, then something's *definitely* goin' on with him," the film affiliate commented. "Money was never a conversation with Charles. That's why everybody wanted to get him for *cheap*," he added with a chuckle. "If you weren't around, he would have been directing movies for peanuts."

Jackie allowed herself a slight chuckle. "Don't I know it," she responded. "But I'll get to the bottom of it."

"All right, keep me posted."

"I will."

As soon as she hung up the line, Jackie exhaled with her head dropping forward as if her neck had run out of muscles. That's how long of a day it had been from putting out fires, and Charles's fires were the *biggest.*

"He dun' pulled me into this shit with him anyway," she told herself. She clapped her hands for effect and barked, "I *knew it.*"

She stood up and shook her head in front of her desk with no idea what to do with herself. "Okay, I'll call Jeffrey first," she plotted. She didn't care what time it was. It was an emergency.

She planned to leave the seasoned attorney a message to call her back, but she was surprised when he answered his phone on the second ring.

"Jacqueline, I'm glad you called," he told her immediately.

Jackie hesitated. "Why?"

"We've had a serious change of events with Charles," he answered.

Her heart started racing as she listened. "I know. How bad is it?"

"Is it just me and you?" he asked her.

"Yes. I'm alone at my office. And I've been getting phone calls all day," she told him.

"I can imagine. Are you sitting down?"

She paused. "Is it *that* bad?"

"Yes."

Jackie sat back down at her desk.

"Okay. I'm seated."

The attorney said, "A young woman has a *tape* on him now. And it's only audio, but it's *crystal clear.* And he's directing her to do some . . . *things.* Now, of *course,* we would argue that's it's not *him.* But if the media gets their hands on it . . ."

Jackie sunk her face into her hands. "Oh my *God.*"

"Yeah, he's really gotten himself in bad shape. And a few of the lawyers have upped their case to full-blown sexual *assault* now. Because he's been *physical.*"

"But it's *consensual,* right? I mean, you *know* he wasn't *raping* these girls," Jackie defended him. "He's not *that* kind of a monster. Charles doesn't even have that *in him.*"

"It doesn't matter at this point. It just keeps getting more expensive to defend him."

"So, what are you saying?" she questioned.

"It's pretty much out of our hands," Jeffrey leveled with her. "He's not a Weinstein at the top. He's a Clay at the bottom. You hear what I'm telling you? You know how this country *works.* So, I would advise you to protect your own career. You can't help him anymore."

"Well, I *knew* that already. He's so *full of it,* he won't even allow me to help him. I just didn't know it was gonna get this *deep.*"

"Oh, yeah, it's deep. And with him calling around asking for new directing jobs without *you,* that doesn't look good for him either."

She said, "I *know,* right. That's what half of my calls were about today. It's like he doesn't even realize that these people are gonna call me. He doesn't even *talk* about the business. So, they *know* something's up."

Jeffrey said, "Yeah. And you didn't know anything about it.

You have to repudiate *everything* the media says. Okay? We have to do this very *strategically*."

Jackie nodded. She didn't have a *choice* in the matter. "Okay."

"And if you speak to him at all, I want you to focus *strictly* on *why* he's asking people for directing jobs and other business deals without *you*. That makes it look like he's doing something on his own. Which he *is*."

Jackie sighed and felt sorry for the director. In just a matter of *weeks*, Charles's career was headed down the drain.

She said, "I got you. I have to steer clear of any talk about his case."

Jeffrey said, "Thank *God* he turned down your offer to help him before you wrote out a *deal* memo. That could have been used to hurt your stance of innocence. But now it'll look like he's out there trying to raise his own money."

"Because he didn't want me to know anything about it," Jackie filled in.

"Exactly," Jeffrey agreed with her. "That's how you'll have to *play it*."

Jackie shook her head again and couldn't believe it. "It seems like just *yesterday*, we were setting ourselves up to do some major film deals. Now *this* happens."

"It's called *life*," Jeffrey told her. "And we can't *control* how everyone decides to *live it*. All we can do is respond to it as best we can to protect ourselves and our loved ones."

In closing, Jackie nodded again. "Thanks for taking my call tonight," she told him.

He said, "I *had* to. That's why I'm still in the office now. It's been a *lonnng* day."

Jackie grinned and said, "Tell me about it."

"Have a good *sleep*," he told her.

"You too."

When Jackie hung up, she thought of calling Charles immediately to test out her responses to him. She was curious to see how he would account for his actions.

She even practiced her controlled tone. "How could you call

these people and not think they're gonna call *me*? I mean, what are you *doing*? What do you need the money for?"

She stood from her chair as if practicing for a scene in a film.

"You've been trying to do films for *free, forever.* Now you're calling around looking for money projects without *me.* What's going on?"

Satisfied with her delivery, she then practiced her response to any conversation regarding his case.

"What? What are you talking about? Explain yourself."

She stopped and listened to his imaginary response.

"Are you *crazy*? Why would I do that? Are you confusing real life with one of these *movies*? What are you talking about? Are you *high* on something?"

She stopped again and shook it off. "Nah, that's too much," she told herself. "Just keep your cool and stick to being boring."

Then she eyed the phone and took a deep breath. "Okay. Let's do this."

She dialed Charles's cell phone number and waited as the phone rang. And rang. And rang. With no answer. His message didn't even click on.

"Hmmph," Jackie grunted to herself. "Did he erase his messages?"

Maybe he did, she mused. *Especially if people started calling him like they know something.*

Jackie realized that Charles couldn't take the pressure of a massive failure. That's why he shied away from the bigger-budget films. He wasn't *comfortable* with them. And she was *right.* Charles preferred to remain in his small niche, where he could control more. He was more interested in becoming a *specialist* than focusing on the big-event movies that Jackie wanted.

But it was too late for that now. Charles's personal life was about to be broadcast on a major level, and not for *good* things. And there was nothing he could do about it.

As Charles's cell phone rang over and over again at his office, the celebrated director with the bright future in filmmaking hung from a long and sturdy rope that was wrapped over a pole near the ceiling of his loft.

He had measured the rope from the pole near the ceiling, climbed up on a tall stool, wrapped the end of the rope around his neck, and handcuffed his wrists behind his back with official police steel, before he kicked the tall stool away with his feet to hang himself.

And it *worked* with his bare feet dangling just ten inches away from the ground.

DARK & MOODY
Reflection 41

"*O*H MY *GOD*!" TAMMY COMMENTED WITH HER HANDS OVER her mouth. She was watching the eleven o'clock Atlanta news with Dark & Moody on the living room sofa when it was reported that rising twenty-three-year-old rap artist Mrs. Melody—aka Melody Anderson—had been found shot and killed in her car that evening.

"Police authorities say it looks like an attempted robbery," the newscasters reported from the scene.

Tammy looked over at Tasha for her response. She understood how much she had riding on the young rapper. Tammy was even jealous of her. Dark & Moody had changed her sound and everything for this girl, or at least on her latest productions.

At first, Tasha was speechless. She couldn't gather her thoughts fast enough, while watching the TV screen without emotion. A dozen different scenarios raced through her head, starting with the phone call she had with Melody hours earlier.

"I can't *believe* this petty-ass guy did that shit!" Melody had snapped over the phone. "If a girl ain't with you no more, then *speed on* and get over it!"

She had been complaining about a past fling who sent text messages and a photo to her and her current boo, BJ, in an obvious attempt to ruin their relationship.

At the time, Dark & Moody had chuckled at the complaint. "That's what happens when you move too fast from one guy to the next," she had commented.

"Well, I don't *appreciate* that shit! It was *childish*!" Melody ranted.

Tasha continued to smile. She said, "I *knew* something was up when both of y'all looked at y'all cell phones at about the *same time* with the *same response*. I just had this *feeling*. And when he asked you to step out in the hallway, I *knew it*."

Mrs. Melody laughed and said, "Yeah, BJ knew you were *snoopin'* on us too. He said he likes you though. He said he can tell you got my back. And I haven't really had female friends like that. They always be on some jealousy shit."

Me too, Tasha thought to herself. *'Cause you're a sexy-ass bitch!*

But while she was getting closer to Melody on the music side of things, she had been able to hold her other emotions in check.had

"Well, don't do nothing *crazy*," she had warned the impulsive rapper. "His ploy didn't *work*, so don't sweat it. Just let him be jealous."

"Yeah, I'll see. I just wanna let him *know*."

Tasha shook her head and spoke out against it. "Girl, leave that shit *alone*, and move on from it. Just focus on your music. We don't need that extra drama. Keep the drama on the dance floor," Dark & Moody told her.

Mrs. Melody got excited again. She said, "I like that. 'Drama on the Dance Floor.' Write that title down for a new song."

Dark & Moody grinned and said, "I already got it. But promise me you not gon' do something *stupid*. Just let that shit *go*."

"Aw'ight, I promise," Melody agreed too fast for comfort.

Tasha paused and *knew* better. She said, "I'm *serious*, girl. Leave that shit *alone*. You have to stay locked in on your *career*. *Laser focused*."

"All right, Grandmom! *Shit!* I got you," Mrs. Melody had complained.

And now . . . she was dead.

The reality began to settle into Tasha's mind, slow and lethally, as fresh tears began to swell up in her eyes. Understanding the pain of the loss, Tammy cried herself and moved in to hug her, but Dark & Moody held up her left palm to stop her.

"Wait a minute. Not right now. Not right *now*," she warned twice. She could feel *anger* boiling up in her spirit.

This motherfucker had something to do with this! she told herself. *Now I gotta find out who it is.*

She stood up and walked out of the room, immediately pulling out her cell phone for BJ's number. She had exchanged numbers with a bunch of the guys at the studio for music purposes.

"What are you gonna *do*?" Tammy asked, hesitant to follow her.

Dark & Moody ignored her again. First, she just wanted to talk to BJ.

He answered her call on the first ring. "Hello."

"This is Dark and Moody."

As soon as she said her name, BJ went off on an angry tantrum of his own.

"*Shit*, man! These motherfuckers out here in Atlanta! It's getting *worse* and *worse* out here. This is *fucked up*!"

Obviously, he knew about Mrs. Melody's murder and was on his way to the hospital as he spoke. But Dark & Moody had other ideas.

"Melody said somebody had texted you a picture to try and throw shade on y'all relationship. Who was that?" she asked him.

"What? You talking about *Gary*?"

"Is that his name, that she used to deal with before you?"

"Yeah, why?" BJ asked.

Tasha started to tell him what she knew and stopped herself. Instead, she asked, "Can you give me his number?"

"Why?" It was a natural question that she couldn't get around.

"I just wanna ask him some questions," she answered.

"About what?" BJ needed to add it all up, but Tasha didn't know if she wanted to include him in on what she was thinking.

"Are you gonna give me his number or not?" she questioned. She was trying to keep her cool with him.

"You think he had something to do with it?" BJ finally assumed.

"I don't know yet. I just wanna talk to him."

BJ calmed down and thought about it. What difference would it make? Melody was gone.

He said, "Aw'ight, I'ma text it to you. And you let me *know* if you find out something. 'Cause I wasn't even *thinking* about him."

Tasha nodded and was full of emotions as she wiped the tears from her eyes.

"Aw'ight. Thanks," she told him.

As soon as she hung up the phone, Tammy was right there behind her, eavesdropping.

"What are you gonna do?" she repeated. "You think her old *boyfriend* had something to do with it?"

Dark & Moody shook her head and walked away toward the bedroom to change back into street clothes from her comfortable sweats. Tammy continued to follow and interrogate her.

"*Tasha,* what are you planning to *do*?" she pressed with more authority. But it didn't work. Dark & Moody had tuned her out with a one-track mind for a blood mission.

She walked into the bedroom closet and pulled out all dark clothes, topped off with a black hoodie, just like the man who had shot and killed Mrs. Melody was dressed. Dark clothes at night made it nearly impossible to identify an assailant.

Dressed and ready to go in a matter of minutes, Tasha checked her cell phone to see that BJ had texted her the phone number. He had even added the last name, Gary Pinkston.

Good, she told herself with a nod. She still didn't have any words for Tammy. Not any *positive* words. Mrs. Melody had become far more important in the hierarchy of her life, where Tammy had been reduced to a meantime girl.

At the front door, Tammy pleaded, "*Please,* don't do something you'll *regret,*" with tears in her eyes. In her mind, she was ready to tackle Tasha to stop her from leaving, but she didn't want to start an all-out fight between them. That's how seriously Dark & Moody took her mission. Only *God* could stop her.

She marched toward her car in her dark assassin's gear and black carry bag as Tammy watched, *helplessly*, from the front door.

"*Please*, God, have *mercy* on her *soul*," Tammy prayed with urgency.

DM made her first phone call as soon as she pulled out of her parking spot. After four rings and no answer from Gary, she hung up and called him again, eager to have a few words with him.

"Hello?" he answered on her second call.

"Did you make that happen?" she asked him. She was prepared for it.

"What? Who is this?" Gary asked immediately.

"A friend of Melody."

He paused. Then he said, "I didn't have *shit* to do with that, man. She just happened to be on the phone with me when it happened," he admitted. There was no way of getting around her cell phone records. But Gary knew that he was *innocent*. So, he was ready to defend himself.

"But you put it all in *motion*," Tasha countered, with fresh tears rolling down her cheeks. "If she wouldn't have been so concerned about calling *you*, she wouldn't even have been out there."

"Aw, you can't blame that shit on *me*. It was just bad fucking *timing*," he blurted.

"Yeah, bad timing for *you too*," she told him before hanging up.

If it's gonna happen, it's gonna happen, she convinced herself. There was no turning back. She was tired of hardheaded, egotistical guys. In the rap industry, that's all she seemed to deal with. Mrs. Melody had been a breath of fresh air. And her fresh air had been snuffed out already.

Pumped with adrenaline, Tasha wiped her face with her right hand and made a second call.

"Hey, what's up? You still selling that *heat*?"

Another pause. "You *serious*? What's going on?"

"Yeah, I'm serious. I got two hundred on me right now," DM told her gun connect.

"You gon' need *three* hundred. That's the smallest I got right now."

"All right. Give me that."

"Cool. Call me when you get here."

It's amazing what a person can do when they put their minds to it. The main ingredients were willpower and courage. In other words, what are you willing to *do* that you won't back down from?

It's all about walking the walk after you talk the talk, and Dark & Moody had finally been inspired to do it, to actually *kill* someone. So, she got Gary's picture from BJ, looked him up on social media, and called around to people she knew with questions on where she could find him.

"Yeah, he live up in the Buckhead area. I've been to his place before. Let me find that address for you."

As Gary had told Mrs. Melody hours earlier, the city of Atlanta was indeed *small*, particularly for the movers and shakers. So, by the time it had turned 1:30 AM, Dark & Moody was sitting across the street from the man's house with a .38 Special handgun in her lap that she was fully prepared to use.

On alert from the craziness of the evening, Gary still had friends over the house and was nowhere near ready for bed. He was still explaining things, while dressed in his day clothes inside the kitchen.

"So, I hear gunshots firing in the background, and I'm like, 'What the fuck is going on?' "

His friend Mike was over at the house as well, the first one to catch Mrs. Melody creeping with BJ.

He said, "That's crazy. That was just bad timing for her."

"Yeah, that's what *I'm* saying," Gary agreed.

Off instinct, he eyed the name TASHA SAMUELS and the number that she had called him from earlier. But he didn't share that story with his guys. He didn't want to look paranoid after her call. So, he kept it to himself. But he still thought about it.

"It's been a crazy-ass night," he commented. "I need to walk out and take me a smoke."

They had freshly rolled marijuana blunts on the kitchen table, and all four of his friends were strapped with pistols, including Gary, who held a 9-millimeter Glock inside his waistband.

Sometimes the circumstances of life can line up too perfectly. Just as Gary grabbed one of the rolled-up blunts to smoke outside on the back deck of his house, Tasha quietly slipped out of her car and headed to the back as well, which often gave you a clearer view of what's going on inside the house than the front. Sometimes doors and windows at the back of the house could even be left open.

And what a surprise it was for Dark & Moody to make it around to the back just in time to catch the man of the hour walking outside in plain view to smoke a blunt.

Oh my God! I guess it was really meant to be! she thought to herself. Why else had everything fallen into place for her sacrifice? So, there was no hesitation.

DM aimed the gun at her target and started firing as she ran forward to get closer to him.

BOP! BOP! BOP! BOP! BOP! BOP!

With much better aim and a closer distance than Melody, Tasha hit the target with three of her six bullets, striking Gary in his left shoulder, his neck, and his back as he attempted to duck and run away.

"SHIT!" Mike yelled on his way out of the house with his own gun. The other three friends followed, all with their pistols drawn, and started firing at the dark object that scrambled back toward the front of the house.

POP! POP!

BOP! BOP!

POP! POP! POP!

BOP! BOP! BOP! BOP!

With no time to reload her six-shooter gun, and a lack of foot speed to make it back to her car with four guys in hot pursuit of her, Dark & Moody realized that it was a one-way mission.

Fuck it! They got me! she panicked as she ran clumsily, while expecting their bullets to rain down on her. And they did, with the first bullet catching her in the leg, then her arm, and her back, and her ribs, until they were able to walk up on her and spray her body into a bloodbath.

DESTINY FLOWERS

Reflection 42

"WHAT THE HELL IS GOING ON?" I ASKED MYSELF AT MY OFFICE. "*Four* of my clients all die in the same damn *week*? What the *FUCK*? And they're *all* from my movie idea!"

I didn't know *what* to think. I was *shocked*! Could you even *imagine* something like that?

NO FUCKING WAY! I thought. It was *unbelievable*!

I just sat at my desk and stared forward. What else could I do? It was obvious that something in my universe had gone very *wrong*. And I had no control over it. I was too stunned to even cry for them. How unlikely was it for all of that to happen so *drastically*?

My office phone began to ring while I sat there and stared at it. Who could it be . . . ?

"Hello?" I answered skeptically.

There was a long pause. Then she said, "You still don't get it yet, *do you*?"

Destiny Flowers! I thought.

Next, there was a knock on the door.

I looked toward the doorway and asked, "Who is it?"

"Open the damn door," Destiny told me over the phone.

I looked at the phone and then back to the door.

"Is that *you*?" I asked her over the line.

"Open the damn door and *see.*"

I froze and panicked. Did I have a *gun*? Did the building have *security*? Did I need to be ready to *fight*? She had just popped up at my office out of the blue? Who *does* that?

"Open the damn *door,* Victoria. You been asking for this for a long-ass *time.*"

I took a deep breath and composed myself. If I needed to be ready to *fight,* then that's what I had to do. So, I stood up and walked to the door, like a *Camden* girl. When I opened it, I stood back and looked her in the face with my hands up like a boxer.

"*You,*" I stated, confused. It was Tyrell Hodge's live-in girlfriend with her expressive eyes and hair. She grinned at me and walked in, as if she *owned* the place. Then she sat down in my client's chair. She wasn't concerned about me *at all.*

She said, "Okay. Talk to me. I'm your *client* now."

I studied her and moved slow, working my way back to my desk, while keeping my eyes on her. I had no idea what this woman was capable of. But she had my same size, even with our heels on.

I sat behind my desk and just looked at her.

She said, "Well . . . what do you *think*? Do I look good enough for you now?"

"Good enough for *what*?" I asked her over my desk.

"To play in your movie," she answered. "And I want one of the *lead* roles."

I paused. "I don't *have* a movie anymore," I told her. "All of the people I had in mind for it *died.*"

"Because you *fucked it up,*" Destiny snapped at me. Her anger was so sudden and acute that it *jarred* me. So, I listened to her in silence, knowing that she had more to say.

"Try'na fuck up somebody's *relationship,*" she stated. "Who even told you you could make a movie in the first place? *I* did. That's *who.* But you think you *know* something. And you don't know *shit* but what I *tell you.*"

She still had *style,* too. She wasn't dressed like a crazy woman.

She had sizzle like a fashionista with her own podcast. But she was still *angry*. So, I didn't move.

"You don't know a *damn thing* about *Camden*," she continued to rant on me. "And you ain't ever been there. But you gon' start having all these ideas and shit, like you more important than somebody, just 'cause you think you a damn *doctor*."

She began to smile, *wickedly*, as I continued to listen and stare at her.

"I'm not a doctor?" I asked her. "I'm not a psychologist?"

At that moment, she had me doubting *everything*.

She leaned forward and pointed to her head with both of her index fingers. "You are a *figment* of my imagination. You are *nothing* without me. You don't *exist*."

That's when I smiled back and gathered my thoughts.

I said, "Yeah, you really *are* crazy." I wasn't going to let this woman walk into my office and tell me I wasn't a real *professional. Fuck her!* She didn't know *me!*

She leaned back in the chair and nodded, calmly. "Yeah, I know. I *been* crazy. And so are *you*. 'Cause you're a part of *me*."

She said it so calmly and straightforward that I damn-near *believed* her. But I *couldn't*. That didn't make any *sense*!

I shook my head and said, "I'm not a part of *you*. I don't even *know* you. I've never seen you a day in my *life*. And *obviously*, you're much *younger* than I am."

I wouldn't give her a day past thirty-two.

She glared at me and said, "Really? Then how did you just recognize me at the *door*, like you saw me before?"

It was a question that I couldn't answer. I seemed to know a lot of things that I couldn't explain. It was like . . . I just had it all in my mind, sitting there.

As I reflected on everything I thought I knew, this woman pulled a gun out of her carry bag, the same colorful gun that Mrs. Melody had.

I drew back in my chair, alarmed by it.

She said, "Does this look familiar to you?"

It *did*, but I had never actually *seen* the gun. So, I stared at it, wondering how I knew.

Destiny smiled at me again. "It's all in your damn *head*," she told me. "Because I *put it* there."

I slowly shook it off. "You can't put things in my *head*. Melody probably *told me* about the gun. Or maybe she showed it to me before."

Destiny started laughing. She said, "Really?" Then she nodded to herself. "Yeah, well, like I *said*, I let you borrow my *shit*, but now I want my *mind* back. 'Cause you dun' got too *powerful*."

When she said that, she leaned forward again with the gun, and I had nowhere to go to escape her. So, I pulled my desk drawer open to see if I had a gun too. But there was nothing inside my drawer. I mean, *nothing*, which confused me. I didn't even have a pen or paperwork inside.

Destiny looked at me and winced. She said, "What are you doing? You don't have anything in there. You still don't believe me, do you? You don't *exist* without me. But *I* exist without *you*. So, it's time to put you *back*."

I jumped up out of my desk chair and dodged right and left, as if she had already started shooting at me. I screamed, "HELP! SECURITY! I HAVE A CRAZY WOMAN IN MY OFFICE!"

I did all of that, just for her to sit there and stare at me. She didn't even *flinch*.

She said, "Ain't nobody coming to save your dumb ass. It's just me and you in here. But you still don't realize it yet. You still think you're more *important* than me. So, I had to *show you*. And you just got all *five* of your clients *killed*."

Five? I counted four, I thought to myself. Then I panicked again.

"Oh my *God*! What did you do to *Tyrell*?" I asked her. Did she really have that kind of *power*? Was she a *witch*? What was going *on*? She had even warned me before it all happened.

"Yeah, you *would* ask about him, wouldn't you? Had a little *crush* on somebody," she said with a smirk. "You thought you was gon' *get some*?"

I ignored her and asked, "What *happened* to him?"

She eyed me, real serene, with the gun still in her hand. And she told me casually, "You got him killed like the rest of them. In fact, you got him killed *first.*"

I didn't want to believe her. And since I didn't *see it,* I *didn't* believe her.

"You're *lying,*" I told her. "You wouldn't have done that. You still *love him.* Why else would you *live* with him for that long?"

I was trying to make it make *sense. Something* still had to be logical. Would she kill everyone just to prove a *point?* I still couldn't *believe it.*

She said, "You're still in here try'na be a *doctor?* I thought you just called me *crazy.* Well, crazy people do crazy *things* . . . right?"

I felt anxious, as if I was ready to fight her. But first I had to get the gun out of her hands.

"How did you kill him?" I asked. Maybe I could jump her and grab the gun while she explained it to me.

But then she rocked the gun in her right hand, as if she *knew* what I was *thinking.*

When she held the gun steady again, she looked me straight in the eyes and said, "I shot him. I shot him right in his *heart.*"

She even pointed the gun forward to reimagine it.

"Why?" I asked her.

She glared at me again. "Because he *deserved it.* He should have *known* how *special* I was when he *met me.* But he started taking me for granted, and only wanted me for *sex.* So, I stopped giving it to him. And he could have walked away whenever he wanted to. But he didn't. Because he wanted to keep *using* me."

"Using you for *what?* It wasn't for *sex.* You wasn't giving it to him. Right?" I asked her.

She said, "But he still *knew* that I was *special.* And I always gave him *ideas* that he would *use* without giving me the *credit.* My ideas would just pop up in his writings, as if he didn't know where they came from. Mother-*fucker.*"

"And you let him *do it?*"

I was still focused on the gun and when I could jump her to get it.

"Like you said . . . I loved him," she admitted. "So, I just kind of . . . held on, like we *do* sometimes when we're trying to figure it all out in our heads. And he didn't want me to *leave* anyway. He was *hooked.*"

With her guard down, I eyed the gun and was ready to make my move. But then she became *fierce* and held it tightly in her hands again.

She said, "But then *you* got him all riled up with that *movie* shit, and your *relationship* talk, thinking you *know* something. So, I'm gon' let you have this *last* reflection before I put an *end* to this shit," she told me with the gun. "Maybe then you'll finally *get it.*"

She pointed to herself with her free left hand and said, "*I'm* the one in control. Not *you.*"

TYRELL HODGE

Reflection 43

AFTER THIS DUMBASS, WANNABE PSYCHOLOGIST GOT TYRELL ALL fired up with her brainiac talk about *movies* and *relationships*, his ass needed to be calmed back down with some damn *medicine*. I swear, they must have missed his ADHD (attention deficit hyperactivity disorder) diagnosis in grade school or something, because he was *definitely* wired for that shit. And every time he got disturbed by something, he would bother *me* with it at *work*.

I knew something was up when he started texting me before eleven o'clock in the morning.

You coming straight home today? You wanna do a lunch date? You bored?

As soon as I read that, I *knew* he was gonna keep bothering me. When you know somebody, you know somebody. And that was Tyrell's MO (modus operandi). He'll keep bothering you until he gets his way, or until you shut that shit down. So, I had to shut the shit down!

Are you driving today? I'm working.

Then he got sarcastic.

All work and no play, wastes your life away.

Once he started with that, it only irritated me.

I'll be fine. I'm working.

Then he started his usual *whining* and shit, with capital letters.

You're ALWAYS working. You don't have any time for US anymore.

The truth of the matter was, I didn't *need* time with him anymore. I had my system, and it included ignoring *him.* And I could get away with it because he wasn't going anywhere. Tyrell was a man of *habit,* and that habit included *me.*

But if I didn't respond to him, he would restart the text conversation later on, and I didn't want to deal with him again in the afternoon. So, I had to close out the conversation.

I'll be home later.

Once I did that, all I had to do was repeat my text.

I'll be home later.

Life was like a constant chess game with Tyrell. And I had gotten *used* to playing it. So, I could checkmate his ass every time now.

Apparently, his ass hadn't planned on driving PDS at all that day, which meant he would be a hundred miles an hour on *me.* But I didn't know that when he was texting me.

So, I got in after five o'clock and realized that he had been at home *waiting* all fucking day for *me,* like a damn *puppy.* But he wasn't a happy puppy. He had a fucking *attitude*!

He went right in on me and said, "Look, if we *over,* then let me *know.* But I'm not playing this *game* no fuckin' more. I'm *tired* of this shit! So, let me know what you wanna *do*!"

I looked at him like he had lost his mind. But he was *always* losing it.

I said, "If you're ready to leave then just don't come *back.* I'm not keeping you here. And I can pay the fuckin' *bills* myself."

He said, "But do you want me to *leave*? What do you want me to *do*?"

I can't tell a grown-ass man what to fucking *do*! If he wanted to leave, then *leave.* If he wanted to stay, then *stay.* Why the fuck was he asking *me* that? So, I ignored him and walked away. I was tired from work and needed to *rest.*

At that point, this motherfucker said, "Don't fuckin' walk away from *me*! Answer the fuckin' *question*! You're not walking away from me tonight!"

Now, that was some *new shit,* right there, because he had *never* spoken about stopping me from walking away before. I wasn't in *jail*! Who the fuck was *he*?!

So, I ignored him again and kept walking. That's when he grabbed me by the *neck. Yes,* the motherfucker grabbed me by my *neck*!

He said, "I'm fucking *sick of you*! If you don't want me *here,* then *say it*! Say what the fuck *you want*!"

Well, I fucking *lost it* myself at that point, and grabbed both of his arms with my nails.

"Get the *fuck off* of me! You don't *deserve* an answer! You don't respect *shit I do*! You only give a fuck about what *you do*! And I'm *tired* of *you too*! So, you can go to your fucking *psychologist* and ask *her* for some!"

He yelled, "I *told you,* I'm not fucking with her! It's *business*!"

"And when have you ever done *business* with *me*!" I yelled back at him. "All you wanna do is *fuck me*! You don't care *nothing* about my *mind*!"

"That's not *true.* I *love* your mind. I love everything *about you,*" he told me with tears in his eyes. "I just want you *back* to how you *used* to be."

"Yeah, when you could get your *way* all the time. But I ain't going back to that shit!" I told him. "I ain't fuckin' *na-eeve* no more."

And this motherfucker actually *cried* after trying to *choke me.*

He said, "You got your way *too.* You got everything you wanted from me. But I can't give you the fucking *world*! *Nobody* can have *everything.* So, you lost your *heart,* and you punished *me* for it. Before I *ever* went to another woman."

"Yeah, whatever." I wasn't trying to hear *any* of that shit after he tried to *choke me.* He was talking to a *brick fucking wall*!

He said, "Aw'ight. If that's how it's gon' *be.* Where you wanna *fake* what you're doing with me. Then we gon' end it right here then."

He went and got this lady handgun that he had given me a while ago for protection. And I never really bothered with the gun. But I was *thinking* about it as soon as he put hands on me. I didn't think he was going to let me get it though, especially while I was still *pissed* at him. But his dumbass went and brought the gun *to me.* Like I had *blind* and unconditional *love* for him like that. And I *don't.* Not anymore.

So, when his ass put the gun in my hands, he had signed his *death* certificate. Because I don't fucking *play* like that.

Then he said, "If you don't really love me, then put me out of my misery." And he stood right in front of the gun with his heart.

At that moment, I knew what that shit was about. It was all about *control.* He was still trying to *control* me. But I was *tired* of that shit.

I told myself, *I ain't going back to that. For nobody! Nobody's gonna control me anymore.*

And I squeezed the fucking trigger to his heart.

POP!

He took the bullet to his chest and grabbed both of my arms, squeezing the hell of out them. Then he fell to the floor. And the first thing I thought about was taking care of this wannabe *psychologist,* who had put all that shit in his head in the *first place.*

"And *fuck* her movie! She gon' get hers *next.*"

And I took care of every character in my head that she wanted to be involved in.

DESTINY FLOWERS

Reflection 44

When Destiny reflected on all of that to let me *see* it and *feel* it, I was honestly *terrified* of her. How could a woman shoot a man in the heart who loved her that hard?

She still had the gun in her hands as I watched her. And if she could do that to Tyrell, I figured I didn't stand a *chance* to reason with her. I had to get that gun out of her hands by any means necessary.

After a moment of silence, with us both staring at each other, she exhaled and stood up.

"All right, let's get this over with."

"Oh, shit!" I panicked and reached to grab the gun in her hands. I was actually *shocked* that I got my hands on it before she could fire it.

Then she headbutted me. "Let it fuckin' *go*!"

But I held on for dear *life* and wrestled it with her.

"I'm not going out without a *fight*!" I told her.

BOP!

"AHHH, SHIT!" I hollered. The gun shot off in the room and burnt my hand, but I still didn't let it *go*.

"You gon' fuckin' *die*!" she told me, as we wrestled around the room, falling into shit.

I shouted, "What are you gonna do, *shoot yourself*? I'm all in your *head,* right? So, if *I* die, then *you* die! Dumbass!" I argued with her.

"We *both* gon' die then," she told me.

"For *what?* You don't have to kill me. Just *control me.* Control *yourself,*" I reasoned.

Then she leaned down and bit my hand.

"Ahhh! *Bitch!*" I screamed, and headbutted her back.

When she fell to the floor, I fell down with her. And the gun was just *inches* away from *her* head and *mine.*

"I let you *borrow* my *shit,* and it's *over*!" she told me, squeezing the trigger.

POP!

WHO AM I?

Reflection 45

I AWOKE AT AN ATLANTA HOSPITAL ON A GURNEY WITH MY ARMS strapped down to my sides and a bandage wrapped around my head. At first, all I saw was lights, blinding me, while stretched out on the table. Or it *felt* like a table. And when I looked up into the eyes of a doctor, I asked him, "What happened?"

He was a clean-shaven Asian man in his thirties, wearing all white. Or maybe he was older than that, because Asians always looked young to me.

He said, "Apparently, you ah . . . created a whole bunch of characters in your head. And obviously . . . you lost control of them."

"Really?"

He nodded. "Yes . . . really."

I stopped and thought about it. I said, "But they seemed so *real.*"

The doctor smiled at me. He said, "They always do." Then he looked serious. "That's why you tried to hurt yourself."

I guess that's why they had me strapped down to the gurney like that. But . . . I didn't believe him. Something *had* to be real. I could still *feel it.* I just had to figure out who I was. And how I got here . . . Then I could start all over again.

Discussion Questions

for *Control* by Omar Tyree

1) When you hear the phrase "psychological thriller" what are the first ideas that come to mind?

2) Do boys have more control over their lives than girls? Why or why not?

3) If you had to rate the level of control that you have in your life from 1–10, what number would you give yourself and why?

4) Do you believe young women gain more control or less when they decide to go along with the wishes of powerful men?

5) Do you think it's harder for wealthy men to control their urges for sex than it is for wealthy women? Why do you feel that way?

6) Compared to women around the world, are the emotions of American women out of whack? Have you noticed any difference in the emotions of foreign women?

7) Do you believe White America owes Black America reparations for slavery? Why or why not?

8) Who is your favorite character to read about in *Control*? Why?

9) Would you like to read more thrillers by Omar Tyree? What did you like about this style of writing?

10) Did this book make you think about the issues of real life, or was it just a fun read? What more did it make you think about while reading?